Fiction

The H

Dunstan Power

The Empty Rope

First published in 2024 by Black Pear Press
www.blackpear.net

ISBN 978-1-916910-17-1

Cover photographs Tim Butler
Cover design Black Pear Press, Dunstan Power

Black Pear Press

Dedication

For Mum and Dad, thanks for instilling a love of story and adventure.

The cruellest lies are often told in silence

Robert Louis Stevenson

January 1990, Southern Patagonian Icefield, Argentina

The ice shards tumbled away from his crampons into oblivion. Better to look up; a few final moves and he would crown the summit.

At last, he stood there, the panorama laid out below him. He said a silent prayer of thanks then whooped for joy into the wind. All around the silver spires gleamed in the late afternoon sun, each one a temptress offering its own adventure. He took out his small camera and snapped some pictures that could never do justice to this place. If only she were with him to share this experience; if only nature hadn't intervened. He looked down at the glimmering Lago Sucia. Perhaps she was watching the peak right now and could see him, a tiny dot altering the skyline? He waved his arms above his head, just in case.

A strong gust tugged at his down jacket, pushing him towards the edge, and the light momentarily dimmed. He squinted into the low western sun, to see a bank of clouds rolling in fast from the Pacific. The sun reappeared and then was gone for good behind a dirty grey blanket that stretched all the way down to the horizon.

A storm, maybe only tens of minutes away.

He crouched and tightened his rucksack straps. Already he could feel the wind speed increasing and the temperature plummeting. He breathed in and drank in the view one last time.

His luck had turned. He needed to get down.

CHAPTER ONE
August 2015, Llanberis, Wales

When the door chimed, the early evening Saturday sun was already flooding into the shop and I was beginning the all-too-short process of cashing up. In the back room I could hear Lottie pacing about, ready to charge up the hills to see the sheep. It had been a slow day and I was ready to join her, an hour stretching my legs on the hills was just the tonic needed before tea. I glanced up from the till to see my visitor, silhouetted in the white frame. She paused for a moment, as though weighing a decision in her mind, before stepping in. I returned to the task of running out the till receipts, but glanced up occasionally to check if my guest was to become a customer, or would melt away with an apologetic smile, as so many did.

I soon knew she wasn't in my shop to buy. It wasn't her age, many of the customers were in their twenties, nor her athletic beauty—that was not unusual in the climbing community, nor the aimless way she moved around the shop. No, it was the furtive expression towards me, as the object of the visit, that gave it away.

She didn't come over immediately, but instead picked her way around the small room, feigning interest in the hats and gloves, headtorches, harnesses and gear hanging on racks along the wall. I joined the pretence, busying myself with packing up for the day, but all the time waiting for the question. The shop was small and she would soon run out of excuses to meander.

Lottie barked from the back room. It was twenty past five and my curiosity was getting the better of me. 'Can I help you? I'm sorry but I need to close up soon.'

She looked up from the thermos mug that had become

2

an object of great interest and flashed a perfect smile towards me. 'I…um…' She put the mug down and slid around the shelves towards the counter. 'Are you Craig? Craig Darwen?' Her American accent caught me by surprise.

'I am.'

'I'm actually after a climbing partner…I was hoping to tackle "Comes the Dervish", heard you were a guide.'

I whistled through my teeth and reappraised her. It was a tough route she was proposing; she was no novice. 'Not sure where you heard that. 'Fraid you met me twenty years too late. Haven't done anything like that for a long time.' I turned around to the cork board behind the counter. 'But I have the number of someone here…'

'No, maybe I'm being too ambitious. Just want to see more of the hills, with someone who knows them.' She had stepped closer, her smile continuing to beam under electric-blue eyes.

I sighed. 'I'm sorry but I just run the shop these days. Been a while since I guided. Who *did* you speak to?'

She looked away, then back at me. 'Oh, a guy I met at Plas y Brenin. He rated you. Said you were a bouldering supremo.'

I felt some colour coming to my cheeks. She had obviously talked to my friends who had told her I only climbed alone and unaided. One of them had no doubt added, 'He's a miserable bugger.' Still though, she hadn't been put off.

'Oh well, I used to do a bit of instruction and spotting for other climbers, but my guiding these days is limited to climbing the likes of Crib Goch; walking, really…Nick here,' I waved a card, 'he can help you out.'

'Well, I guess the shop is closed on the Lord's Day and I think Crib Goch would be grand. How about tomorrow

3

then?' She was grinning now.

I tried one last line of defence. 'I don't usually…'

But she didn't seem to be listening, instead rooting inside her buck-skin handbag. 'Here—' She drew out a sleek pen, leaned across the counter and scribbled on the back of a leaflet advertising the local mountain railway. 'My number. I'm Sarah, Sarah Hughes.' She held out her hand which I shook, entranced. 'I'll come over at nine.'

'I'm not free,' I called after her, but she had turned and, with a chime of the doorbell, was gone.

It was a Saturday and Saturday was pub night. I left Lottie on the sofa, which we shared in the flat above the shop, locked the side door and set off across the footpath behind down to the pub. It was a beautiful evening; the lush green hills were bathed with a golden light falling through high Cirrus clouds. I passed the campsite that was packed as always at this time of year, thin columns of smoke rising from a hundred barbecues, and walked on into the village.

The Queen's Head was August-heaving; locals and tourists jostling for tables whilst the hassled bar staff pulled pints and weaved between the oak tables laden with empties and steaming plates of food. I pushed through to the public bar, beer in hand.

Sean from the climbing centre was at the end of the table sitting with one of the student instructors, Gwynn. Sean gave me a wink. Bemused I squeezed in on the bench next to him. 'What's up?'

'Who's your secret yank? Is this who you've been holding out for all these years?' he said with raised eyebrows. Gwynn grinned.

'What you talking about?'

'Had some wee lassie asking about you this afternoon.

4

Pretty good climber. Certainly brightened up the afternoon.'

'Ah.'

'So, you *do* know who I'm talking about! Distant cousin? Gwynn here took quite a shine to her.' The young man dutifully blushed, furthering Sean's pleasure.

'I've no idea,' I said. 'She told me you had recommended me. What did she say exactly?'

'Wanted to know if you did guiding, seemed to know your name though. Was very keen to meet you. Asked a few questions about your past...' He nodded knowingly and the two of them laughed.

'Yeah, yeah,' I said, dismissively. 'She didn't spend a lot of money in my shop, that's all I know.'

'God, no wonder you've never found Mrs Right, you mercenary old bastard! I really bigged you up. Told her you were the bouldering king, had climbed every crag in the two valleys. Just not to ask you to rope up! She wanted to know about that, why you only climb alone. I told her you didn't like other people.' Sean laughed at his own joke.

'I do like other people, just not you bastards!' I said and lifted my pint in salute. I wasn't about to tell these nosey-parkers about my potential assignation with the mysterious Sarah tomorrow.

'What, you mean you never climb on ropes?' Gwynn asked.

Sean laughed. 'Ah, the young lad doesn't know about Mr Darwen's legendary frostbite injuries!'

Gwynn frowned, looking at us in turn, as if to see if he were the butt of another joke. 'But you climb okay, I've seen you?'

His frown faded in embarrassment as I held up my right hand revealing my truncated index finger. 'I'll trust my weight hanging on this, but not taking responsibility

5

for a partner.' I took a long draw on my pint.

'Man of integrity our Craig, some vow he made long ago. Rumour has it his toes are a mess too, not that I've ever cared to look. We're not allowed to talk about it, are we? Doesn't bother me as long as he buys the pints and manages the club kitty. On that note, Craig, it's your round.' His glass was empty.

Gwynn said, 'How did you get frostbite then?

'Don't believe a word he tells you, young man. Full of shite. Just got a bit too cold once.'

Sean turned back to Gwynn and nodded across the table to me. 'Shame though, as judging by today, and Miss Lycra, he's missing out.' He winked at me.

I stood up and collected his glass. 'You're a bloody letch, Sean. If Meg was here, she'd have your bollocks.'

Sean laughed and I turned to the bar reflecting on the conversation. Who was this woman and why had she lied to me? I was intrigued, but there was something about this interruption in the pattern of my life that made me distinctly uncomfortable.

That night, as I closed my eyes, images of freezing rock clouded my mind. I pulled the duvet tighter, but still shivered as though an Antarctic breeze was blowing through the room. I heard the door creak open. I looked up to see a shadow slowly slip through the door.

'Lottie?'

A weight fell onto my legs. The collie lay down across the foot of the bed, my protector. It could mean a face licking at six am but for once I didn't chuck her out.

In fact, when I awoke that Sunday morning, Lottie had long retreated to her basket, tired of my tossing and turning. My head throbbed; I'd hardly slept. I rose early,

6

determined to get away from my flat on the off-chance the tourist turned up. I had shoved the leaflet in my pocket when I got back from the pub, telling myself I would call Sarah and explain why I couldn't walk with her. The trouble was, I wasn't sure myself. I had nothing planned for the day, the forecast was excellent and surely her company couldn't be so bad? But I knew something wasn't right.

However, I was too late. As I drew back the lounge curtains, I saw her, leaning against the bonnet of a white Lexus soft-top, studying a map. She looked up, that smile again, and waved. Her long blonde hair was tied in a plait draped lazily over one shoulder. She was wearing a base-layer and three-quarter length trousers, more cut for running than a gentle ramble. But maybe she didn't have a gentle ramble in mind. I decided to keep quiet about what Sean had told me in the pub, that I knew she had been slightly misleading me. Whether this was deliberate or not would no doubt become clear.

I waved back and turned to Lottie, who was eyeing me expectantly, ready for a long walk. 'What do you think? Oh, what the hell.' I ran down the stairs and opened up the shop front.

'Morning! You're keen,' I said, as I opened the door.

'It's a beautiful day, I didn't want to miss a moment!'

I let her in saying, 'I'll make some sandwiches, you okay with egg and cress?' She looked a veggie, the sun-dried Mediterranean tomatoes with couscous type, but that was beyond my larder.

'Oh, thanks. But no need.' She patted her slim rucksack. 'I think I'm prepared.'

'Oh, okay, give me a moment.' I returned upstairs to get my things together. In the bathroom, I checked myself in the mirror. The haggard face stared back. Old enough to be her dad, with too much worry and experience written across my brow. My hair was shaggy and long, cut rough above my shirt collar, no technical underlay for me. I tried to make a bit of an effort, but a shave and a comb were no substitute for youth. But then who was I kidding? She wasn't interested in me in that way. However, there was something about the look she had given me when she had entered the shop the day before. Some sort of recognition perhaps?

I splashed water on my face and after patting myself dry, re-entered the shop with my rucksack.

'Sorry, I forgot to ask, how much for the day?'

Her question took me by surprise; I had forgotten my guiding was in a professional capacity for a moment. 'Oh, a hundred and forty for the day…I should have said. I hope that's okay?'

She answered by placing a belay device on the counter. 'I'll take one of these too.' She had plucked it off the rack whilst I was out back. It was the most expensive I had, a Doug Swanson. 'You've got quite a bit of his stuff I see?'

'Well, it's among the best, not sure about the harnesses, prefer DMM, but his gear is all top notch. You American? Do you get SummitSeeker over there?' SummitSeeker was a Swiss outdoor equipment brand, founded by Doug Swanson, which marketed their top line under his name.

She smiled as though at some secret joke, and passed her gold card over. 'I'm over from Vancouver actually, and yes, SummitSeeker has reached us too.'

I felt myself redden as I rang the purchases in. 'Right, you ready? Don't mind dogs, do you?'

'No, love 'em.' On cue, Lottie trotted out and licked her hand. She gave her a scratch under the ear. 'Grew up with a couple of labs myself.'

8

'She's a rescue dog, failed sheep herder. You'll see why when we get up there…We didn't discuss a route. What sort of thing are you after?'

She shrugged. 'I've got some climbing booked later in the week. I'll let you choose. You mentioned Crib Goch?'

'Nice pronunciation! You know it? It's a classic ridge walk up to Snowdon.'

'Sounds perfect.'

'You do realise you don't need a guide for this?'

'Stop it, Craig, I want the company.' She placed her hand on my forearm as she said this and I breathed in deeply.

'Okay, well, um, thank you.' I felt like a teenager. This was ridiculous. I stepped behind the counter and checked the contents of my rucksack.

'You have waterproofs and something warm? The weather can change quickly up here.'

'You betcha. Gore-Tex pack-lites and a fleece.'

I wondered how she had fitted them all into the tiny aerodynamic rucksack, but asked no more, instead sneaking a spare extra fleece and hat into my old frame rucksack, just in case.

We drove up to Pen-y-Pass in my ancient Fiesta. The sun was illuminating the russet ferns along the valley floor. Above us dark crags glinted like steel daggers thrusting up into the opal sky, waiting to be conquered. I reflected it would have been criminal not to be out with the weather this good, whatever the company.

We were just in time to catch one of the last spaces in the car park. The tarmac was already full of walkers setting out on the popular Miners' and Pyg tracks. Around us climbing gear clinked, Velcro ripped and buckles snapped into place. We looked around at the groups of walkers

9

standing, chatting and drinking from those ubiquitous paper coffee cups. Their ranks were being ever-replenished by the nearby youth hostel. I muttered an apology. 'I had forgotten how busy this place gets.'

'Heh, it's fine. It's beautiful up here.'

She was right. For me, Snowdonia is one of the loveliest places on earth. It is the crown of Wales, a set of wild, rugged mountains, enclosed by the sea to the north and west and gentler, little-visited hills to the south and east. The colours change throughout the year: greens, blues, russets, white snow and baked gun-metal slate. The weather is infamous for its rainfall, but on a day like today the gloomy drizzle that could set in for weeks would be forgiven and forgotten by those who took to the hills.

We joined the busy Pyg track, keeping a smart pace, and I was grateful when we were able to break away onto the somewhat quieter Crib Goch ridge. As we felt our way over the boulders, we made small talk. She was over visiting a friend in London but had decided to try out some 'Brit rock' to see how it compared to her native British Columbia. It sounded like she had already charmed one of the boys down at the outdoor centre in Plas y Brenin into taking her for some exclusive one-to-ones. Even on the phone she would have been irresistible to those kids, but I didn't fancy their chances, she was out of their league—I knew that without meeting them. She was out of all our leagues.

The ridge grew steadily into the knife-edge it is famed for. The ground tumbled away on either side of us. On one side we could see tiny walkers, of all shapes and sizes, making their way up the simpler paths, whilst toy cars ambled their way down the Llanberis Pass on the other. Sarah moved gracefully across the rock, with the confidence of a gymnast. From her poise it was clear she was a confident climber, though it was impossible to know just how good from what was a straightforward scramble. Together, as a threesome, we summited the first peak after only an hour and a half.

'Looks like we've got time for the whole horseshoe,' I said as we supped in the view. 'Unless you want an extended stay in the café up top, that is?'

She grimaced at that suggestion. 'Let's give that a miss.'

It was at lunch time that she struck. We were sitting by a cairn, high on the western peak of Y Lliwedd, having cleared the hordes on Snowdon's summit. The number of walkers had dropped right away and I finally felt as though we had the mountain to ourselves.

'Craig, I've got a teeny confession to make.' She was sitting very close, and her voice took a new tone, the bubbly edge replaced by a low seriousness. 'It wasn't only because of your guiding I came into your shop.'

I paused. I had known something was coming. 'My rugged good looks, right?'

'Um, I—'

'Go on.' I put down my sandwich and looked her in the eye.

'Well, Craig. Um. This is how it is. I'm working in the film industry. I didn't mention that…right?'

No, she hadn't mentioned that.

'Well, I'm working a project. I did a pitch, got a little funding. I'm putting together quite an ambitious project. I'm hoping it will get picked up by one of the studios. I'm close, real close.'

'So, it was my good looks then?'

'No…' She appeared confused for a moment, then broke out into a smile. 'Craig, I'm sorry I didn't tell you this earlier. I guess I wanted to get to know you a bit and to speak to you somewhere where—'

'I couldn't run?'

'I suppose so.'

'Couldn't you have just phoned?'

'I…' She looked away, out towards Snowdon's peak. 'I want you on-board, Craig, and I thought it may be too easy to say no over the phone. I think I was right; you didn't even want to come walking with me—right?'

I knew where this was going. Maybe not exactly where, but I knew the general direction. There was only one reason why an American would be speaking to me about a film. Only one reason. But I wasn't going to make this any easier for her. After all, this was not going to be easy for me.

'So, I think you need to tell me where I come into your project. You've come a long way.'

'Okay, listen, I'll do you the pitch, right?' She stood up and looked around, brushing her hands off on her trousers. Lottie pricked up her ears and sat up to double the audience size. 'Okay, my ten second pitch…In 1990 two climbers set out to make a small piece of history, by creating a new route on an infamous Patagonian peak. On Sunday 14th January disaster struck leaving one man alone with his unconscious friend. Only a truly remarkable feat of mountaineering could rescue them both. This is that story.'

My jaw was hanging loose and I said nothing. Sarah blushed. 'I'm sorry, it's not polished, I…' Her voice faded away and she slowly retook her seat.

We both stared out across the valley. I started to pack my lunch away.

'C'mon, Craig, this could make you famous. More business for the shop? We've got a great compensation package lined up for you, six figure sum. You look like you could do with an extra buck or two.'

12

I swung my pack onto my back, said, 'Come on, Lottie,' and started my descent.

'Craig! Craig...' I heard the running steps behind me and my arm was grabbed. 'Craig, I'm sorry. I should have said when I came in. 'C'mon, hear me out.'

'A great climber died that night...It's not a piece of...Hollywood! Bloody *compensation package?* Who are you people?' I shook her hand off.

'Please, Craig, stop. I've come a long way.' The energy had left her voice. 'Please?'

I turned around, 'You've forgotten your sack.'

'Sorry. Oh yes...Just wait.'

I continued on, fast down along the ridge, aiming to put as much distance between us as possible. No way was I going to be part of some trashy reconstruction of those events, turning our tragedy into Los Angeles dollars. So what if she'd come a long way to talk to me? She could go a long way back. I heard her calling my name, but soon I was alone with Lottie. A stiff breeze from the north had sprung up and, in the distance, I could see the dark anvil heads of cumulonimbus clouds threatening to spoil the day. I stopped and looked back. She was nowhere in sight, and I reluctantly recalled my duty as a guide. I had some responsibility to make sure she got down safely, but I didn't want to walk alongside her or talk. I sat down in a dip in the ridge and waited for her to catch me.

When she appeared she was walking fast, jaw set, but her features relaxed on seeing me. She came over and sat next to me, avoiding eye contact. After a while, she said, 'I'm so sorry, Craig, what I said back there was truly crass. Can we start over?'

Lottie came over to me and I scratched her head. 'I'm sorry, love, but the story's not for entertainment. I'm sure you mean well…maybe you can find another project.'

She remained silent then said, 'Look, Craig, I read that book when I was sixteen. It changed my life.'

'It changed your life? Really?' I turned to look at her, half expecting a smile, as though this were a joke, but her expression was dead set.

'Yes. I was starting out climbing back then. It was a bit of fun, something to do, hanging out with my friends. The book totally changed my perspective; the lengths one human would go to save another.'

'Still don't see why someone has to make a film about it. It was a long time ago. Surprised anyone's heard of it.'

'That's my point, it's a story I think needs to be told to a wider audience.'

I sighed and looked north again. 'Weather's not so clever now. Let's get down.' I stood up, put out my hand to her and pulled her to her feet. 'Why don't you tell me about your project and maybe I can suggest something else you can do with it?'

At that her face lit up, perhaps a little too quickly for my liking, and as we descended, she began to tell me about it. She had thought it all through, every scene, every set, every camera angle. She wanted to make a film that mixed talking heads documentary with reconstruction of the climb and climaxed with a return by the surviving climbers to the scene of the incident, Mount Fitz Roy in Patagonia. A place I'd spent a quarter of a century trying to forget.

When she finished, I said, 'Sounds like you have it all figured out. I don't see you need me.'

'C'mon, Craig, there are two sides to every story. I need to hear your voice.'

'You do realise I remember bugger all about that incident? You're wasting your time. Read the book, that'll tell you more than I know.'

'Join the project and I'm sure it'll come back to you.'

I grimaced; surely even this girl could understand that was the last thing I wanted.

The descent down to the valley was spent with a blow-by-blow account of how the film would work and where I fitted in. I was needed as a talking head and for the final return trip, as well as to give guidance on the reconstruction set pieces. These were to be filmed in the Alps. I knew where without her telling me. I didn't want to give her any hope I would take part, but there was one big question that needed asking.

'So, is *he* on-board?'

'Yes.'

'Did he know you were coming to see me?'

'Yes. Of course. He wants you to be part of this.'

I hadn't seen him for a quarter century. But I saw his name every day—Doug Swanson, the purveyor of the most expensive gear in my shop. Every day in this little way, the divergence between our lives was rubbed into my face. He had saved my life and then got rich on telling the story. Now I lived off selling his equipment. Crumbs falling from the table.

CHAPTER TWO

We parted amicably though Sarah was clearly disappointed with my decision and was refusing to accept it was final. She thrust a business card into my hands, saying, 'You've got my mobile and email here. Call any time. I really hope you join us.'

The card was notable for having no company name or job description on. I made a show of pinning it to the cork board by the till and waved her goodbye.

I tried to get the whole encounter out of my head that evening, flicking through countless TV channels, looking in vain for diversion, but I couldn't get my mind off her proposition and the events that had brought her to my door. I stayed up much too late and took a whisky nightcap, but it didn't help. That night I dreamt I was immobile, tied up in a coil of slimy rope on a dark, freezing mountain side. I tried to free myself but as I did so, the rope sliced through my fingers and then on looking down I saw I had no legs. I screamed and a bearded man appeared, dressed in mountain-rescue red. He picked me up and carried me gently to a cliff edge, before tossing me into the blackness.

I awoke with a start and sat up, hands tightly clenched. I was soaked in sweat and my quilt was twisted tight around my legs and torso, like a shroud. I threw it off and went to the kitchen for water. It had been many years since I had had a nightmare about the incident, but now the events of the past were rushing back through my brain, like the southern wind that gripped those Andean peaks.

I let Lottie back into my bedroom for company. She jumped up beside me and with a yawn, stretched out and closed her eyes. Her calm was infectious and I drifted off. I slept fitfully for another few hours but as soon as there

16

was a hint of daylight, I stumbled downstairs. Lottie wasn't happy to be woken up and readied for the outdoors, but perked up once the door was open and the scent of the mountains came flooding in. We passed through the snicket at the side of the house and into the lower field behind. The sheep were on higher ground, so I let her run free. She was sharing my torpor though, and chose to trot alongside me, with the occasional half-hearted sniff of a promising rock.

I felt a real urge to climb high and escape the confines of the valley and within an hour we were on top of Mynydd Perfedd, horribly ill-equipped, but at that moment I didn't care. I sold safety every day, but it was overrated. If the weather was out to get you, no amount of gear would help.

I sat, looking down at Llanberis in the distance, thinking back to the Andes. It had been the effective end of any real mountaineering on my part; the conclusion of an all too short career. Whilst Doug had gained everything from the incident, I had had almost everything taken away. And when the taking looked like it could only end in my destruction, I had made a final retreat to here, the fortress of the Welsh kings. Here I had remained, undisturbed for two decades until now. Even those kings had been defeated eventually though.

The street lights had all gone off down below; I needed to get down to open the shop. It was a Monday, not normally busy, but first thing in the morning was the time to catch those early starters who had forgotten some vital piece of equipment. We trotted back down the narrow path together, Lottie leading the way.

I got back just in time to open up. The post had come early; the usual collection of bills, two of them red. I knew what that meant, but added them to the burgeoning in-

17

tray; I would deal with them later. Those idiots wouldn't leave their base in London, or wherever they presided. However, stocking the shop was becoming more difficult these days with a couple of the suppliers being difficult. I was hoping for a good summer. One good season would see them alright. But it was already August.

The early starters didn't come that day. The first time the door opened was after eleven, when an elderly couple came in to buy walking poles. They took a map too, but that wasn't going to cover the bills for the morning. The hours ticked by and I looked across at the window displays wondering if I should change over yet to some of the autumn stock. The weather had been proving fickle, perhaps a bit of rain would help bring them in?

However, looking through that glass just rubbed the truth in; there were few passers-by, particularly outside of the weekend. The shop had been a good little enterprise when I had taken it over, but the arrival of the internet and competition from chain outlets had hurt me, more than I wanted to admit. I still had loyalty from the local clubs and some regulars, but the game was changing, and perhaps too fast for me to last until retirement. In fact, retirement seemed an ever more unlikely scenario, at any age.

I looked over at the cork board. Her card, bright with embossed gold lettering, sat calling me, requesting my action. I went to pull it off the wall and throw it away but stopped myself. Maybe one day it would be useful?

The steady rhythm of my life ended two weeks later. It was eight-thirty on a Monday morning and I was eating my breakfast when I heard the staccato clunk of van doors being slammed shut. I stood and peered out of the window. There were two of them, in cheap suits and DM

18

boots. The driver was the older of the two, with a lightly trimmed grey beard and a shaved head. His associate was younger, but as heavily built. The driver picked a clipboard out of the car and started to make notes whilst his associate produced a camera to take photos of my car and the shop.

I cursed to myself and told Lottie to stay where she was. Their occupation was clear enough, who had sent them exactly, wasn't.

There was a loud banging on the shop door and I trotted downstairs, calculating what approach I could take. I wondered about slipping out of the back entrance, but when I glanced over to the door, I could see the silhouette of one of the men through the frosted glass.

I breathed in deeply, pulled up the shutter and opened the door. The boss was standing there. 'Yes?'

'Mr Darwen?' His accent was southern, a grating, Home Counties nasal twang.

'Yes, that's me.'

He handed me a thick brown envelope. 'Mr Darwen, we're here on behalf of SER Ltd, to claim settlement of their overdue invoices and to recover any surplus stock belonging to them.' He took a step forward, as though to force his way in, but I kept my hand on the door handle. 'May we come in? We don't need a public show, do we?' He cocked his head to one side and raised his eyebrows. His colleague had appeared at his shoulder, but said nothing.

'Hang on.' I shut the door in their faces and retreated back into the shop. I heard the letter box open, and the man's voice, 'We'll wait for you, Mr Darwen.'

I trotted up the stairs into my small office. The desk was strewn with letters, some open, some not. I grabbed a lever-arch file and leafed through to the SER invoices.

19

The last one was from over a year ago. The last paid one, that was. Maybe there had been others. I had been distracted and had got out of the practice of opening all of them. I had no idea what I owed them nor even if I had any of their stock left. I looked at my watch, 8:45, Sue would be here soon; I couldn't have her see this.

Once again, the sound of firm knocking on the door rattled up the stairs. I grabbed the phone and dialled my mate, Lewis, who ran the fishing tackle shop down the road.

'Lewis?'

'Craig, what's up? You been burgled?'

'No, why would you think—No, never mind. Look, um, I'm in a spot of bother. Owe a bit of money. They've sent some people round, bailiffs or something. God, I don't know what to do?'

'You faced a county court judgement?'

'No, course not.'

'Then tell them to fuck off.'

'What?'

'Tell them to fuck off. They're debt collectors not bailiffs. They've no legal rights. If you don't let 'em in, they can't do nothing. Can't touch you. Honestly, mate. Had some bother meself a couple of years ago—' More banging from downstairs, '—settled it with the company. Problem solved. You let 'em in and they'll strip your shop, believe me.'

'What about opening up?'

'Maybe better to have the day off, mate. Sorry, gotta go, got a trip going on this morning. Good luck with the bastards.' He hung up.

I drew in a big breath and returned to the front door. The two men had backed away, the boss was on his mobile, whilst his colleague had lit up. When he saw me, he tapped his boss on the arm and pointed in my direction. The boss mumbled something into his handset and then returned to the door. 'So do you have it, sir?'

'Have what?'

'The two thousand, three hundred and seventeen pounds you currently owe SER?' Each number was spat out slowly, as though he'd assumed I might have a low IQ or deafness that would prevent me understanding what he meant.

'No, I don't. Goodbye.' I shut the door and pulled down the security shutter.

'We'll be back tomorrow,' the voice shouted through the shutters.

I looked back into my darkened shop. I was going to have to do something. Get those finances in order. I needed some time, but I needed the shop open. No, those men would lose interest, Mondays were rarely busy anyway, I could lie low for a few days without it costing me. I had just enough time to catch Sue before she left her house. I called and told her not to come in, saying that I was planning to shut the shop for a week due to a death in the family. I could tell from her voice she was far from convinced, but I assured her that I'd pay her as normal and would get in touch when I was back.

I peeked out through the upstairs window. The boss was on the phone again, his partner on his second cigarette. The boss looked up and I pulled back from the glass, hoping he hadn't seen me. They climbed into the car and drove off, leaving the small car park empty save for my old banger.

I flopped into an armchair. My hands were shaking. I closed my eyes and leant back into the foam, asking it to support me. A moment later and a wet tongue was lashing my cheek. 'God, yes, Lottie. Let's get out of here.' That

21

would solve the issue of what to do, for now.

When I returned to the shop over two hours later, with a dirty but happy canine partner, Sue was sitting on the wall outside. 'Heard you had a visit?' she said.

'News travels fast.'

'Bad news faster,' she replied. 'Want to talk about it?'

I'd known Sue for over ten years. She had been my shop manager-cum-shop assistant since I had placed an advert in the local rag, after a particularly gruelling Easter weekend. Times were different then; Amazon had only sold books, not walking boots. She had been in her mid-thirties, with a couple of kids at the local secondary school. Her husband had walked out on her the previous summer, something she seemed less than upset about. The change in her life had come at a time when she was already looking for a new career direction, but had been struggling to find a role that fitted with her family commitments. 'Sick of kids,' she had said in explanation as to why she wanted to work in a shop rather than back in her chosen profession as a childcare assistant. As the only applicant who seemed to be beyond puberty, I hired her. We had got along very efficiently over the years. She had a relaxed, engaging and proficient manner with customers, and an eye for store layout. I had come to rely on her for much of the running of the business, but had kept the finances and stock ordering to myself. Of her social life, I knew little other than her kids had left home and she was seeing a man called Damon from Betws-y-Coed. Sue and I didn't socialise.

So, when we climbed the stairs to my lounge that morning, it was a new chapter in our relationship. I collapsed into the sofa and she took a chair by the table and looked down at me. 'You're skint, aren't you?'

'Yes,' I sighed. 'That's about the size of it.'

'I'll make a brew,' she said and proceeded to locate the mugs, tea bags and milk as though she lived there.

'I'm really sorry, Sue. I don't know how much longer I've got.'

'How much?'

'What, how much do I owe? Problem is, I've no idea.' I slowly stood up and went over to the office door, which I poked open with my foot. 'Take a look.'

She wandered over and stuck her head in. 'Oh dear.'

'That's the long and short of it. God, I used to be so on top of it. Sort of been sticking my head in the sand.'

'I had noticed, saw the takings down, saw you had stopped stocking Karibou—'

I tried to interrupt her but she held up her hand. 'It's alright, love, it's not your fault. Shops like this are going bust up and down the country. Bloody internet.'

'You realise I probably can't employ you…for a time anyway.'

She laughed. 'Don't worry about me, love. Think you've got bigger fish to fry. Let me help you sort this mess out.'

I tried to object, but she said, 'Come on, Craig! You helped me out when I was in a hole. I couldn't get work anywhere and you took me on. I've loved working here. All the interesting people—'

'Yes, some of them are certainly that!'

'Exactly, and the not so interesting ones. And I love Lottie.'

I'd never stopped to consider whether Sue liked working for me. She just turned up and did the job. We rubbed along, worked as a team. But her endorsement made me feel a little better. 'Do you know anything about finances?'

'Probably about as little as you, but I'm willing to get stuck in and see where we're at.'

'Thanks,' I said. 'Don't think I can bear to re-enter the cave.'

Sue spent the next three days working through the accounts. I couldn't recall an exact moment I'd lost control. For years I had run a steady ship, but over the past twelve months the bills had slowly mounted up. One by one, a letter at a time, a cancelled rep's visit, a freezing of credit, demands for cash up front, a tide building and building until it overwhelmed me and I turned my back on the hard reality.

After an initial reluctance to go anywhere near the office, as though it held a toxic substance that could strike me down, I slowly started helping. My overwhelming feeling was of embarrassment, then fear, then relief we were at least taking action. We phoned up the suppliers and got updated invoices, spoke to the bank and assessed the tax position. I avoided asking Sue for any sort of running total, but the final figure came soon enough.

It was every bit as grim an outcome as I had feared. I had managed to run up combined debts of over sixty thousand pounds, spread over a dozen suppliers. I owned the shop outright, I had that in my favour, but the business was rapidly heading towards bankruptcy. I had loans secured against the shop and it was only a matter of time before they were called in. My visit on Monday was surely the start of many.

Sure enough, the very day we finished going through the accounts, I received a call from the bank asking me to visit, along with a letter calling in my overdraft. I had a month to comply or they would take legal action.

I cooked tea for us both on the Thursday evening, doing my best to concoct a beef casserole complete with a salmon starter, as way of a thank you. Over a bottle of plonk, we talked over the figures.

'Unless you've got a rich relative, I think you'll have to sell the shop,' Sue said. 'I talked to a friend of mine, a bank manager—It's okay I didn't name you. Seems as though you could probably write off debts and rent the shop back off them and have enough spare cash to keep going.'

'But for how long?'

We went silent. The thought of selling my only real asset when I was ten years from retirement age was profoundly depressing. Sue broke the stillness. 'You do have one rich friend, don't you?'

For a moment I wondered who she was talking about, but then I snorted—him again. 'Hardly a friend. Just someone I knew once.'

'Come on, he talks about you in that book—'

'Didn't know you'd read it.'

'I bought it before I came to your interview—'

'It was hardly an interview!' I said. 'Anyway, how did you even know—?'

'Everyone knew, you idiot. It's a small town. And yes, to me it was an interview. It mattered and I wanted to know more about you and climbing generally. I remember it being inspiring at the time, but one of the boys said you didn't much like talking about it.'

My elbows hit the table as I put my head in my hands.

'You want to tell me about it, love? What happened?'

I flopped back in my chair. 'Truth is, Sue, I don't remember much. You know, I had this girl come into the shop, asking me about it only a few weeks ago. She's making a bloody film. Wants me in on it.'

Sue threw her hands to her mouth and gasped. 'A film?

Craig, that's wonderful! How exciting! Why didn't you tell me?' Then she read my expression. 'Tell me you didn't say 'no'?'

'Told her to piss off. What right they got, raking over the past?'

Sue frowned. 'Sorry, love, I don't understand? I read the book, you got nothing to be 'shamed of.'

I took a swig of wine. 'She wanted me to recount it all on camera. Can't remember a thing about it, just get the odd nightmare, that feeling of cold and pain... When I came back from that place, I swore I'd never climb again. Needing rescuing like that. I don't even remember the accident. It's like a blanket came over my head half way up that mountain, blacking it all out. Then I woke up in hospital with some nightmares for company. That book didn't shed much light, neither.'

'So, you sell outdoor gear and teach climbing?'

'I couldn't do nothing and climbing was all I knew. Got into a bit of bouldering by myself, but partnering, no. A climber with an aversion to rope. Ridiculous! I know, bloody pathetic. I've made myself join that club, sell the gear, instruct and belay on the climbing walls, but mountaineering, forget it. I don't want to trust someone else and no one should have to trust me. Partners can let you down.'

'You didn't let anyone down?'

'Let *him* down, didn't I? Now I've let you down.' I spread my arms. 'Look, I'm in this little flat above a bankrupt shop with my sole, loyal employee who I need to lay off.'

Sue said, 'Craig, you gave me a job when I had no hope and you've been the best employer I could have wished for. Don't be frightened of help and support. You need to take that film offer up. Answer to a maiden's prayer. How

26

much were they offering?'

'Forget it, I'm not going with a begging bowl to anyone, least of all him. And no, I don't want to talk about it anymore. Spent years forgetting it.'

Sue looked at me pointedly. 'Listen, love, you could lose everything here. You need investment. I think you should consider it. The money could clear these debts at the very least.' She took my hand and with a softer voice said, 'Come on, and with that publicity, you could get on the internet, niche a bit more, there's still plenty of customers, you could be driving around in a Merc?'

'What have you been reading?' I asked.

'There was a lady in the Mail last week, made a fortune selling jewellery online from her lounge. Got her whole family working for her now! Come on, you could use your reputation, make a go of it.'

'I'm too old.'

'Don't be defeatist! I'll help you and don't worry about my pay; I can get by for a bit.' She stood up and put on her coat. She laid her hand on my forearm and said, 'I'm sure you'll work something out. You've survived worse.' Then she kissed me lightly on the forehead. 'I'll see myself out.'

As I watched her descend the stairs, I felt a prick of a tear in my eye at the thought my days of working with her had surely all but come to an end.

I couldn't sleep that night. I lay in bed staring at the ceiling, trying to see a way out. Of course, there was perhaps a solution, but it was unpalatable. I didn't want to trek around film locations, I didn't want to go over that accident, but most of all, I didn't want to be reunited with *him*. But as the hours ticked by, the inescapable reality of my situation became harder and harder, and my attitude towards working with Sarah softer. Maybe the film's pay-out would be enough to get me through this hole, she had said 'six figures' after all? With that amount I would never have to see him again. I had no interest in being up on the big screen, but maybe the brief fame could give my shop a lift as well. We could do some marketing off the back of it, set up a website perhaps, like Sue had said. Across the room on a bookcase, his book, *The Empty Rope,* sat nestled amongst a motley collection of novels. I hadn't opened its pages since that first read but it had remained on a shelf in my bedroom as a narrow, paper reminder of what had happened. I was in no rush to open it again.

And yet, at four a.m. I climbed out of bed, turned on the light and padded over to the bookcase. I picked the book off the shelf but didn't open it, instead nestling it in my hands. Other than for the edges that were tinged a light brown, it could have been new, such was the pristine condition of the cover. The front showed an abstract painting of the Fitz Roy massif, whilst the back had blurb about Doug's heroism under a vanity shot. I didn't re-read it but instead pulled out a holdall and tossed it in followed by a random collection of travelling clothes. I descended the stairs into the shop and pulled Sarah's card from the cork-board.

With one email, one set of problems ended and another began.

CHAPTER THREE

It was a week later when my Ford Fiesta pulled into the late-afternoon heat of the *Aire de Bonville*, a truck stop a short hop from Chamonix off the A40. It had been a long and tiring journey, through an overcrowded England, over the Channel to Calais and, following a sleep in a lay-by, south and east through the autoroutes of France, my wallet lightening with every *peage*.

Chamonix lies in the west of Europe's Alps, within France but close to the border of Switzerland to the east, and Italy to the south behind Europe's highest mountain, Mont Blanc. It's the proximity of this peak that has made this small town the home of Alpine mountaineering, a magnet for climbers from all over the world who come to sit in its cafes whilst only a few miles from them men and women test their bodies to the limit against rock and ice.

And now I was nearly there for the first time in a quarter century. I parked up and wandered into the prefab cafe where I bought a coffee and croissant. I felt like shit, my body ached from the hard seat, I was sleep deprived and for sure no one was going to brave my B.O. to take up one of the plastic seats anywhere near me. Despite being late September, it was unseasonably hot, and the smog seemed to glisten in heat above the black tarmac outside.

I sipped my coffee slowly. The time to turn back had passed me by, not so much on boarding that ferry but months before when I had started to ignore the red headed post piling in through my door. I had been in trouble for a long time, I just hadn't faced it. I hadn't liked Sarah's approach but she had offered me and my business a lifeline I couldn't refuse. I looked out of the grimy window through the haze to the foothills beyond. This was the edge of the Alps; I'd soon be at my old home. A couple of truckers were smoking outside sharing a moment before mounting their cabs to go onto Switzerland or Italy. They were probably keener to get on with their professional journeys than I was with mine. My croissant was crumbs and my coffee, dregs. It was time to go.

I only travelled a few miles down the road before pulling into another rest area. The motorway had swept through the lower hills to suddenly reveal Chamonix's main attraction. Mont Blanc sat in front of me, a monolith of white and black, its lower slopes hidden behind lesser rock. It looked harmless; a simple, gentle, if long climb. Distances can be deceptive. The last time I had been up there I'd had to abort, albeit not on my account. It should have been easy, but back then I had a partner and you were only as strong as the weaker climber.

I rummaged through the glove compartment to find the address of my hotel. I had printed out some directions to an underground car park behind the Aiguille de Midi lift. Sarah had arranged it all, I just needed to get down there. I had refused her offer of a flight, fearing it limited my means of escape. At least the hotel promised to be a luxurious stay away from whatever the filming involved. Sue was minding the shop and Lottie in my absence. I had been promised this first meeting would only take a week whilst talking heads were captured and my advice was sought. That was all, one week. I put my car into gear and set off once more—no more stops, no more procrastination.

The hotel proved easy to find and I wasn't disappointed on entering the wide, marbled reception area. A sleek, besuited receptionist, Marcel, took my booking, with a smile. Behind me, stylish euro-couples passed by wearing embroidered bathrobes, on their way to the spa. I hadn't packed any trunks.

Marcel smiled at me. 'Your first time in Chamonix, sir?'

'No...But it's been a while.' It was probably before he was born. He passed over the inevitable form to fill in, at the bottom of which was an eye-watering day rate.

Seeing something in my complexion, or perhaps the hover of my biro over the signature box, Marcel said, 'I believe the bill is being covered by your employer?' He rustled through some documents out of sight below the desk and removed a letter. 'Yes, SummitSeeker S.A...Sign here.' He pointed to the box and I dutifully filled it in.

'Merci.' He slid a crisp, white envelope, marked with a familiar logo, across to me. 'Sir, you were left this message.'

I tore it open, to reveal an embossed card.

'Hope you had a good journey. Meet me at the Le Republique this evening at 7:30pm and I'll brief you. Sarah xx'

I looked at my watch; I had less than two hours. So much for my quiet night in to recover.

A quick shave and shower later, I crossed the Place de l'Aiguille du Midi and the gushing grey glacial flow that was the River Avre and entered the Rue du Dr Paccard, home of Chamonix's shopping centre. I felt myself smile as I passed old haunts. Many of the restaurants and shops had changed hands, as was inevitable in the time that had gone by, but the sense of a small slice of Switzerland within France remained; if anything, the opulence had increased. My pace quickened as I reached the Place Balmat. Here was the shop where I had first learnt my trade. In the 1980s it had been a fiercely independent climbing boutique, ruled over by the indefatigable

31

Alberto. Arriving there, I was disheartened to find just another glass-fronted designer outlet stuffed with overpriced labels. At some point it had been defeated by the march of the chain stores, like so many others. I felt a small glow of pleasure that my own enterprise had somehow managed to outlive it, before reflecting that perhaps its owner had sold up and was now living in luxury on the shores of Lake Geneva. I walked on.

Le Republique was a large, modern restaurant which sprawled out across one side of the Place du Mont Blanc. As I looked for an empty table, the meeting point struck me as a bit odd. It was a tourist hot spot, jammed with families with young children mostly, stuffing steak-frites and cokes down their sunburnt faces, efficiently served by the young staff. Hardly the stylish bistro I would have expected her to frequent. At least my early arrival suited me as I wanted to lay eyes on my companions before they saw me, as though that could give me a small amount of control.

I was not sure if Sarah intended for me to eat before or after we met, but my appetite was light, as my insides tightened at the prospect of my forthcoming encounter. I selected a table inside and as far from the entrance as possible and ordered half a litre of 1664. I made short work of that and a second was soon weaving its way to my table. The drinks did little to calm my anxiety which was increasing by the minute. My mind raced with the prospect of the briefing. I knew nothing about film-making, how long I was required, the whats and the wheres—

'Craig!'

I almost knocked my drink onto the floor as the greeting rang out. It was bang on 7:30 and Sarah was crossing the restaurant, her mouth set in a wide smile. She was wearing a sleeveless summer dress, with her hair flowing loose over her tanned shoulders. Her passage between the tables was closely watched by a number of the fathers, eyes straying from their toddlers' bad behaviour. One cast his envious eyes over to me, before his wife tapped his arm.

I stood and held out my hand in a greeting, but she pulled me forward into a hug and kissed me on the cheek. I mumbled an 'of course' then quickly hoped she had not heard me.

'So, how was your journey? Can't believe you drove! All that way in this heat!'

'Thought I would make a bit of a holiday of it,' I said, sitting down. 'Gave me a chance to revisit some old haunts on the way.'

'Well, I'm glad you came and agreed to join our project!' She reached into her handbag and pulled out a couple of tickets, dropping one in front of me. 'Your timing is perfect, we've got a little excursion tonight, to give Doug a surprise.'

I frowned and picked up the card. *The Empty Rope*, a talk by Doug Swanson. 8pm, August 31st 2015, Salle des Alpinistes, Chamonix.

'That's right, he's giving one of his talks here, tonight. Thought we could surprise him by sneaking in the back. You could heckle.'

I looked up. Her eyes twinkled conspiratorially.

'It's some sort of little fund-raiser he's doing for the mountain rescue team here. Think he likes to keep in with the French. Village politics, that sort of thing?' She was speaking at a volume most of the room could hear, and she still had the attention of a few of the other tables. I wanted to move on.

'Where is this place?' I asked.

She smiled again. 'Across the square.' She nodded towards what looked like a bookshop. 'They do lectures upstairs. Nice and cosy.' She held her hand up to summon a waiter and ordered herself a beer. Her voice then dropped and she leaned towards me. 'Got one question to ask before the big meeting; why did you change your mind?'

'Oh, fame, glory?' I tried a smile.

'No, really?'

'Um, I don't know. A weak moment I suppose.' She would never know just how weak.

She sat back. 'Oh well, thanks again. I mean, we could do it without you, but it would only be part of the story and, well, it would have been a real hole to fill.'

I hadn't been described as a hole before, but I nodded and sipped my beer. 'How's the film going?' I asked.

'Awesome. We've shot most of Doug's commentary and a lot of close up climbing. Still got the big stuff to do though. Your timing's great.'

We descended into small talk about the town's hotels. From the sound of it, she wasn't a fan of the French way of doing things, and had already encountered some of the legendary rudeness within the hospitality industry, who were nearing the end of a tiring high season.

At ten to eight, she tapped the table and said, 'Ready?'

I nodded.

CHAPTER FOUR

The Salle Des Alpinistes, turned out to be a large first floor function room with its own ground floor entrance. A signboard outside listed the talks, films and plays the location was used for over the season. Life for it seemed to stop on October 1st. Sure enough, Doug's talk 'The Empty Rope [Anglais]' was listed for 8pm tonight. We showed our tickets in the foyer and went up the stairs.

I let Sarah push through the double doors on the landing above and I ducked my head as we took up back row seats. The room was like a smart village hall, set out for about a hundred people sitting on folding chairs. At the front was a low stage with a large screen across which was projected a classic image of the beautiful granite pyramid that had changed our lives, gleaming against a crystal sky.

The room was already crowded with a collection of climbers, both vicarious and real, some dressed for the occasion as though they had just descended Mont Blanc. I was grateful there was no sign of Doug. I slouched low, then felt Sarah's hand on mine. 'I know this is hard, but don't be nervous.' I pulled my hand away and sat up straighter, feeling a little patronised.

'I'm okay,' I said and that was the end of the conversation.

At eight o'clock prompt, a young man stepped onto the low stage and tapped the microphone. He spoke in French, with what I understood to be a welcome and an apology the talk was only in English, then said, 'Ladies and gentlemen thank you for coming tonight to hear from one of our most loyal supporters, and probably the only one we have not had to rescue!' A ripple of polite laughter broke around the room. 'Our speaker tonight needs no introduction. A mountaineer, author, entrepreneur and resident of our beautiful town. Today SummitSeeker Outdoor Equipment has offices in ten countries and a turnover of fifty million euros. They sell to climbers, theme parks, emergency services, and the military. All this success started from humble beginnings here in Chamonix and we are ever grateful he has chosen our little town as his residence.

'Tonight, Doug will tell us the story of how it all started. Looking around, I'm sure many of you have not only read his books but dangled from one of his harnesses. Doug is going to tell us the story that established his reputation—The Empty Rope…And I have heard a rumour…' he paused and searched the audience, before fixing on Sarah, 'that he is about to turn the book into a film!' He raised his hands and clapped, with the audience joining in. A few faces turned to see the young lady beaming beside me. I sank low in my chair.

She whispered into my ear, 'He wasn't supposed to say. Last thing we need is crowds following us around.' But she carried on beaming, enjoying the first critical reaction to a film that was still in its genesis.

'Ladies and gentlemen, Doug Swanson!'

The applause resumed as a figure stood up from the front row and bounced onto the stage. He turned and looked out across us, blinking in the stage lights. I surveyed my old friend for the first time in two decades. He was small, that hadn't changed, nor had the wire of his now grey hair, curling around his ears and neatly cut to project an image of stylish outdoorsman. He wore a black polo neck, a poor choice in my view, as it revealed the start of a belly probably from too much claret and not enough climbing. His face was heavily tanned, etched with thick lines, like crevasses on a glacier. These didn't mask the thin scar that ran down his left cheek; it was a souvenir, a badge of honour, an advertisement to others to trigger him to recount this story. His wrist sported a chunky watch, a Rolex probably. He was still handsome, but those looks were in retreat, like the ice we had once crossed in the valleys above.

I glanced across to Sarah. Her smile had disappeared, replaced by a look of intense concentration, as though preparing to hear the story for the first, and only, time. Doug's eyes darted around the room, and they paused briefly as they passed across us, but he made no sign of recognition. That was Doug, always the professional.

He began to speak.

'Mesdames et Messieurs thank you very much for allowing me to speak this evening in aid of a charity very close to my heart. Thank you to the Alpinist Club of Chamonix for hosting this talk.'

Behind him the screen lit up with a beautiful vista of impossibly steep golden granite spikes cutting into the blue cloth of the sky.

'Mount Fitz Roy, ladies and gentlemen. It's not the highest mountain in the world, anything but, sitting at a mere three thousand, three hundred and seventy-five metres, five hundred short of our local friend the Aiguille du Midi which you can ascend by cable-car! It isn't the hardest to climb, the furthest south, the coldest. In fact, there is a long list of what it is not. But to my mind, what it is, is the most beautiful peak in the world. We will never know who first laid eyes on this wonder, but the Argentine explorer, Francisco Moreno came upon it in 1877 and named it after the captain of Charles Darwin's Beagle, Robert Fitz Roy. It has a distinctive outline that is instantly recognisable to any who have ever seen it and to those who have viewed my wonderful slide collection.'

Doug paused and grinned, flashing a set of perfect teeth, letting us know this was a joke, that he wasn't really that vain. I looked around at the enraptured audience. Every seat was taken, by the young and old, tanned tourists and indulgent locals alike. I wondered how many times these people had read or heard this story, but whatever the number, he had them captivated already.

'The peak was first conquered on February the second, 1952 by Lionel Terray and Guido Magnon, fellow Frenchmen, who had made their name climbing the mountains that surround us tonight. They ascended the south-east ridge, which is regarded as a celebrated conquest given its isolation and the technology of that decade. Since then, many have topped the granite spires, though fewer do each year than summit Mount Everest.'

The slide show clicked to an image of a much younger Doug with curly locks in front of the Fitz Roy spires. I recognised the photo. I had taken it.

Doug continued. 'The nearest village to the Fitz Roy Massif is El Chalten. These days it's a town, with restaurants and lodges, but back then, it barely existed, with a single hotel, the Hostal Laguna Sucia, to stay in. The ride there was bumpy and slow and the weather worsened, so by the time we arrived, we seemed to bear the brunt of a full storm. Our driver laughed at us, "This is good weather! Welcome to Patagonia!" '

He explained that the only other guests at the Laguna Sucia were a recently married couple, Bob and Cassie Green, from the United States. They were on a three-month extended honeymoon, trekking and climbing their way around South America. However, during the trip Cassie discovered she was pregnant forcing a change of plans. Bob now had to conquer the Franco-Italian route solo. This route was the first successful ascent of Fitz Roy and whilst simpler than some other routes, would be a serious challenge for a solo mountaineer.

Doug put a map up showing Fitz Roy with routes overlaid. Our route came in from the west, Bob's from the east. The lines were short, over contours that were so close together as to merge into a thick line.

'When we arrived at El Chalten, they'd been there a week already, waiting for a break in the weather. Bob had conquered Fitz Roy a couple of years earlier in a team of four but now had plenty of solo experience and a detailed plan laid down. Craig and I had one ear as to whether we were likely hinder him, or vice-versa, but other than starting from the same town, our routes had nothing in common.'

The picture of the hotel was replaced by one from the inside of his book, and it made Sarah sit up. It was of three young men, smiling in the sun. It was probably one of the only photos of the three of us together.

We all looked lean and fit with beards grown through lazy disregard for our appearance. The third man stood slightly apart from Doug and me, who had arms across each other's shoulders. He wasn't wearing sun glasses and his hazel eyes seemed to bore down the camera lens, through the projector and into me. Doug and I were here in this room, older and heavier. This other man would never have that privilege. I shifted uncomfortably in my plastic chair, which had suddenly begun to feel a whole lot firmer. Doug was going to have to get into the difficult bit. The reason all these bums were on seats.

'Here's Bob, Craig and me on that morning, raring to go. We took provisions to last us a fortnight, the majority of which would be stowed at the Fitz Roy base camp. Bob and Cassie decided to join us until they needed to split off for his route. She was planning to camp at the base and watch him, something that sounded far too nerve-wracking for me. I wasn't to know at the time how grateful we would be later for her courage.'

Yes, Cassie, where's your clothing brand, your outdoor equipment stores? I checked my thoughts; I was letting bitterness get the best of me. It wasn't Doug's fault that only he had prospered from these events.

'The walk to Fitz Roy is one well worth taking. When we reached Lago de Los Tres, the small glacial lake at the base of the Torres valley glacier, we set up camp. Cassie and Bob had left us a few hours earlier, with shouts of 'Good Luck' and promises to meet back at the hotel in three days' time. The weather had chilled right off and the clouds were now teasing around the peak. We were aching to get going, but decided to spend the next day surveying the routes.

'This evening, before I came here, I had a look on-line at the routes now listed for Fitz Roy. There are thirty-one, probably more. Some are incredibly technical and daring, many have been climbed solo. In 1990 there had been only a handful of ascents however, and most were climbed on fixed ropes. Whilst this gave us a great opportunity to break new ground, it was also intimidating. There was a real possibility we could find ourselves hitting a dead end, or overreaching ourselves technically. However, we had two powerful weapons—youth and overconfidence!' Another image appeared of a young Doug sprawled in a snowdrift, a huge grin on his face. A snow fight long forgotten.

'The next morning, we woke up to the sound of rain on the tent. It wasn't what we wanted but we were short of time so decided to carry on and ascend the glacier, hoping for an improvement.

'Our plan was to start up a route called the Supercaneleta,' he said. 'This is regarded an ultra-classic, a route created on the second ascent of Mount Fitz Roy in 1962. It's a huge chimney that rises 1600 metres up the west face of the mountain. We picked this because at the time it was the only one known to be climbable alpine-style, rather than with fixed ropes. However, we intended to follow a variation up an adjacent crack that spurred from the top of the chimney up to the summit. We naively saw the variation of splitting off the route and heading directly to the top as a combination of the best of the old but with a new challenge.' In the background the west face of the mountain was shown with our planned route marked in bright red. A view that was burned into my memory.

'Crossing the glacier was where we left any semblance of being tourists, or trekkers, behind. We donned our crampons, clutched our ice axes and felt firm ice beneath our boots for the first time. I was a rock climber first and foremost, not happy with ice climbing where I could avoid it and Craig was the same. However, we were hoping, perhaps naively, the amount of ice climbing required at that time of year would be minimal. We had incredibly limited information, compared to the realms of reports that can be easily accessed over the internet today, but had learnt that in the summer the route was predominately a rock climb with some frozen waterfall sections. Patagonia being Patagonia though, flaky, slippery rime ice is always a problem for those of us who like our rocks dry!

'Where the glacier joins the rock is what is known as a bergschrund, a meeting of the ice and the rock. Crossing this divide can be tricky, but on that evening, we found an established traversing point close to the base of our route.

'The drizzle persisted through that day and we set up

41

camp in a shallow cave. We stripped down our gear to the minimum, stashing spare food there, either to be consumed whilst waiting for a window, or on our return. Craig broke out a pack of cards and so began the first of many games of contract whist.

'That night the winds picked up. We were well sheltered but could hear the gusts howling over the glacier below. Our trips outside were kept extremely brief and we were soon wearing all our layers as we huddled in our sleeping bags. We joked the weather was sure to be better higher up.

'Once again, Mother Nature did a complete about-face overnight and we awoke early to dazzling sunshine beating across the glacier. We ate our porridge and mapped out as much of our route as we could see. We had nothing like the detail or even climbing anecdotes we were used to from the Alps, but we felt very prepared.

'And then we were off. Weather windows were notoriously short at Fitz Roy, so for speed across the easier sections, we simul-climbed, that is we moved together, one of us placing protection and the second removing it whilst also climbing up the rock. It isn't the safest method, that's true, but sometimes time is the main enemy. We alternated the lead and as we grew more confident, extended the time between changing pitches by drawing out our use of protection. The weather held all that morning and we ascended quickly. The climbing was beautiful, with exhilarating views, which only got better. I believe that morning was probably the most enjoyable few hours of climbing that I've had; challenging, but not too technical, with views unmatched anywhere. By two o'clock we'd reached the junction of the Supercanaleta and our direct route to the summit. That was when we hit our first problem.

'I was seconding Craig and found him eating a cereal bar on a wide ledge. He was scanning the rock wall above with a puzzled expression on his face. 'Do you think that's it?' he asked. I checked my altimeter. We were now at about the altitude we should have been leaving the Supercanaleta but I hadn't been paying attention to our progress, waiting instead for the call from Craig. He was right to stop and take stock though, we didn't want to miss our chance to add a small piece of history to Mount Fitz Roy's route-map.

'I sat down and joined him in staring up at the rock. The crag which had looked like a certain route for us wasn't obvious. 'What do you think?' He nodded towards the only possible gully, veering at ninety degrees from our line. It was in heavy shadow, and so I couldn't make out any detail about what lay inside. I checked our time. We still had enough to comfortably make it to the top and back to a bivvy point before it got dark. We were an hour ahead of our schedule.

'Our route notes were very brief and shed no light on whether this was our target or not. So, we set off, Craig leading and me seconding. I think I knew we'd bitten off more than we could chew early on. The gully was almost vertical, narrow and packed with rime-ice which was flaking away in Craig's hands as he climbed. We didn't climb together, but I belayed him from a static point, unsure of how he would progress. As he moved, chunks of ice and rock rained down the gully. After fifteen minutes or so, he tied himself in and called for me to climb. It was every bit as bad as it had looked. The rock quality was atrocious compared to the superb granite we had ascended on up to that point. I have to confess to being very slow on that first pitch, and also not being totally convinced by some of the protection placement I

43

encountered—Craig had clearly been struggling to find suitable cracks and had run out of camming devices for the larger holes that peppered the face.'

Not convinced by the placements? My fist clenched.

I stood up, whispered, 'Excuse me,' to Sarah and without waiting for her permission exited the room. Outside the air was cool. A couple walked past, swinging a tired toddler between their arms. The sun had gone down and the town was growing quieter. A ripple of laughter came from the room above, something in the accident was clearly amusing. I walked away, down the Rue du Dr Paccard, back towards my hotel. I'd feel better after a good night's sleep.

'Craig!'

I looked back to see a red-faced Sarah. She had run after me and was panting from the exertion.

'Come back. Doug's expecting you!'

'Sorry, just a bit tired.'

'I know it's hard, it'll be better once you catch up. Sorry, I shouldn't have sprung that talk on you.'

A breeze tugged at my collar. The temperature had dropped fast since dusk. How I longed for bed. 'I'll be fine tomorrow. It's been a very long day. You go back, I'll see you tomorrow.'

Sarah stood for a moment then put her hand on my forearm. 'It's okay, Craig, you'll get to say your side of the story. I'll make sure of it.'

I looked at her expectant face. She really didn't understand me at all. 'I'm sorry, it was rude of me to leave.'

'You coming back then?'

I sighed. There was no point in delaying the inevitable. I nodded.

'Thanks,' she said and took me by the arm, perhaps to prevent me making another bolt for it.

We walked back to the hall and quietly entered again at the back. Doug was still speaking.

'Craig and I travelled back to England two weeks later. The experience transformed my life. I had come close to death but had survived and I realised how serious a business mountaineering is. It transcends the notion of a mere sport. It can lift the spirit to incredible heights but can also destroy it. I had to take what had happened and use it as a positive experience, one that would shape my life, not allow it to destroy me. I vowed to carry on climbing and to make some bold decisions. I got engaged, founded a company and set to improving on the equipment I had been using—I had tested it in an extreme situation and it had been found wanting. I knew I could use my experience to improve upon it. At that time, I had no idea of how successful SummitSeeker would become, but I also had lost any fear I had previously had of going into business. Coming close to death and surviving had given me that chance.

'Thank you all very much for coming out tonight and for listening. Fitz Roy these days is much more accessible but still a formidable challenge. Since we climbed, many more have lost their lives on this beautiful rock. The weather is still as bad as ever and the rock is as steep, but maybe there is someone in this hall who will sit on top of it one day. Thank you.'

I breathed in deeply, feeling my heart race. Before me was not one, but two encounters I had been avoiding for the last twenty-five years.

CHAPTER FIVE

When the applause had died down, and Doug had taken a selection of easy questions, he made a pitch for the mountain rescue charity the event was supporting. It was a presentation guaranteed to put the faint-hearted off climbing for life, full of stretchers being winched up to helicopters and orange bodies being carried down through fields of scree. Then, following a final thank you from the organiser, he retook his seat, ready to sign copies of his book, T shirts and post cards.

The audience began to disperse, as the host clucked away packing up and thanking Doug, until eventually only myself and Sarah were left. When the host had finally gone, Doug came marching down the aisle.

'So, Sarah, you really did manage to tempt this reprobate to take part in our little project. Craig, it's so good to see you!'

I stood up slowly, feeling every year of my age, but unable to check the smile that had appeared, unrequested, on my face. I made to shake his hand, but he grabbed it and pulled me into a bear hug. 'Craig, Craig! Why has it been so long? It's crazy, man. Linda will be delighted to see you. C'mon, let's go for a drink!' He stepped back and looked at us both. 'Yes?'

I said, 'Sorry, Doug, I'm bushed. Great talk by the way...brought it all back. I need to go back to my hotel—'

'Sod your hotel, man! You're both coming over to ours tonight! We've plenty of space. I'll give Linda a call, she'll be thrilled to see you, we weren't expecting you until...' He tailed off, then said, 'Well, we weren't sure, what with everything, but...well, it's great!' He put his arm around my shoulder and steered me towards the door.

46

In the foyer he turned to Sarah and said, 'If you don't mind sorting old Craigy-boy out, I'll motor on back up to the ranch and let the lady know.'

Our orders had been given. Doug turned heel and almost jogged out into the street, to wherever his Bentley or Mercedes would be parked.

Sarah turned to me. 'You'll love his house. I've been staying there since we started shooting.' She looked up the street to where a 4x4 was pulling away from the kerb, then said, 'He's what they call a "force of nature," isn't he? Was he always like this?'

I cast my mind back. 'Yes, I think he was.'

Half an hour later the little convoy of my Fiesta and Sarah's small hire car, drove into the drive of *Valois*, Doug's less-than-humble abode. It had transpired he lived a good half an hour outside of Chamonix, above the Swiss village of Finhaut (for 'tax reasons' according to Sarah), set away from the tourists; their hotels and shops, restaurants and gondolas. Sarah had offered me a lift, but I didn't want to be dependent on her or my hosts for transport; I might need to escape. So I went back to my hotel, retrieved my bag and car then followed her glowing tail lights out of the town.

The Chamonix sprawl ran the length of the valley; empty ski chalets and concrete apartments thrown across the former farm land. Somewhere amongst them, at Argentière, were my former lodgings; a cheap boarding house shared with a collection of casual workers from around the continent. It had been scattered with ropes and climbing gear, half unpacked suitcases and a permanent odour of drying clothes, but it had been home. Perhaps I would look it up whilst I was over here.

We continued east, climbing up to Vallorcine and

across the border before rising out of the valley floor, through thousands of winding feet of tarmac. Sarah drove aggressively and I struggled to keep up, with tyres squealing at each switchback turn. To one side was a plummet into a vast, dark gorge, its bottom invisible in the night-time. I hated to imagine what this journey would be like in the depths of winter, but perhaps that time was spent on a yacht?

I parked up next to a pair of Range Rovers and stepped out onto the gravel. Away from the pollution of the valley far below, the cool mountain air was heavy with the scent of cedarwood and pine. There was none of the dampness of the mountains of my home.

'Did you enjoy that?' Sarah said as she climbed out of her car.

'I'm sure it's very scenic in daylight,' I replied. I stood back against the car, not wanting to step away across the gravel. Despite the challenging drive, my heart was beating faster now than it had all evening.

The lodge was built into the side of the mountain, with the parking and entrance at the top. It was an ultra-modern construction of timber (no doubt sustainable) and steel, lit up tastefully in welcome to us. From where we stood, I couldn't see how many floors it was spread over, but the number was surely greater than three. Sarah took hold of my elbow. 'Come on, Craig. You'll love it here.'

White lights marked out the edges of the pathway and guided us to the heavy wooden door. I put my hand up to rap the chrome knocker, but before I could do so, the door fell open and there was Linda.

For a moment we stood, staring at each other.

Sarah broke the silence. 'Hi, Linda, I guess Doug warned you?' Linda looked surprised as though she hadn't noticed the young woman was there.

'Oh, yes.' Her trance was broken. 'Craig, so lovely to see you. It's been such a long time.' Her voice had climbed a social class. Gone was the south Manchester lilt, instead there was estuary English. In so many ways she had changed. Of course, she had aged, we all had, but it was an affluent ageing. The years had been good to her; the chestnut pony-tail had been replaced by a fashionably short ash-blonde bob, with a fringe accentuating her beautiful eyes. The jeans and T shirts had been supplanted by designer chic and the gentle oval face had gained some weight and a natural tan. However, there was a sadness too; I could see it, if only through a prism of wishful thinking.

I kissed her on the cheek. 'Good to see you, Linda.'

Two large hounds bounded out to greet me.

'Oh, shoo!' she said, trying to grab them. 'Sorry, you don't mind dogs do you?'

'Love them. Missing my collie already.' I leant over and gave them both a scratch behind the ear. 'I can see yours are equally useless as guard dogs.'

The hounds ran back into the house, tails wagging.

She led us downstairs to the lounge. Sarah took a seat on one of the large, leather sofas, whilst I gave myself a tour of the exhibits. The second floor down was almost entirely open plan, with a huge glass vista looking out over the valley. For now, we could just see pinpricks of light marking out the wealthy inhabitants on the other side, and car headlights spinning back and forth like fireflies.

The walls around us were set out like a trophy cabinet of conquered peaks and awards. There was a framed copy of that book, a suited Doug shaking hands with someone, then pictures of down-jacketed, goggled mountaineers, arms raised in triumph. Of family and kids there was no trace except for one studio picture of a younger Linda, with arms draped around Doug's neck. It was the most artificial image of them all.

I felt Linda standing next to me. She spoke in a low voice. 'We've got a lot of catching up to do, haven't we, Craig?'

'I'm not staying long,' I heard myself say.

'That's a pity.'

'Guys!' It was Doug, announcing his entry. He clasped a bottle of Bollinger in one hand and four glasses in the other. 'This calls for a celebration!' Champagne flutes soon clinked and bubbles fizzed. We flopped into the deep leather, smiled, laughed and commented on the joy of being together. Sarah and Doug dominated the conversation with talk of the timetable for shooting the film, the youngsters who were playing us in the climbing scenes, and anecdotes about the film crew. But it was the silent Linda who I was interested in. She sat on the sofa close to her husband, a sacramental unity, and laughed dutifully at the showman's jokes. However, her glances stolen towards me told a different story. At some point, we would need to talk, in private.

Linda popped in and out, and after a while called us into the dining room. The wonderful scents that had wafted in from the kitchen turned out to be from a delicious venison stew. The conversation meandered onto to the joys and stresses of alpine living, the strange customs of their Swiss neighbours and his 'small' yacht on the Med. Of the son Doug had mentioned in his talk, there was no word. Perhaps it had been a piece of poetic licence, but I chose not to ask.

Doug waited for a clear pause in the flow to pounce. 'So, Craig, how's the business going?' His question was at once concerned and patronising under a mask of innocence. He had probably credit checked me that very afternoon.

'Great thanks, not like your empire though.'

'Ah,' he smiled, 'but no doubt without its stresses and strains. I envy you, a nine to five lifestyle in my favourite Snowdonia.' Proprietorial, even with my own county.

I forced a grin. 'I don't remember seeing you in Snowdonia?'

'Really? No, I suppose it's been a while. We've got too comfortable in our alpine hideout, haven't we, Linda?' He squeezed her hand and she nodded. 'But I, we're, hoping this is the start, the rekindling of our friendship. I'm dying to hit those walls with you again, Craig.'

Did he mean climb with him? That wasn't part of the plan, surely? I started to gather my words to say something to this effect but was silenced as he raised his glass. 'More bubbly? It won't keep!' He seemed to be single-handedly ensuring this wouldn't prove a problem to concern them the next day.

'We could use a silver spoon,' Linda said.

'Tosh!' Doug stood up and refilled Sarah and my glasses. 'No space in the fridge for half-drunk champers!'

Linda appeared to suppress an eye-roll, then said, 'Let's move back to the lounge. Coffee anyone?'

'No thanks,' I said; a caffeine hit was the last thing I wanted.

'A whisky then?' He was already heading for the drinks cabinet. He started to pour two large glasses out. 'Sarah?'

'Oh, no thanks, Doug. Not my thing.'

'Bourbon?'

'No, really. We've got an early start. I'll take a de-caf, Linda?'

It didn't look like I had permission to duck out, and a crystal glass was thrust into my hand. 'Fifteen-year-old Laphroaig. I had a share in the barrel.'

The liquid burned down my throat as I sipped. Doug collapsed into an armchair and a footstool rose under the weight of his legs.

'So, Sarah, I've never asked. What got you into film-making?' Linda said as she re-entered with a couple of steaming mugs.

'Well, my mom, really. We used to do these treks out, you know, to the backwoods and she always had her camera. Always going for that shot—wildlife mainly, but she sure loves the outdoors still. Probably out in some hut up a mountain right now.'

'What about your dad? Doesn't he mind?'

'Oh, mom brought me up. Never knew him.'

There was a pause, then Linda said, 'I'm sorry about that, but it sounds like your mother more than made up for it.'

'Yeah, she did that alright.' Sarah smiled. 'She's great, I'm sure you'd love her.'

'Oh well, maybe we'll meet her one day. At the premiere perhaps?'

'Maybe.' Sarah smiled and sipped her coffee.

I stood up. 'Sorry, but it's late. Long journey and all that.' I grabbed my bag.

'You can't leave all that whisky, Craig! Come on, we have catching up to do!' Doug said.

'No, you're very sensible, Craig. I'll show you your room.' Linda pulled me up by the hand and we descended pine steps to a lower tiled floor and a guest room that wouldn't have been out of place in a five-star hotel.

'It's good to see you, Craig. Really.'

'You too, Linda.'

'We'll catch up tomorrow.' She gave me a small peck on the cheek and then was gone, her footsteps light on the boards. I stood, watching her ascend, wishing the twenty-five years back again.

I tried my best to sleep, it should have been so easy given the exhaustion of my long journey. Perhaps it was the whisky, the heat or the unfamiliar, dry air, but each time I closed my eyes, pictures of mountains and howling winds reappeared as they had not done for decades. A number of times I got up and paced the cool tiled floor but I couldn't go off. I unpacked my clothes and tossed the book onto a desk which was neatly laid out with pen, paper and blotting pad as though expectant of a visiting author or businessman.

Eventually I gave up the fight and crept back up to the empty lounge. The huge windows showed the same scene, though with even fewer lights now visible across the deep valley. I was alone.

'Craig?'

I spun around. Linda was standing at the door wearing heavy pyjamas.

'Sorry. I couldn't sleep,' I said.

'Is your room not—?'

'No, nothing like that. It's great, far better than the hotel down in the town and that was good. No, probably the whisky—never did agree with me.'

'Oh.' She flopped into one of the deep armchairs and nodded towards the windows. 'Not a lot to see, is there?'

'I'm sure it's beautiful,' I said, taking a seat on the sofa. 'Done well for yourself.'

'Yes,' she said, though she sounded unsure. We sat there for minutes, staring out at the white dots of headlights carving through the darkness on distant hills.

'I didn't ask, Craig, is there someone in your life...?' Her voice tailed off.

'You mean a Mrs Darwen? No, no one like that. Just

53

my dog.'

'Ah, I'm...sorry. I mean that you haven't found someone.'

I had found someone, years before. Only she had left me for someone else. But I didn't want her now feeling sorry for me. 'Oh, don't be. I've seen people. Just not met that special one. I'm happy, Linda.' I then remembered something from the talk. 'Doug mentioned a son in his talk—football matches?'

Linda looked blankly at me and shook her head, 'No, we...You must have misheard him.'

'Yes, of course.' I hadn't misheard, but perhaps he had been talking metaphorically? I wondered if that had been a decision or fate. Either way, it was none of my business. She stared at me as though deciding whether to say something more. I remembered her sitting like that in my student flat, feet curled up under her thighs, so many years before.

'What are you up to these days?' I asked.

'Oh, this and that... I work in the local tourist information, helping hikers find somewhere to hike and skiers somewhere to ski, that sort of thing.'

'Using your geography degree?'

'Well, not exactly... But it gives me something to do. Helps with village life.'

The silence returned for a moment. I asked, 'Do you ever climb?'

Linda laughed. 'No, no, 'fraid those days are long gone. I leave that to you boys. Not sure I've done that since we last met...Gardening is more my thing these days, oh and the dogs.'

'Oh... well I suppose much the same for me.'

Linda fixed her eyes on me, then leaned over and patted my hand. 'I don't think so, Craig.' She yawned and stood up. 'I'd better get back to bed... Don't want to be missed.'

'Yes, sorry if I woke you.'

'You didn't.' She threw me a tired smile and left the room. I walked over to the windows and once more looked out into the blackness of the night.

In the morning, I awoke to the sounds of heavy footsteps criss-crossing on the floor above, as though a team of police were searching the room. Sounds of French and English voices drifted down the stairs, but it was the delicious aroma of fresh croissants that got me dressed.

The voices were coming from a cavernous room hollowed out into the hill, illuminated by large skylights.

'Ah, Craig!' Doug looked up as I entered, a broad smile across his face. 'Meet the troops!'

The room was full of people, with Sarah as the only other familiar face, Linda being nowhere in evidence. A large mahogany table was strewn with maps, clipboards, binders spilling out paper and photos, as well as iPads and a laptop. Amongst the stationery was a transatlantic mixture of muffins, croissants, orange juice, and coffee.

Sarah pointed at a plate. 'Help yourself, welcome to chaos.'

Doug chuckled. 'Don't believe a word of it, Craig; Sarah is the most organised American I have ever met.' He winked at me, then raised his voice. 'People, without this man, you wouldn't all be standing here. The climber who taught me everything I know. The great...Craig Darwen!'

I felt myself redden under the scrutiny of ten faces, but was rescued by a giant of a man, stood at the head of the table. 'Hi Craig, I'm Piotr, Sarah's D.O.P.' He resembled a James Bond assassin, with the slicked back blond hair, muscular physique and East European accent to match.

55

'Better known as the chief cameraman,' Sarah said, 'as is Mike, he's his assistant.' She pointed at a younger man, who looked hardly old enough to have left school, let alone shoot a film. 'Lloyd, he's A.D., Ruth, Production assistant...' The list went on with the little crowd nodding, saying hi, then returning to their croissants and the subject matter on the table, '...and Rick, he's director.'

Rick was in his fifties, moustache, grey hair and a runner's build. He came round and shook my hand. 'Glad to have ya on board.' Another yank, but with a nasal, Californian accent. 'Ya had us worried we were goin' to have to write you out.'

I smiled, not sure if he was serious or not. 'I'm sure it'll be fun,' I said.

'No, making a film stinks like a pile of rhino shit. It destroys your life. Fun it sure ain't. But relax, ya just need to do a little talkin' and you can fly on home and wait for the red-carpet night.' Rick remained deadpan and all I could do was nod.

Doug slapped Rick jovially on the shoulder. 'You'll get used to Rick. Sarah found him, he's the best. Let's give them a few minutes to sort out what they're doing.'

'What *are* they doing?' I asked, as Doug led me into the lounge.

'Planning meeting. There's a tight schedule and the crew like to meet up here, away from the actors, each morning...You know, get into the groove.'

'Lot of people.'

Doug laughed. 'Oh, this isn't half of them. Seem to have half a valley full down there. And that's only the first unit; wait until we meet the second unit in Patagonia.'

I blanched. 'Patagonia? I thought—' And then I realised I hadn't really thought anything. Nothing beyond earning some money and getting back to my shop whilst some of the summer season remained. I was familiar with the talking heads thing, maybe I had thought a couple of days would do it. But a couple of days wasn't going to repay sixty grand. The money—we hadn't had that discussion. Now didn't seem like the time.

He looked into my eyes. 'Don't worry, you won't need to climb, but they want us on the original set, to take us back there and to see us tell the story in that wilderness.'

'I need to get back to my shop, just got cover. And my dog…'

'Craig,' he patted my shoulder, 'don't worry about your dog. With the money we'll make on this film, you'll be able to buy a thousand dogs.'

Before I could explain the problems with that statement, we heard Rick's raised voice. 'Okay, boys and gals. You know what you're doing? It's the big shots today, the chopper eats money. Remember, best behaviour with the princesses. Don't want any tears before bedtime. Let's get down there.'

Doug nodded towards the door and said, 'C'mon, come and see a bit of Hollywood in the making.'

I followed obediently as the team filed out to a collection of 4x4s they had arrived in, and got into Doug's immaculate Range Rover. It was probably worth more than my house, judging by the interior cream leather and state-of-the-art gadgets. Doug frowned as I sat down. 'Sorry, Craig. Do you mind?' He nodded towards the window; Sarah was walking towards the car. 'The lovely Sarah and I need to talk things over. Curl up in the back and have a rest. Thanks, mate.'

I felt the heat rising up my neck but dutifully moved to the back seat making way for the young producer. I reminded myself of the money; focus on the money, that was the only reason I was there. The sooner we got this over and done with and I got back home the better.

As we set off, Sarah turned to face me. 'So, Craig, what do you think so far?'

'I was hoping you could tell me a bit more about what the plan is? I could do with letting my cover know when I will be back.'

'Sorry, Craig, it's all been such a rush since you turned up and I didn't want to bore Linda with it all.'

'Yeah, she's heard enough about it,' Doug said with a chuckle.

'Can I be back next week?' I asked.

'Um…Got to be honest, Craig,' in my experience, that phrase usually preceded a lie, 'we're a bit behind schedule.'

'Bloody weather, poncey actors,' Doug said.

Sarah gave him a playful punch on the arm. 'Behave yourself, mister.'

'Okay, poncey climbers.'

They both laughed.

'How long then? Sorry, what is the schedule?'

Sarah said, 'So we were hoping to wrap up all the close-up climbing shots in Chamonix this week. Just got the accident left to film and a bunch of helicopter shots, but the weather hasn't been playing ball with us. We've got some of the interviews with Doug but we need to capture yours and then—'

'We go to Patagonia,' Doug interrupted. 'Free holiday in lovely Argentina. You and I are filmed re-walking our footsteps, then we shoot a whole load more distant climbing shots with some speedy climbers down there and we're done. It was deemed too difficult to film the whole thing there. Dodgy weather, remoteness, poor facilities— sure you remember. And why pay the money when you have perfectly good rock at the end of a local cable car?'

I was going to say they had never mentioned Patagonia,

but I realised I had asked nothing and so could be surprised by nothing. I sat back in my seat. I had nothing to rush back to, only Lottie and she was being well cared for. I just had to put up with this, play along and collect the cheque at the end, then I would never have to see these people again, nor talk about the bloody accident.

'So where are we actually off to this morning?' I asked as the convoy joined the valley road and turned west.

'You'll like our film set; I think you know it...'

The Petite Aiguille Verte; yes, I knew it well. My first test of Doug to see what he was made of. A little, accessible mountain, but a mountain nonetheless with its own foibles and challenges. We drove down the winding road, a noticeably less daunting experience in the daylight, and back into France and Argentière. On the way down Doug explained today's shots involved a helicopter taking high views of the climbing, and as such was very expensive. It was the first time I had heard him talk about money.

We arrived at the large Grands-Montets cable car car park at nine am to find it already crowded with trailers, vans, a few hatchbacks and people hurrying around carrying black bags and metal poles. Above us the large gondola was climbing up the steep valley wall, a sight not usually seen in the off-season.

Doug saw where I was looking. 'They opened it especially for us. Bit easier than hiking up there.'

I nodded towards the packed parking spaces. 'Is this all your crew?'

Doug grinned and nodded. 'Welcome to Hollywood.'

More like the circus coming to town, I thought. So many vehicles in the name of filming two men on a lonely mountain-face.

The car park, that in winter would be rammed full of

59

skiers, would normally have been empty in October, and even only lightly populated in the summer. Only the piste maps and ski hire office served to explain its scale. It was a scene that couldn't have been further from the wind-blown slopes of Patagonia.

As Sarah jumped out of the car, Ruth, the production assistant, ran up to her, her face flushed. A brief excited conversation followed and they marched off towards one of the trailers, collecting Rick on the way. Doug frowned and we followed in their wake.

Inside the trailer there was a commotion. The Winnebago was the size of a small house but was already packed with a number of the crew whom I had met at Doug's house, as well as others who I did not recognise. All seemed to be talking at the same time in raised voices.

'Okay, shut it!' At Rick's command the trailer went silent. 'Now, what the fuck's going on?'

'This bloody shit gear! You risk our lives!' The speaker was a young Frenchman, lean, tanned and fit, the archetypal climber. He was dangling a climbing harness in front of him. 'Why are you making us use this shit?' Behind him was sitting another climber, almost a clone of the first. His arms were crossed tight across his chest and he was nodding in agreement.

Rick glanced around the room. 'Right, everyone out. Sarah, Doug; you stay. The rest of you, get on with setting up.' No one moved, apparently entranced by what was happening. 'Go! We have choppers in two hours, we need to be in position. Go! And shut the door behind you.'

With that command, we all dutifully left, with me wondering what on earth it was all about.

Piotr stepped out behind me. 'Bloody prima donnas,' he said. 'Always have to be the centre of attention, even when not on camera. Surely, we could do better than those idiots? Hope you're not going to be like that.'

'What's going on?' I asked.

'Oh, you wouldn't have expected climbers to be obsessed with health and safety, would you...Well maybe you would? Seems stuffed full of pompous show-offs.' He looked at me. 'Sorry. These guys answered an advert in *Climber* magazine. They're acting you and Doug.'

'I'd gathered that,' I said, still none the wiser.

'Well, Doug's supplied all gear for the film. Latest stuff, all properly safety tested. We were told it was the best, no one going to question the great Doug. Apparently though, the climbers aren't happy with some of it. Say they're not product testers.'

I was bemused. I didn't know much about film-making. Nothing, in fact. But I did know about gear and one thing I knew was that serious climbers liked to use gear they trusted. Safety was everything. Of all people Doug and I understood that. Gear had saved my life and now we made our livings selling it. Professional climbers loved to test new gear; they gained bragging rights when they were offered the first samples from a big brand like SummitSeeker. But to force climbers to try out new products they weren't used to, whilst making a film? Well, it made little sense. These guys would have their own gear for sure, stuff they trusted. It seemed unnecessary, and risky.

'Maybe there is a misunderstanding?' I said. 'He's not using prototypes, surely?'

Piotr cocked his head and appraised me. 'Why do you think he's making this film?'

'He was asked, wasn't he, like me? The book—'

The trailer door burst open, and Doug, Rick and Sarah marched out, with the two climbers in tow. Rick pointed at Piotr and jerked his thumb for him to follow.

'Sorry, got to go. Catch you later.' He rushed off to join the party who were climbing into a black truck, further down the car park. It screeched off in the direction of the cable car station.

I was left wondering what Piotr was hinting at. Surely a studio had asked him to make the film of his book? What other reason could there be?

The door slammed shut as Doug jumped into the Range Rover, shaking his jacket off. 'Well, that was a fucking disaster, wasn't it?'

The rain pounded on the windscreen as it fogged up. Above us, the mountains were cloaked in mist, obscuring all but the lower reaches.

'I'm sorry,' Sarah said.

'You're sorry? We're all bloody sorry, c'mon, Sarah, you know how much this thing is costing.' He pulled out a hip flask and took a swig.

I saw Sarah put her hand on his knee. 'Oh, Doug. Don't get mad, these things happen.'

'Yeah, but they don't all cost fifty grand,' he growled. 'Sorry, don't mean to take it out on you.' He squeezed her hand before she quickly withdrew it.

I sat in the back, like an infant whose presence had been forgotten by his parents.

We had all gone up in the cable car that morning and everyone had got into position for the grand arrival of the helicopter. But then the clouds had lowered and opened up on us, drowning the prospect of the aerial shots and shooting for the day, but not before the chopper had been in the air, burning money. We had shivered, pulled our hoods up and then retreated back to the station before admitting defeat. I did wonder why Doug was so bothered about the cost. Surely Fox, or Universal, or whoever, was picking that up?

'It's not as glamorous as they make out, that's for sure,' Doug said as we pulled away.

'Don't worry about the money, you'll get it all back, and more,' Sarah said as we drove off.

So, Doug had put money in. A few questions I didn't even know I had were being answered.

It was time for some naive questions. 'I thought the studios paid for this?'

I saw the muscles tense in the back of Doug's neck. Sarah answered for him. 'Not at this stage, Craig. We have a group of investors. Once it's done, we'll put it into the festivals and one of the distributors will pick it up. That's how you do independents.'

'You'll get paid,' Doug growled, clearly reading my mind better than Sarah had. But it sounded like the money was more tenuous than I had realised. I wished I had signed a contract, but I couldn't bring myself to ask for one now. Maybe later.

When we got back, I went downstairs to get out of my wet clothes and shower. I was surprised by a knock on the door, not long after I emerged. I opened the door, hoping for Linda, but it was Doug, wine glass in hand. He pushed past me into the room and shut the door behind me.

He sat down on the bed and put his hands on his knees. 'I think we need to talk, Craig, iron a few things out.'

I nodded and took a seat.

'I realise this is all a bit new to you…'

'What?'

He looked sideways. 'Film-making, that sort of thing.'

'But not only the film-making?'

'I suppose so.' He walked over to the window and

63

stared out. 'Okay, I realise we didn't part on the best of terms. Not on your Christmas card list. I know that. I'm sorry about what happened.'

'The accident was a mess.'

'I don't mean about the accident and you bloody know it.'

I did. He meant Linda. But I wasn't going to admit I cared, not to this man.

'You've done well for yourself,' I said.

Doug snorted. 'Well enough. Can't buy everything though…'

He turned to look at me and leaned back against the wall as though I was threatening him.

'Let's cut to the chase. You need the money.' He held up his palms. 'You're right, I've done well for myself, and I'm sure you're happy with your life…And I don't want the boat rocked. Things are going well right now. Film coming out, new products, we're winning the market and all that. Linda and I….Well, that's another story. She's been good to me, but… things are a bit tense right now.'

'What's this got to do with me? As you said, I'm just here for the money, then I'll be gone,' I said.

'Bloody northerner, always calls a spade a spade, eh? Well, I know you and Linda were close—'

'Doug, what the fuck's this about?'

He glanced away. 'You might hear things, see things, I don't know. Everyone's under a lot of stress right now. Let's just get the job done and you can go home.'

'Or I won't get paid?'

He finally looked embarrassed. He took a deep gulp of wine. 'That's harsh, Craig. Who do you think I am?' I didn't respond, it would have been ugly. 'Do it as an old friend. For old times, yeah, even if not for new?' He had regained his composure. 'Play ball and we can all get on with our lives. I'm sure this will do wonders for your business as well as mine.'

'I haven't actually got a contract, Doug, and Sarah never mentioned me flying to Patagonia, surely—'

He stood up and patted me on the shoulder. I was that child again. 'Don't worry, it will all be sorted. Good chap. Dinner's at eight.' And with that he left.

It was pizza for dinner that night, brought up from the village below through driving rain by an unfortunate delivery-man.

Linda put her head around the lounge door. 'Wet day then?' she asked, with a smile.

I followed her into the kitchen, where she began to unpack the pizzas onto a tray.

'Sorry about the cuisine, not very "haute" tonight.'

'It's perfect, thanks.'

She looked up at me. 'How was today? Did you enjoy the filming?'

'Not really, if I'm honest. I was a bit of a spare part and the weather was foul.'

'Like Doug's mood?' She cocked her head to one side and met my gaze. 'I'm not sure how much he's enjoying it. It was supposed to be his big project but—'

'I thought it was Sarah's?' I said. She frowned and started to parcel out the food. At that moment Sarah walked in. She wore skinny jeans and a polo neck and looked straight out of a clothing catalogue for all that.

Linda glanced up and smiled. 'Oh, sorry, I didn't offer you drinks.'

'Really, Linda, you shouldn't be putting yourself out. I bet you'll be glad when we've all skedaddled.'

'Not at all.' Linda avoided eye-contact with either of us as she reached for a couple of wine glasses.

'I'll stick to something soft, thanks,' I said, but Sarah opened the fridge and helped herself to an open bottle of Shiraz. Linda excused herself and went to call Doug.

Sarah appraised me over the top of her glass. 'Nice lady.'

I sucked in a breath. 'Yes, she is. She hasn't changed. Doug's very lucky.'

Sarah took a slow sip of the wine and sat down at the kitchen table. 'Doug's under a bit of stress right now, Craig. He needs your support. You know that, right?'

'I'll make the film and then go, don't worry.'

'I'm not worried, Craig. I know you will. We just wouldn't want any domestic issues to throw things off-course.' She raised her eyebrows, as though I were the transgressor.

At that moment we were rejoined by Linda and Doug. Doug had showered and changed and appeared considerably more relaxed than when he had paid me a visit. He patted me on the back. 'Enjoy today, old man?'

'Foul weather up there,' I said. 'What's the forecast?'

Sarah stepped in. 'The rain has come in so we are going to switch to doing the talking heads up here. I'll be interviewing you, but my voice will be on the cutting room floor. It'll just be you telling viewers how it was. Doug, you might want to take some time out.'

Doug frowned. 'Really—can't they shoot anything outdoors? Doesn't that mean a lot of dead weight sitting around? It'll be bloody snow soon and that would really foul things up.'

'No choice. Rick called me up twenty minutes ago. We've got rain for a week; the choppers will be useless. Best to use the time and get Craig done.'

That sounded good to me, even if she made it sound like a chore for her.

66

Doug walked over and poured himself a large glass which he downed in one. 'I ought to call Rick.'

'Don't worry, I've got it all covered. You relax.'

But Doug didn't seem relaxed now. He frowned and stared into his empty wine glass. 'I could do with a few days back in the hot seat, I suppose. Shouldn't leave Martin running things too long, may go native.'

'Martin?' I said.

'He's second in command at SummitSeeker and I'm sure he's doin' just fine,' Sarah said. 'You stay on set. You deserve to see this thing through after all your hard work. Martin would call if there was trouble.'

'I don't know, Sarah,' Linda said, 'Doug has always run a tight ship up there. Surely a few days off wouldn't hurt?'

'Those bloody R&D issues—' Doug added, but then he raised his eyes and remembered I was there.

'I'm not sure I'll be a lot of use with these interviews, Sarah. Can't recall a lot, you know that,' I said.

She looked over to me. 'Don't you worry, we'll lead you by the hand through it. All you have to do is say what happened. We'll do the rest in edit. There'll be some repetition, for sure, but we'll lick it in a couple of days. That's all Douggie took.'

I saw Linda grimace at the moniker, but she held her tongue and thrust a plate at her rival. 'Help yourself, Sarah.' She doled out the other plates, took some pizza and walked out of the room. The other two seemed not to notice, with Doug still mulling over something and Sarah giving me her attention.

'I should probably have read the book, genned up, you know,' I said.

'Oh no, quite the reverse, Craig. We want your recollections. Doug's story was fine from him.'

Doug seemed to wake up at that. 'Wear your best shirt,

a million people are going to see it.'

I stuffed down my pizza in the kitchen and excused myself. Doug and Sarah had started talking over the film schedule once again and Linda was in the lounge watching TV. Downstairs, I sat at the small desk and picked up the pad of paper. Perhaps if I started writing, more would come back to me. More of what I remembered, not what Doug had written in his book. My mind, however, was a blank. I stared at the wall for ten minutes and scribbled a few notes about Chamonix, Calafate and the hostel. I looked down. It was pathetic, how could I remember so little, even after hearing his recollections?

My copy of *The Empty Rope* sat on the desk next to the pad. I didn't want to read it, but perhaps its photos might inspire me? I opened it up and froze. Across the first page, in a blood red pen, was written 'Liar!' The hand was unfamiliar and on flicking through the following pages, there were no other marks. I glanced around the room, and opened the wardrobe as though the vandal might be standing there, red pen in hand, grinning at me. But I was alone; just me and the book.

CHAPTER SIX

I picked up the book and turned to the events that had made me walk out of Doug's talk. It was time to confront them.

The Empty Rope, by Doug Swanson, Chapter Five

We started to climb up our new route, our little piece of climbing history. Craig was leading, being the more experienced climber in what we knew would be a big challenge. And a challenge it was. Almost immediately we hit problems; the quality of the rock was terrible, crumbly with cracks packed with rime-ice. Stones and ice-shards rained down as he climbed, not only from his boots but also onto him from the canyon above, as the ice thawed out.

His first pitch took about fifteen minutes and then he tied in and I started to climb. It was as bad as it had looked. I was already tired and very slow, climbing right at the limits of my ability. Some of the protection that I removed as I climbed looked very dubious and I doubted would have stayed in place on a fall. Craig had clearly been struggling to find good placements and was short of the camming devices that we needed for the large holes.

However, when I finally reached him, exhausted, he wasn't checking out the next pitch but was staring out across the valley. 'We need to get a move on,' he said, nodding at something. I tied myself in and turned around. I saw instantly what he was looking at. Wisps of clouds were surrounding Cerro Torre's almost impossible peak, and behind it, cumulus pillows were rising over Chile. Even as we watched, they grew higher and darker.

We made the decision to simul-climb again. We weren't familiar with the way the weather moved in those mountains, but had seen enough alpine weather to know how quickly things could change, and Fitz Roy had a reputation all of its own. And that's where it went wrong. We had made two poor decisions, firstly to leave the Supercanaleta and secondly to simul-climb up a dangerous, uncharted route.

Craig took the lead once again and initially moved quickly up the rock, allowing me to follow. However, soon I felt a shower of small stones and ice raining down on me. Curses rang down from above. I called up to Craig, but he was at the height of concentration, placing gear. He called back something about 'shitty rock'. I wondered whether to stop and belay, but looking back across the valley, saw how the cloud was rising. It was touch and go whether we would make the top before it reached us.

We climbed on and our luck held for maybe fifteen minutes, it's impossible to be sure. My confidence had returned, as I could see Craig near to the top of the gully. I was halfway up when I encountered a small piece of protection, a hex, that was well off the route. Good placements were clearly in short supply. I called for him to stop while I leaned out and disconnected the quick-draw, and then tried to tug out the device, but it wasn't budging. I took out my nut-tool and tapped away, but the device was well stuck into the crack. I tapped upwards harder and harder and suddenly it yielded. Somehow the momentum tipped me off balance and I slipped. I careered across the gully like a pendulum and smashed against the opposite rock wall, this winded me, before I swung back again. The rope jerked and I dropped further, spinning in space, my nut-tool fell from my wrist and clattered down hundreds of feet. For a moment, I hung there, in shock, unable to steady myself. I was slowly rotating as the rope uncoiled itself.

Finally, I regained composure and started to try to get a hold on the rock. I called out as I did so, but heard nothing back. I looked up but was rewarded with ice particles showering down into my face. I managed to grab a hold and pulled myself into the rock face. I climbed up to a tiny ledge in the edge of the gully feeling a huge relief as I recovered my balance. I took out a nut, hastily jammed it into a crack and clipped myself in. I was safe, for now at least.

I checked myself over. My face was wet, and putting my hand to it, I realised it was not just ice, but blood too. Probing with my fingers, I felt a gash across my cheek. I was bruised on my left side too, but nothing more serious. I called out to Craig a few more times, but could hear no reply. I tugged on the rope, but he didn't respond. It didn't take an expert to know this was not a good sign.

And so, I did the only thing I could. I climbed up the gully, removing protection if possible, but leaving anything that gave the slightest argument. As I climbed, the tension remained on the rope, without me taking it in. Either Craig was climbing, or he was a dead weight.

That tension suddenly relaxed when I was near the gully top. The climbing had been hard and messy, I wouldn't have won any prizes for style, nor thanks for the amount of gear I had left behind. What I saw though on reaching it, confirmed my fears. Craig was lying on a narrow shelf, some ten metres below me on the other side of a flake of rock, across which the rope was running. He was clearly unconscious, and in a precarious position. Had it not been for that shelf, he would have dropped a metre for every metre I gained. I cursed my stupidity at not tying the rope off sooner to prevent his fall, and this is what I did immediately, without any surety of my next move. The wind had picked up now, and outside of that gully we were both exposed to it as it rattled around the mountain. The sky had darkened too. There was no doubt a storm was imminent. I remember my teeth chattering, not from the cold but from an intense fear I had never felt before. I realised right then how reliant I'd been on Craig—he had been the leader, the trip had been his idea, he was undoubtedly the better climber but here we were with me having to rescue him.

Once I had tied off the rope to make him safe, I took out my rope and abseiled down to the ledge, calling to him repeatedly, hoping he was alive and conscious. My thoughts were scrambled, I couldn't process the situation we were in. How had we gone from such a fantastic and safe morning to this mess? I think I said at least one prayer, probably the first since I had left primary school. The answer was a roll of thunder.

But to my relief Craig was breathing when I reached him. I took some deep breaths and reminded myself of distant memories from a mountain first aid course. He was clearly unconscious. Though we were both helmeted I could see he had taken a blow to the side of the head, where there is less protection. Blood was dripping out onto the ledge even as I stood not knowing what to do next.

The first drops of ice-cold rain woke me up. Getting off that mountain, by myself, with an unconscious partner might be almost impossible, but perhaps he would come round, and improve our odds. Looking around, I couldn't see anywhere better to camp out. So, I set up our tiny tent on that ledge and pulled him inside. It took me what felt like an hour and by the time we were in, the sky was black and the tent was being buffeted by the wind and fierce volleys of rain or hail. I don't think I've ever been so scared as I was at that moment. I was totally exhausted and all but beaten. I couldn't afford to try to brew up in the tent, it was too cramped, but whilst I ate a cereal bar, Craig suddenly and quite unexpectedly, opened his eyes. I had kept talking to him, wishing he would come around as I put the tent together, but more in hope than expectation. He mumbled gibberish then passed out again. I tried to get some water down him, but it was useless.

However, this moment made me pull myself together and really assess what I could do. My altimeter said we were at about 2700 metres. In terms of kit, we each had a pair of skinny lightweight sixty-metre ropes, food and water I could stretch to a couple of days, a small stove, sleeping bags and what remained of our climbing gear. Somehow, I needed to abseil us both down the face and get him to safety.

Whilst Fitz Roy is a challenging mountain, famed for its steep faces, this did have a small advantage. That is, the most difficult thing to do with an unconscious mountaineer would be to traverse across the face with him. I figured perhaps I could knot the ropes and abseil straight down and minimise the traverses. If I left him there, he would be dead. Perhaps he would come round. His gash looked nasty, but that brief moment of consciousness had given me some hope.

The storm continued all night. I didn't sleep, though I was sorely in need of it. I tried to picture how I could get down. Tried to remember the Supercanaleta pitches we had come over. Were there overhangs, traverses? Craig drifted in and out of consciousness, sipped water I offered him, but never seemed coherent. It was clear he was not going to be able to belay himself down the face.

Morning came eventually and with it the storm relented. I must have drifted off to sleep for part of the night, perhaps catching ten minutes at a time before the wind shaking the tent would wake me. The daylight was a relief. I shook Craig gently and he muttered my name. He was barely lucid but was still with me. I opened up the tent to find inches of snow covering the ledge and our gear sacks. I had decided what I would do. Craig was in a bad way, and I wasn't great; I was cold, wet, tired and shivering constantly. We had insufficient provisions to last more than a few days even without Craig's injuries. I brewed up and tried to get some of the hot tea down Craig hoping it might rouse him, but he took little in. We needed to get off the mountain as fast as possible. I pulled Craig from the tent and packed up the gear, then tied our ropes together, with stop knots at the end. I attached him to me with a sling and tied the belay device above us, through on another sling, so that he hung free of me. I then made sure the protection was good and set off down. I had estimated the number of pitches I had left, and I figured I had enough gear to be able to ditch them as we descended and to get down.

It was exhausting work. The first pitch went better than I could have hoped, though the weight and poor positioning was difficult. However, as each pitch went on, I grew more and more tired and my hands became numb. I had added a prusik below the belay, to slow control my descent, but moving it became more and more tedious, and as ice formed on the rope, I wasn't sure it was helping. Halfway down, the weather worsened once more. A gale blew in from the west, then came a wall of hail and snow. I began to grow careless, and on one pitch had to re-climb to release a trapped knot. I cursed myself, Craig, the weather, the mountain, everything. I swore I would never set foot on a mountain again if I survived.

When I finally reached the end of the chimney, I was too exhausted to celebrate. The danger was far from over, but perhaps the worst was past. However, now we were off the vertical sections I knew I was incapable of traversing with Craig's dead weight. I needed help. I packed Craig into a fluorescent orange survival bag and promised him I'd be back.

The wind had dropped but a mist had descended obscuring any landmarks I may have picked out to navigate against. I set off to find our route across to the glacier. It seemed to have entirely disappeared, replaced by an endless crevasse. I was totally exhausted and so when I stumbled across our cave, where we had slept in what seemed to be a century before, I took shelter.

I woke the next morning to find Cassie Green reviving me with a brew. Bob hadn't returned and, given the storm, she was extremely worried. The weather had cleared and she had spotted Craig's orange survival bag from down below on the glacier. She had climbed up searching for Bob, at great risk to herself, and had rescued the frostbitten Craig then followed the tracks to my cave. She must have been bitterly disappointed not to find her husband but she never let on. I'm eternally grateful to her that she found us, but it's a tragedy that Bob has never been found to this day.

Cassie stayed on the glacier, caring for Craig and hoping against hope for her husband's return whilst I made my way back to the hostel to get help.

I never went back to the mountain. The Argentinian military ultimately rescued Craig and flew him up to a hospital in Rio Gallegos, whilst I recuperated for a week. Craig had suffered some frostbite in his toes and on one of his hands, and had a fracture to the skull. The medics were amazed he had survived. I was luckier and got away with little more than exhaustion and a scar. Cassie was brought down off the mountain a week later, practically dragged down, according to the hoteliers. She and I shared one miserable dinner together. She had the grim task of dealing with the Argentinian police over Bob's status. I wish I could have helped her, but she was getting far more valuable support than I could have given, from Marco and Rosa who ran the hostel.

Poor Cassie. I needed to stop feeling sorry for myself; she was the real loser in this story. I thanked Doug for reminding me of this. I wondered what she was doing now? Maybe she did a lecture circuit in whatever place she lived in, recounting her story, after all she had ultimately rescued me and Doug. Somehow though, I doubted it; after all, it wasn't her gear hanging in my shop.

I'd find out soon enough just how right I was.

CHAPTER SEVEN

The next morning found me sitting in front of a green screen in a downstairs meeting room that had been turned into a studio. Bright lights shone down from two sides and two cameras pointed at me, to allow different angles to be used in the film.

I had stayed up making notes but then had slept badly, trying to remember as best as I could what had happened, what had led to all of this. Of all the places in my mind, Patagonia was one I least wanted to revisit. So much had changed since before we set off on that trip, and yet so little since I returned.

Sarah sat on a high stool in the shadow of the cameras. She was to be my interrogator, not Rick, who had also disappeared for a few days with the majority of the crew. 'He's an outdoors sort of guy,' Sarah had said by way of explanation. But I wasn't sure, I thought she wanted to do this herself. Just her, Piotr, a makeup woman, and a lad who was some sort of dogsbody.

'So, Craig, this is how this works. I'm simply going to ask you questions and you talk. This is about you and Doug. No one else. We want you to tell it how it was. Everything. Don't worry if you think it's irrelevant or repetitive. Let's get it all out there. We'll probably need retakes, but that's for later. We want your memories, not Doug's. We need perspective, that's why you're here. Forget about Doug, forget about Wales. Let's go back to 1990. Feel free to add a bit of poetry in. Spice it up.'

'Spice it up?'

'I don't mean lie. Say how you felt. Emotions—it sells the film.'

Emotions. They were none of her business.

I started to talk but she interrupted. 'Sorry, Craig, hang

on.' The clapper board came out and we were away.

1989—Chamonix, France

Craig hung the last of the head torches on the rack. He stepped back and appraised them. They were all aligned perfectly, as Alberto always insisted.

He looked down from the mezzanine across the shop floor. The display stands were now full of lightweight rain gear, hike boots and camping equipment. The winter left-overs, not shifted in the spring, were stored, ready to sell in three months' time. But now it was all about sunshine and summer tourists.

It was nearly his lunchtime, and a precious half hour of freedom. The others, the French, liked to take turns in the back room, reading books, the paper, a magazine. A hurried affair. For Craig though, he needed the walk along the banks of the Avre, to one of the parks perhaps; a chance to stretch his legs and see the mountains, to remind himself each day exactly why he was there. It wasn't to push overpriced Gore-Tex.

Craig was deep into training as an IFMGA qualified guide. It was slow going and expensive but by next year he should be exam-ready and the need to work in a shop would be gone. He could get a job with one of the schools somewhere in the Alps and actually get paid for his hobby. He still needed more leading experience across some of the big routes and practice in instructing, and he desperately needed to improve at skiing. On his previous assessment though he had been told his people skills weren't in line with his technical ability. More like not French enough. Maybe that was why he was now struggling to find a reliable partner to notch up the rest of his qualifying routes.

The shop was busy, as was normal in late June. He

spotted an anomaly; a bit too old to be a student, too young to be on a coach tour of the Alps. He was perhaps in his late twenties, sporty build and bouffant hair. Craig watched him move around the shop, playing his people-spotting game to relieve the mid-season boredom.

Definitely not French, so few were given the high prices compared to towns a short drive away. Northern European, Dutch or British perhaps? The man had a swagger about him, but somehow didn't fit in. His clothes were unusual, new looking but not a brand Craig recognised from the last two seasons. Perhaps he was North American? He had now migrated to the climbing equipment and appeared to be checking out the more serious end of the offer.

Intrigued, Craig jogged down the stairs. Close up, the man appeared less assured. He had freckles and sunburn under the auburn quiff, rather than the designer tan of so many that graced the store. His blue eyes were darting across the rack of anchors. He picked a couple off the wall and started to read the labels.

'Can I help you?' Craig asked, guessing on English as the correct choice.

The man turned to face him. 'Thank god, a Brit. My French is bloody awful. I'm after a couple of micros, need to replace some I lost last weekend.'

His voice smacked of a private school in southern England to Craig's ear. Not posh exactly, but privileged. Probably thought he didn't have an accent. Craig's mind jumped forwards to other assumptions about who was paying for this man's leisure, but then his eye fell on the logo on his jacket; an intertwined D and S. The jacket was cut well but there was something almost home-made about it. It was light, presumably breathable cloth, designed for low weight and protection from an unexpected shower; double stitched all round, probably taped seams. But one of the arms didn't quite match the other, as though the manufacturer had run out of cloth part way through. Not the sort of garb the well-heeled would typically wear—they preferred a brand that would convey the size of their bank balance.

'Your jacket—not seen one of those before?'

The man smiled, exhibiting a perfect set of teeth. 'That's because we haven't met before.' He held out his hand. 'Doug Swanson.'

Craig shook it. 'Craig. Nice to meet a fellow Brit and a climber at that. The jacket?'

'Ah,' another broad grin, 'DS, my brand. Sort of a joke really, just my hobby, making gear. The boys always took the piss out of me for it, but whose hands can you trust more than your own?' He looked back down at his jacket, as though he were trying it on for the first time. 'This one is a fave, though a bit of a balls-up to be honest. Ran out of Pertex part way through. Very fond of it though, saved me from a few lashings.'

'Have to say, that's a first. I won't try to flog you a new one then. In Chamonix long?'

'Got here last weekend, but to be honest, man, I'm after someone to climb with. Chap I came down here with pissed off home yesterday, romantic issue. Didn't even say goodbye.'

Craig wondered what would have made a climbing partner leave at such short notice, but he couldn't pass up this opportunity. 'I do a spot of guiding if you're interested?'

Doug put down the gear he was holding and his eyes widened. 'Well, this must be my lucky day! I was about to head up to the guides' office, but you've saved me the walk! What's your rate?'

Craig fished out a crumpled business card from his pocket and handed it to Doug. '£50 a day, including kit. That's if you need any?'

At that moment Craig spotted Alberto, back from his early lunch and on patrol. 'Here, this is what you're after,' Craig said loudly, picking one of the micros and handing it to Doug. Alberto had turned his back and was wandering away.

Craig dropped his voice. 'I can meet you after work if you like and we can take it from there? Look, you need to keep this schtum, I'll explain later.'

'Okay, mum's the word,' Doug said, tapping his nose.

The sale was made, as was the rendezvous in Bar Louise that evening. Craig's assumptions about Doug were reasonably accurate. He was indeed from the Home Counties, but was not the private school boy he had thought him to be but rather the product of a local grammar school. Through beer, jokes and most of all war-stories, the two measured each other up. Doug was clearly an experienced UK climber. He had been primarily a walker who had come to rock-climbing at university in Sheffield. They had both spent many weekends on Stanage Edge, probably at the same time, perhaps in ear-shot of each other's curses and roars of triumph in previous summers. Doug had gone from a history degree into a soulless telesales job, selling car insurance. He hated it.

'But I learnt a lot about people,' he said, downing a fourth beer. 'Can spot a lie at a hundred metres.'

'I climbed the North Face of the Eiger.'

'Bullshit!' Doug banged the table. 'See, I told you! Nose for it. But I will—and the bloody Himalayas. This is just the start, you watch.'

'Okay, you got me. Anyway, enough of this bollocks,

Mr Himalayas. What experience you got on ice?'

'Two winters in Aviemore.'

'Skiing? Don't think that qualifies.'

'No, ice climbing. But you, why all the cloak and daggers in the shop? How do I know you're not going to drop me to the bottom of the nearest crevasse and steal all my gold?'

Craig looked around the bar, no one was paying them any attention. He liked this guy, time to take a bit of a chance. 'Look, I'm in training.' Doug's eyebrows raised, and Craig held up his palms. 'I know, it sounds dodgy. I'm qualified in the UK, just not over here yet. I'm a bloody good climber and as safe as anyone in this valley, you'll see, but it's a slow process and to be honest I need to get a load more routes under my belt this summer and a bit of practice with training. Got some exams coming up. Go up to the guides' office and you'll get some frog who'll charge you three times as much.'

'And I'm guessing taking me out isn't entirely above board...? Or is it the charging for the service?'

Craig answered with a swig of his beer.

'Right, I'm shopping you.' Doug made to stand up. Craig spat out his beer and almost leapt across the table to restrain him.

Doug burst out laughing. 'Relax, man. I'm pulling your leg.'

'Don't joke about it. I get caught and I'll be kicked out of the valley for good.'

'Why are you taking the risk then?'

'I need the money. I'm sorry. Shit, I think I've had one too many beers.' Craig stared down into his glass. 'Look, it's up to you, I think we can both help each other out, just keep quiet about it either way. This is my life.'

'Oh, don't worry about that; we're going climbing and

you're leading, Mr Guide.'

Craig breathed a deep sigh. 'Thanks. Okay, you up for a stroll on Saturday?'

Saturday came and that afternoon the two were sat just down from the peak of the Petite Aiguille Verte. Doug had made easy work of the popular NW ridge, though by the summit he was clearly struggling with the thinner air.

'Nice view,' Doug said as they stared out across the valley to the peaks beyond.

'Nicer in winter,' Craig said. 'Sorry if that was a bit easy.'

'No, it was fun. Thought I was a bit fitter than that though.'

'You need to acclimatise to the altitude; not a problem back home, but it's not the Himalayas here either—a few trips will see you right. If you're up for it, I'll take you on something lower but with a bit more bite tomorrow.'

'I probably need to conserve the cash, man. Sorry.'

Craig waved away Doug's words with his hand. 'Forget that. I've booked a few days off and the forecast's good. As long as you pay for the cable car.'

Doug grinned. 'Think I can manage that.'

'That's sorted then,' Craig said. 'Don't worry, you'll get used to the thin air.'

Doug flopped backwards onto the ground. 'Give me a few days and you'll be begging me to slow down.'

The next two days were spent tackling progressively tougher routes. Craig made sure the step-ups were large as Doug seemed to take each new challenge with ease. On the third day he allowed Doug to lead, who made light work of the test. Craig was finally convinced he had a partner to bag some of the big routes he needed for his qualifications.

As they drove back to town on that third day, Craig

asked, 'So, what are your plans? Shame I need to get back to work.'

'I think I'll stick around; still the odd thing that needs climbing round here.'

'Okay, so you free Monday? That's my next day off.'

'Of course.'

'Great, I'll put a plan together.'

Craig dropped Doug at his hostel and headed back to his flat to get planning. He had a list of targets but most were multi-day trips, which would be impossible once the holidays were in full swing. He hoped Doug would stick around long enough to join him on some of his projects, but that was unlikely, or even if he did, it would only be because he had integrated himself into a team whose timetables didn't revolve around the retail calendar.

However, to Craig's surprise and delight, by that Friday Doug had found a sales job in a competing shop, easing himself into a vacancy with his charm and knowledge of clothing. 'Watch me, I'll outsell you!' Doug joked on the eve of his first day.

'We'll see.'

The summer season took off after that week; schools closed across Europe and families flocked to the Alps, to hotels and second homes, youth hostels and tents. Tourists crowded the streets and squares of the small town, filling the shops and cafes. Time off was limited to one day a week and Craig and Doug made sure on that day they were up early and on the rock. There was no opportunity, however, for any of the longer routes; that would have to wait until the autumn. The summer was all about earning and saving money to spend later in the year.

The August weeks ticked by slowly; a roundabout of work, fitness training and the precious day of climbing to keep skills up. In the evenings Craig made his plans for the low season; a selection of big routes he needed for his application. With fair weather he could have it all tied up by the following Easter, but then he had told himself that the year before.

Finally, September arrived; the first scalp would be the big one, Mont Blanc.

Doug had been talking about it all through the summer. He knew he had already climbed much tougher routes, but he had the need to bag the mother of the Alps, the peak that looked down upon all the others. It was psychological, a tick box, it had to be done. However, as a serious mountain that claimed fatalities every year, Craig thought it better they should team up as a four for the challenge.

Craig was a peripheral figure in the local climbing club, but even so, his absence had been noted. He was keen not to entirely abandon the hard inroads he had made into the local clique and so he invited two of his French acquaintances, Frank and Eric, to join him and Doug. Both were, like him, training to be guides and needed to build up big route experience. Sometimes it seemed like everyone in the valley was in the same situation.

So, on a dry and cloudless September afternoon, the four men set out on the Cosmique route from the Aiguille du Midi cable car over Mont Maudit. They had picked the route to avoid the traffic jams from the tramway route and because it offered a bit more technical challenge.

As the cable car carried them up, Craig watched Chamonix shrinking below them. It was the end of his third season, two more than he had originally intended. He was competent at selling, and he rubbed along well with his colleagues, but it was hardly his life's ambition when he had made the journey southwards two years earlier. Would Doug fall into this lazy trap? He was also looking down at the same scene, but Craig doubted Doug was aspiring to spend his life behind a shop counter. Doug was a go-getter; that much was clear. He always wanted to compare sales figures and talked endlessly about the great peaks of the world, when there was so much to explore within easy reach. No, Doug wouldn't last more than a season here before he went on to better things. At least Craig knew he was the better climber. For now.

They reached the top station at two o'clock and after a brief visit to the viewpoints headed down onto the glacier to the start of the path. They were just about to leave the tourist area when Frank said, 'Where's your mate?'

Craig turned around; Doug had been behind him a moment before with them. He wandered back up and found Doug, sitting down, fiddling with the contents of his rucksack.

'What's up?'

Doug didn't answer.

'You okay? The guys are keen to get on. Eric's worried we may struggle at the refuge.'

Doug looked up and grunted, 'Thought Frank had booked?'

'So did I.' Craig couldn't read Doug's expression behind his mirrored glasses, but he could see he was pale. 'Look, we won't have a problem; Eric's just a bit of a moaner; he's well pissed off with Frank.'

Doug didn't answer, instead standing up and shouldering his bag.

'You sure you're okay?'

Doug just nodded and so they turned and rejoined the others. The four descended the arête to the glacier below and made the easy walk to the Cosmique Refuge. Doug seemed fine, if a little slow and so the earlier blip was forgotten. As Craig had anticipated the refuge was only half full. The climbers there were mostly the serious variety, which was promising for congestion on the following day.

Early the next morning they started out to ascend Mont Blanc du Tacul, the peak lying between the Aiguille du Midi and Mont Blanc itself.

Frank and Eric led off with Craig and Doug following. The climbing would be fairly straightforward, if steep, but from a technical perspective, none of it compared to some of the routes they had already tackled together. At breakfast Doug made a big show of enthusiasm, but Craig could sense a nervousness in his movements and his fixed grin.

It was still dark as they walked out into the frigid air. Voices of another group carried up the mountain ahead of them, and the beams of headtorches could be seen dancing across the cliffs at the start of the ascent.

Frank and Eric set off on a fast pace. They had eight hours to the summit followed by a descent that would also take many hours on tired legs.

The first peak was reached by a steep glacier climb, technically easy but with plenty of danger from seracs and crevasses. They roped as two pairs. Initially Doug and Craig kept up with the others ahead of them, but Doug was soon slowing. Craig asked if he was okay, but received a rebuke for his trouble and so they pressed on.

A thousand feet of ascent later, Doug seemed seriously off the pace. They were now lagging well behind with Doug wanting to stop frequently. By ten o'clock Craig knew they were never going to get to the top of Mont Blanc with ample time for the descent, having only just reached the north-west shoulder of Mont Blanc du Tacul.

Frank and Eric had stuck around as the worst of the crevasses had been navigated but now Craig could see they were very fidgety. Their conversation stopped as Craig arrived.

'I think your Doug has the altitude illness,' Eric said, nodding down at Doug ascending below them.

Craig didn't reply but watched as Doug made his final weary steps to the group and sat down heavily in the snow.

'Doug?' Craig said.

Doug took a swig from his water bottle. His face was grey and moist with sweat. Doug looked up at his partner. 'I'm bushed. Head's going to explode.'

Craig glanced over at the other two who were looking on. He crouched down and said in low tones, 'Are you up to descending with just me?'

'I don't know, you're the fucking guide.' Doug threw his bottle into the snow next to him.

Craig looked around. The sun was now hot on his skin and reflected in tiny diamonds off his breath. Every peak was beautifully, perfectly illuminated, yearning to be climbed. Such days of freedom in the Alps needed to be seized and devoured. But they would have to descend. At least he had conquered Mont Blanc before. It wasn't a serious ascent, more of a badge of honour for Doug, but Doug's expletive had neatly answered the question for Craig. He turned to the others. 'Sorry, guys, another time.'

Frank said nothing but glanced back at the peak of Mont Blanc glistening in the sun.

Eric said, 'It's okay, Doug, we go down. This mountain will be here next week!' He patted Frank on the shoulder and murmured something in French.

'Thanks, guys.' He looked back at Doug. 'Right let's get down to some thicker air.'

Craig had seen people hit like this when guiding a number of times, usually with unfit tourists. However, he had not before had a fit mountaineer suffer so badly. Whilst it was true they could have spent some more nights at altitude ahead of this ascent, the pair of them had been climbing at over two thousand metres for a couple of months now. It was as though Doug had hit a wall. He was now heading to be a liability and needed to descend.

Two hours later Craig and Doug were in the cable car. The descent had been uneventful and Doug had partially recovered once they had reached the glacier. The conversations had been very sparse, each man lost in his own thoughts. When they reached the Cosmique hut, the French pair had announced their intention to stay another night and ascend Mont Blanc the following day. They shook hands and parted. Eric and Frank wouldn't be joining Doug on a mountain any time soon, that was for certain.

Craig watched Doug staring glumly out at the valley below.

'Let's give it a go at the start of October, we can get you acclimatised before that.'

Doug didn't reply.

Craig sat back. They both knew Doug might not acclimatise. They read the books, the magazines, swapped the anecdotes. Some people just didn't. Maybe Doug was going to have to change his life's plan. That was something Doug had probably never had to do before.

They walked out of the cable car station into a busy Chamonix lunchtime. Any climber looking on would sense the smell of defeat but Craig didn't care, they had made the right decision and he could write this one up as part of his evidence. For Doug though, something more significant had passed.

They shook hands.

'Friday?' Craig asked.

'Yeah, see you there.' Doug turned and walked away.

Friday night meant climbers gathering in Bar Louise.

Craig joined Eric and Frank on a corner table. 'Did you make it?'

Frank said, 'Yes. It was beautiful.'

'Sorry about, well you know, but thanks for coming down with us. Know that must have hurt.'

Eric batted away the statement and asked, 'How's your friend?'

Craig glanced around the bar, Doug wasn't there, which was unusual for him as he had quickly settled into the local scene, propping up the bar and entertaining the locals with his climbing anecdotes. Sometimes Doug had left with one of the female members of the club, not always the same one. Perhaps he was entertaining Juliette or Sylvie this evening? Craig took a long gulp of beer at the thought. He'd been celibate for nearly two years now but perhaps that was about to change; he had Linda visiting at last this weekend. God, he hoped she would stay this time.

'You say your friend can climb?' Frank said. 'Didn't look good to me.'

Craig put his glass down. 'I wouldn't have brought him up there if he couldn't. He's great on rock, I mean really good. It's the bloody altitude.'

Eric nodded. 'Not able to adjust?'

'I don't know. May need a bit more time. Looks like I'll need a new partner for the high routes though. Buggers my training schedule.'

'This guiding takes away all the fun,' Eric said. 'You can make more money selling shit to tourists.'

Craig said, 'I need to get more experience; it's going to take years at this rate.'

'Why don't you join us next weekend? Aiguille du Grepon?' Frank said.

'No, got other plans.'

Eric and Frank exchanged glances.

'Ah, other plans! I believe this is the friend you have visiting. Maybe your *mademoiselle* might want to join us?' Frank said.

Craig felt himself blushing, much to the amusement of the others. There was no way he was introducing Linda to this bunch of letches to see her spirited off on one of their arms.

At that moment Craig felt a tap on his head. He looked up to see a grinning Doug holding a rolled-up magazine.

'You seem pleased with yourself,' Craig said.

'Move over.'

'It's okay, I'm going,' Frank said, and left for another group.

'Suit yourself,' Doug said, taking his stool. He threw the magazine down on the table, theatrically. 'Voila.'

The cover showed a dramatic granite peak with the title, 'Patagonia special.'

'It's technically solid with hardly any established routes, not like round here. And it's low! Look, every Tom, Dick and Harry round here wants to be a guide, you're all training for the same thing, you'll all be competing with each other. This will give you an edge. It's a new world, a new market, it's the future!'

Craig picked up the magazine and started to leaf through the pictures. He had seen pictures of the granite spires before; the rock formations promised a drama not found in Europe.

'I'll leave you two crazy English to your dreams,' Eric

said, standing up.

'C'mon, Craig, you said you were in a rut. This will make a name for you. They can't refuse you your certificate with a few of these beasts under your belt.'

Craig sat back and looked at Doug. 'Do you think we're good enough?'

Doug raised his glass. 'We will be.'

How long had I been sat there? We had paused a couple of times for a drink of water and for fresh powder to be applied but my back was aching from sitting on the high stool in a fixed position.

'I need a break.' I stood up and stretched. We were there now, at the story. I was sure most of what I had said would be junked, but she had let me talk. She could decide what was important. I went out to the toilet and then climbed the stairs to the lounge. Outside the clouds hung heavy on the valley and the spruces waved in the wind. Autumn.

'How's it going?'

I turned to see Linda framed in the doorway. She stepped into the lounge and dropped into an armchair. 'She grilling you?'

I smiled. 'Something like that. We've reached the business end.'

'Fitz Roy.'

'Yes.'

'Do I figure in the story?'

I broke her gaze and looked back out at the panorama. 'Do you want to be part of this film?'

'It's not my story,' she said.

'I don't think it's mine either.'

'Hi, Craig, you ready?' I turned around. Sarah had come up the steps into the room. 'Sorry, hi, Linda. The cameras

96

tend to disappear for lunch for hours around here. Like a union thing. We need to push on.'

'See you later,' Linda said with a wave and I followed Sarah downstairs. I was back in the hot seat. Makeup was dusted up again and off we went.

'Right, Craig, where were we?'

'Let's talk about Patagonia.'

CHAPTER EIGHT

After the interrogation, I needed to get out. The Q&A had been a disaster as I'd feared. Sarah had started with the easy stuff, Buenos Aires, the flight down to Calafate and the difficult four-by-four beyond that. Our humble accommodation. Describing the beauty of the region was not difficult and Doug had already done this more than justice with his slide show.

But then it got onto people. Doug and me, Bob and Cassie and most of all, the four of us together. But I even survived that, and our trudge up the glacier to the start of the Supercanaleta. Beyond that, my recall was sketchy to non-existent. It was bloody cold and the views were good, but as for the accident...

By three o'clock we were all pretty pissed off and in need of a break, so it was a great relief when she finally gave up for the day.

'I'm sorry, I'm going to need a bit more than this to work with,' was her final comment before I quit the studio.

I mumbled a reply about trying to write down more before almost running back up to the lounge.

The weather was still foul; the cloud had descended over Finhaut and into the depths below, submerging the house in a damp, clinging mist. I donned my raincoat and boots and marched out into the open air. *Valois* sat above the village, as the highest bastion of civilisation. Above us was only forest, rock and road up to a nearby dam. I set off following a set of signs for a hiking path which disappeared into the surrounding woodland. Walking along it alone made me realise how much I missed the uncomplicated company of Lottie and her unconditional love. As the rain battered my hood, I quickened my pace, until I found shelter amongst the fir trees.

I took a break once I was sheltered from the downpour and pulled my jacket zip higher to keep the wind out. This wasn't cold, not real cold, the type that creeps through your limbs like an avalanche carving through a forest leaving only death behind. This was just a cold to challenge a rambler's clothing. Sarah's interrogation had not been hard, they were only questions, reasonable questions, but somehow talking it through had brought that ice back, that insecurity then helpless surrender. Yes, I did remember more and she knew it. How, I had no idea. I was no liar, no salesman, not like Doug. But my memories were shadows, fleeting dreams and nightmares. Ice, cold, wind. Pain. His bearded, frosted face, his hands moving noiselessly in the howling gale, the icy lips mouthing words I couldn't hear. Falling, falling. Sleeping, waking. Cold, wind, darkness. Hardly a story to be listened to over a mouthful of popcorn. Doug's version was much better.

She would make me do it all over again, of course. Probably three or four times. More pauses, more emotion perhaps, some smiles and laughter, grimaces, tears? It was supposed to be entertainment, after all.

I heard the barking of dogs and peered out through the trees. Someone was walking a pair of hounds into the meadow below. A familiar figure. I stepped out from the tree line and waved. 'Linda!'

She looked up towards me and waved back then quickened her pace up the hill. She was a welcome sight.

'Bloody awful weather!'

'Thought you were a hardy Welshman now!' she said, with a grin.

'It's always sunny in Wales! What are you talking about?'

'The palm trees of Bangor?'

'Of course, they're set above the coral reefs. Maybe you have a special wind down here?'

'We do, the Mistral, but that's Provence. This is just shit weather. Let's keep walking.'

It was good to hear Linda talking more like the lass I used to know. 'What've you been up to?' I said.

'Not a lot, I don't work Wednesdays. I saw you rushing out. Thought you might need a local guide. Wouldn't do to have one of the stars getting lost on the hills, would it?' She smiled and brushed the wet fringe away from her forehead.

'Shall we get out of this rain?' I said. 'But not the house…Please.'

'Oh dear,' she said. 'There's a surprisingly good bar at the top of the village, they even take dogs. C'mon, sure the dogs won't mind getting out of this.'

I followed her through the grass and back down to the village. The square was deserted and with half of the chalets shuttered up for the low season there was not a soul in sight. It was therefore a relief to see the bar was open, better still, it was empty.

Once we had seen to the dogs and removed our soaking coats, the proprietor brought us a couple of coffees with regulation biscuits which he laid in front of us with a grunt.

'Service with a smile, I see,' I said.

'Oh, David's pretty friendly by local standards. They keep themselves to themselves round here, too many tourists. He's actually a sweetie under that bushy moustache.'

There was a word I hadn't heard in a while. I wondered if Doug was a sweetie. Actually, I knew the answer to that one.

'So, what's she got you doing?'

'Who, Sarah?'

'Yes.' She took a sip of her coffee, inspecting me all the while. 'What do you think of her?'

I broke eye contact. 'In what way?'

There was a pause, then she said, 'Oh, Craig, have you got a crush on the little blonde bombshell?'

'You are joking? I'm old enough to be her dad!'

She took another sip and said into her mug, 'Hasn't stopped Doug.'

I didn't want to get embroiled in their domestics. 'She seems to know what she's doing. Must be a talented girl to get the funding to make a film at her age.'

Linda snorted. 'That's one word for it. Can't see what he sees in her. She'll be some washed-up, sad wraith in a few years, once she's finished shagging her way to the top of whatever grubby heap she's climbing.'

I was taken aback at her ferocity but part of me felt pleased, a sense of schadenfreude perhaps. 'I'm sorry, didn't realise it was like that—'

'D'you know who she is?' Linda interrupted, her tone becoming even more strident, 'Some film studies student! Came over two years ago for a marketing job and started pitching a film project straight at him. Landed a bullseye with his vanity. Persuaded him it will boost sales, move the company to the top of the pile and him to the top of the top. Make a legend of him. The old fool fell for it hook, line and sinker. By the time I met her, I could see he was smitten already, but she was stringing him along. Probably still is. Not sure I care.'

'Linda—'

'No, no…Sorry.' She raised her hands. 'Didn't mean to involve you. Just can't believe she's under my roof now. That's all. I'm waiting for him to finish his Hollywood infatuation and for her to move on. Believe me, she will once the film is picked up. I'm sure there's someone else she can sleep with to get it distributed.'

I took a breath, not sure how to continue. 'If there's anything I can—'

But she held her palm up. 'I'm sorry, Craig. That was…unseemly. I was asking you about what you got up to this morning. Tell me about the filming; what you think about it.'

The conversation had switched direction as quickly as a mountain breeze. Her outburst had raised a host of questions about their relationship, but that was none of my business—was it? I decided not to probe.

'My side of the story. Corroboration and all that. Talking heads. Probably mostly going to be binned.'

'Was it fun?'

I smiled and sat back. 'You know I struggle to remember much. Couldn't at the time and it was decades ago. My memory isn't improving.'

'So, what did you say?'

'Just what happened. Like Doug said. I want to get it done with and get home.'

'Don't you want to go back there though, to see it again?' She smiled.

'I can think of other places I would rather go to. Pretty much anywhere in fact. Perhaps not North Korea, but—'

'That bad? Really?' She leant forward and dropped her hand onto mine. 'Come on, Craig, don't you want to at least spend a bit of time catching up with me after all this time? And Doug? He was your best friend.'

'You were my best friend,' I said, before I had thought it through.

Her hand pulled back, but then retook the coffee cup. She broke my gaze. 'I know…I've missed you, Craig. We were a good team.'

I took a deep breath. 'Sorry, didn't want to dampen the mood. Think the weather's done enough of that. I've moved on, honestly, Linda. Just, all this, it's brought the accident back to me. It was no fun, you know that.'

'Just the accident?' She shot a look at me. 'Why did you cut us out, Craig? You didn't even come to the wedding? Surely you could have done that?'

This was not the conversation I had been expecting, but sooner or later, it had to come out. Today was as good a day as any. 'I'm sorry, Linda. I was a bit messed up.'

'I don't want an apology, Craig. Had enough of those at the time. But an explanation would be nice.' Her adopted cut-glass accent had dropped back to her soft northern tones.

'The accident. It was hard on me, think I lost more than a few brain cells in that fall. I...Look, climbing was my passion. I lost it on that mountain, a man died, left a widow. Your hero saved me.'

'You don't seem that grateful.'

'He got his reward. You both did.' I stared back at her. Her jaw dropped. 'I beg your pardon?'

'You heard what I said.'

Her chair shot back and she glowered down at me whilst roughly pulling on her sodden coat. 'You've no idea, Craig.' She threw a twenty euro note onto the table, gathered the dogs and walked out without another word.

I watched her leave as the rain beat on the window then dropped my head into my hands. Why the hell had I said that? Couldn't I have kept my gob shut for a few more days and enjoyed her company again? I didn't know what Linda wanted from me; I didn't even know what I wanted from her.

CHAPTER NINE

I slunk back to the house an hour, two coffees and a whisky later.

To my relief, Linda was not in evidence but the dogs greeted me at the door. I needed to apologise but didn't know how. Maybe she would calm down given a bit of time? I went down to my room and changed out of my clothes, then called Sue to see how Lottie was doing. The weather in North Wales sounded considerably better than I was experiencing and when Sue put Lottie on the phone, she panted a greeting to me which brought a tear to my eye. I was such a ridiculous fool, making this film in a foreign land with only a dog back home missing me. Perhaps this episode was the kick up the arse I had needed to get my life back. I still hadn't confronted Doug and Sarah about the contract; it was long overdue, particularly if they wanted me to make this absurd trip back to Patagonia.

I had a quick shower then went in search of Sarah. I found her with Doug in the studio room downstairs. They were talking in hushed tones that went silent when I walked in.

Doug managed a thin smile. 'Craig, nice walk was it? We were wondering where you had got to. You okay to carry on this afternoon?'

'Sorry, needed a bit of air. Pretty hillside you got here.'

'Not Snowdonia though?' Sarah added.

I ignored the question. 'Sorry to disturb you, but I need this contract sorted out. I'm obviously covering the business at the moment and—'

'Craig, Craig, don't worry! We won't let you down,' Doug said.

'No, Doug, Craig's right. Sorry it's been so hectic. It's

unprofessional of us,' Sarah added. 'I'll call the office now, get it sorted. Excuse me, Doug.'

'Thanks,' I replied to this entirely unspecific promise.

I was left with Doug who said, 'Some better news, the forecast has improved. We think we can do the chopper shots tomorrow, catch up a few days. Wrap it up before the week is out.'

'Oh, great,' I said, attempting to inject some enthusiasm into my voice. 'Do you need me?'

'Come on, Craig, can't you at least pretend to be enjoying this?'

'It's a bit unfamiliar, that's all. Missing the dog.'

Doug didn't seem to know if I were joking or not. 'You tempted to get onto any rock over here? Maybe a little taste when it dries out?'

I wasn't, wet rock or dry. I asked Doug about whether he had done his talking head and it turned out his story had all been completed weeks before, as part of the preparation for the storyboarding of the rest of the film. They were now waiting for the accident close-ups to be completed and then the French film unit would be disbanded. My fears were confirmed that the interview process had taken many shots and I needed to make sure my clothes were the same for each take. 'Give your wet stuff to Linda, she'll throw them in the wash,' he assured me. I wasn't so sure that was where she would throw them.

We made some more small talk about the film and then he left me, ostensibly to track down Sarah.

What the hell was I doing here? Was it honestly the money that had brought me out? The idea of further days knocking around the house, another interrogation; I couldn't stand it. I needed the money but I didn't need to stay here watching the Swanson soap opera. Linda would understand, even if Doug didn't. I went down to my room

105

and packed my things, then left a note for Linda giving my apologies, saying I thought perhaps they could do with a bit more space.

I sneaked out of the house, like a burglar laden with swag. Only one of the hounds seemed to notice and even it turned its back on me without so much as a sniff. A few days, that's what I needed, seeing the old haunts. They could call me when I was required.

The call came sooner than I expected. I had booked back into the hotel and spent a boozy, but very welcome night in my own company, celebrating my minor escape with a thick steak and a couple more beers than were necessary. That, and the resurrection of my terrible French which seemed to improve with each glass, formed the best evening I had had since my return to Chamonix.

I awoke to much finer weather, a clear sky and light easterly wind. No doubt another attempt at the helicopter shots would now be made. I didn't want to run into the film crew, not today, but I was secretly intrigued by the process and so drove down the valley to Les Praz after breakfast and took the Flégère lift up the opposite side of the valley. I found a pleasant spot, a small cafe up top which commanded a clear view of the peaks to the south. To the west stood the massif of Mont Blanc which ran eastwards to the Aiguille Verte and Les Drus. What a difference the night had made, clearing the clag from the skies to reveal the full glory of the range. The glaciers glinted in the sunlight and white ribbons of water drew thin lines across every expanse of grey. Once the rock was dry it would be perfect climbing weather. There was no doubt the film crew would be seizing this opportunity.

I set off on a walk to Les Chéserys lakes, but when the opportunity provided itself, stole a glance across to where the filming would be taking place. Sure enough, at eleven o'clock the sound of a helicopter ascending the valley greeted me. The black shape then proceeded to criss-cross back and forth and hover for the next couple of hours, putting down at least once. The weather held out. Doug would be happy.

My phone rang at three by which time I was descending on the path down to Chamonix. It was Sarah. 'You need to come back, Craig. It was naughty sneaking off like that.'

Before I had a chance to express my indignation, she added, 'There's been an accident.'

An hour later I was back at the chalet. Linda answered the door and pulled me inside. A hubbub was coming from the lounge; Doug, Sarah, Piotr, Rick, all their voices appeared to be speaking at once.

I started to speak, 'Look, Linda, I'm really sorry—'

She touched her fingers to my lips. 'Forget it. We both said things we shouldn't have.'

I was amazed at the ease of this forgiveness 'Oh, um, thanks,' I said. 'Sarah called, didn't say a lot. An accident?'

She took my hand and led me into the kitchen and shut the door. 'One of the climbers fell—he's okay, a broken leg and some bruising. It could have been a lot worse.'

'What happened?'

'No one's entirely sure. He was trying to replicate Doug's feat,' that would be the abseiling with an injured, unconscious climber, I presumed, 'he slipped, or some protection popped out, I don't know. He was shouting and screaming a lot, blaming Doug and the gear.'

'That's unlikely.'

'I know, more like his incompetence, I'm sure, but either way, he's off the film, as is Francois. He's refusing to carry on.'

I groaned. This would surely only mean more time out

here whilst they found replacements, if that were possible at all. 'I'd better go and see them all.'

'Wait a moment.'

'What is it?'

'They're going to ask you to climb, to take Francois' place. Doug's already agreed to step in.'

'What?' This was the craziest thing I had heard since my return. 'Can't they hire someone? The valley's full of climbers, can't throw a stone without hitting one.'

'There's no time. It's the budget…'

I sat down on one of the stools. 'Why are you telling me this?'

'Doug needs you, Craig.'

Ah, here it was. It was all for Doug.

She held up her hand. 'I know what you're thinking. He's a bit of an idiot at times,' I smiled at that, idiot wasn't my choice of words, 'but underneath that bravado, he cares about you, as well as the film. He won't force you, but…'

I stood up. 'Thanks for the warning.' I'd made up my mind.

I entered the lounge and the room went quiet. Sure enough, almost all of the crew from the breakfast a few days before were there, huddled around maps and laptops. Doug caught my eye immediately and feigned a smile. 'Craig, so good to see you.' He put his hand on my shoulder. 'We need to have a chat.' He shot Sarah a look and steered me into the dining room, shutting the door behind him.

'I know, you want me to climb. I'll do it, but I want twice the fee, paid up front. No more stalling.' For once, Doug was speechless. He sat down and looked at me. I added, 'You do realise I haven't climbed anything more than a scramble for over twenty years?'

108

'I didn't, no,' he replied weakly. 'Linda told you?'

'Never mind that. I'm sorry, Doug, but I need to get on with my life. Let's cut to the chase, I'm skint, you're rich. You need my help; I need your money.'

'Craig, you seem really angry.' There was a knock at the door. 'Just a moment,' he called back.

'Yes, I'm angry. It's not your fault, but things haven't been great recently and I feel, quite frankly, manipulated.'

'Manipulated?'

'Yes, by your girlfriend and you.'

Doug shushed me. 'Keep your voice down! Get a grip.'

'Do we have a deal, Doug?' I asked.

He looked towards the door. 'Okay, yes, but for God's sake, lighten up. This is supposed to be fun.' But it didn't seem like he was having much of that himself. 'Sod it. Come on, let's go climbing.'

'What? It's nearly five?'

But Doug had a solution.

An hour later I was hanging off a rope in a small, local climbing centre, top-roped on a wall that would barely count as a v. diff and loving every moment. We had left the house without a word to the others with Doug's assurance Sarah would sort it out. 'We need to blow our cobwebs away, I think,' he had said as we descended the hill. The boot of his car was full of climbing tackle, a mixture of factory samples and his own tried and tested gear.

The hall was empty except for a couple of school kids who were making very light work of the only overhang the room offered. They hardly gave the two middle-aged men a second look as we entered. They were surely unaware they were in the presence of the great Doug Swanson.

The wall was built up along one side of a sports hall;

109

orange, blue and pink handholds arranged as a random patchwork above thin crash-mats. A collection of ropes hung down from the top of the wall, ready to be tied into, with route and grade descriptions chalked up on blackboards. One end of the wall was the easy stuff, the other the hard. We pulled on our harnesses. Doug slipped his on effortlessly, whilst I managed to tangle mine like a beginner on an Outward Bound course. Fortunately, Doug didn't seem to notice and soon I had it pulled tight, secure around my waist. It was uncomfortable and only offered as much security as my partner would give. Doug was standing, hands on hips, surveying the suspended ropes. I headed towards the easy end, but Doug pulled me back. 'C'mon, Craig. I'm sure you can do better than that.'

I grabbed one of the ropes and tied a figure of eight, trying to recall the last time I had done this. Doug was watching me, 'Making a bit of a meal of that aren't you?'

'I'm a bit rusty. Just do bouldering these days. Do you trust me?'

'Craig, c'mon, I'd trust you with my life.' He patted my arm. 'But I'll check your knots.' He winked, but check them he did.

I climbed first, the large, easy holds presenting little challenge. As I ascended the rope jerked through the karabiner above, which rattled against the wall. It felt unnatural to me, restricting my movements without offering any comfort. I reached the top and held on.

'Let go,' Doug called from below.

For a moment my hands gripped the holds. The rope was tight above me.

'Let go, I've got you.'

I let my arms flop down and leant back. I didn't fall. I was safe.

He let the rope out quickly and I was lowered, landing

softly on the floor.

Doug raised an eyebrow. 'What was that about?'

'What d'you mean?'

He tossed his head towards the top of the wall. 'You shoot up there like a pro then freeze like a beginner.'

'Keeping you on your toes.'

Doug didn't seem convinced and we swapped over so he could climb. 'You okay?' He was looking at my hands. I followed his stare. My hands were shaking as I threaded the rope through the belay device. I clipped it into the karabiner and took hold of the rope.

I could feel his eyes on my belay device, checking it was set up correctly. 'Don't worry, I've got you,' I said.

He grunted, then said, 'You really are rusty, aren't you? Never would have thought it.' He shook his head. He walked towards the wall and I pulled him in. I felt the heat of the orange nylon run through my hands.

'That's me,' he said as the last slack in the rope disappeared.

'Climb when ready,' I said.

'Climbing.' He lifted himself off the ground and I tightened the rope. My hands swapped, below the belay device to above it, feeding the rope through, keeping the tension on, keeping my partner safe.

'Let it out a bit!'

I looked up. Doug was flat against the wall. 'Give me a bit of slack, mate,' he called.

I loosened the rope and he continued slowly up the wall. At the top he let go without warning, but I held him tight, the rope locked in the belay device.

'Any time when you're ready,' he called.

I slowly let the rope out, and he descended, finally landing in front of me.

He looked at me quizzically. 'Think we both need a bit

111

of practice, me with the climbing, you with the belaying.'

'It's the frostbite,' I muttered.

Doug stared at me, an eyebrow raised. 'So, you can climb, but can't belay? Think we both know the truth about that one, Craig.'

I made to say something but no words came out.

'I'll do another while I'm on. Work that injury of yours off.' He turned back and before I could take the rope in, was almost running up the wall. My hands worked quickly to catch up with him but barely had him protected when he threw himself backwards, halfway up. He fell a few metres before I had arrested his fall, my body jerking forward with the strain. 'You mad bastard!' I shouted up at him.

'Think we're both getting over our deficiencies nicely.'

I lowered him down. I was sweating and breathing hard. Doug walked over and put his hand on my shoulder. 'I trust you, Craig.'

I looked away, feeling a mixture of embarrassment and anger at his stunt. 'I should have let you hit the mat. Then we could have seen how much you trusted me.'

Doug smiled. 'Sorry about that, old man. It was naughty of me but I knew you wouldn't let me down.' He untied himself. 'Let's try something harder.'

We took it in turns to climb and to belay. After the crags of the Llanberis pass, the walls were technically easy; no moss or moisture, with colours to show the way and most of all, a rope to guide you back to earth when you reached the top or if you fell. The rock shoes Doug had thrown me barely fitted, but I didn't care. Soon I was twenty, thirty years younger, tied into that rope and I couldn't wipe the grin from my face. We spoke little, working our way across the wall, steadily increasing the grade of each ascent. From the top of the third climb, I called down, 'The view's great from here!'

'The weather too!' Doug called back. 'Why can't they centrally heat the mountains?'

For the first time since Sarah had entered my shop my mind felt free. All the cares remained down at floor level as I worked out where the next hold should be or how much longer I could stay in a position, or whether a particular feature counted as the route I was supposed to be on or was 'cheating'. It had very little in common with exposure on an alpine cliff but at that moment was all the better for it.

We carried on in that vein until we were kicked out by the manager of the sports centre who had let us stay on an hour beyond closing as it was, being a close friend of Doug's like everyone else it seemed. I had lost track of time, only the pain in my legs, arms and hands told me how long we had been climbing for. 'Mont Blanc tomorrow?' I said as we loaded the car.

Doug smiled. 'Welcome back, Craig.'

CHAPTER TEN

My mobile rang at six the following morning. It was barely light and my body was feeling more like I had been in a street fight than on a climbing wall.

'We're on.' It was Doug.

'What?'

'On camera, the weather's clear we need to get it in the can today. You up for it?'

I didn't feel up for going down the stairs at that moment, but this was never going to get any easier. 'Okay.'

'Great, I'll pick you up at seven.' He hung up.

I flopped back into my soft pillows and cursed. I was awoken again by the phone at eight. 'Monsieur? Your driver is here.'

Shit. I threw on a base layer and the nearest thing to climbing trousers I had with me and pelted down the stairs. Doug was sitting out in his Range Rover, the engine running.

'Took your time,' he said.

'Are you going to tell me what we're doing?' I asked as he accelerated east along the valley. 'No Sarah?'

'She went ahead with the crew at first light. Lots to do today, we need it all wrapped up. A lot of the guys have other jobs to push on to. Should've been finished by now.' He pulled out onto the Route Blanche and put his foot down. Weather, the accident, perhaps my late decision to take part, had all resulted in a big slip in the original schedule, and with it presumably a lot of additional costs.

'Don't worry, Craig. We'll get it done today. Now the A-team's back doing the climbing.'

I looked out at the clouded peaks; perhaps they would stay shrouded and we could get a bit more practice in at the climbing wall. I wasn't ready. Maybe Doug was, but I wasn't sure about that either. Next to me, his hands gripped the wheel tightly. For all his bonhomie he was as worried as I was. The weather was still playing games, but probably was good enough for the chopper to fly and to pick up the distant shots of the rescue.

'What exactly are we climbing?'

'Oh, the frogs never finished the rescue abs. Need us to do them again. Probably have to scrap the whole of the last day. Too many continuity problems.'

He sounded like a regular Steven Spielberg. 'So, what does that mean for us?'

'Just an abseil, easy stuff, you'll get a brief when we arrive. They'll cut and paste it in with the previous scenes. No one will be any the wiser.'

I tried to relax. It did sound straightforward, the sort of thing you do in the Scouts, albeit with the addition of a film crew. Doug had been true to his word over the contract and when I had returned to the hotel after our sport-centre climbing, an envelope bearing the SummitSeeker's letterhead was waiting at reception. I tore it open in my room and read it. The figure was generous, with a cheque enclosed for fifty percent. The contract stated the balance would be paid on the signing of the distributor contract. I didn't know what that meant, but no doubt it would take a few months. The cheque I had in my hand though was enough to clear my debts and to last out the year. It had all been worth it.

Doug made no mention of the money and so I chose not to. 'So, it's just an abseil?'

'Like I said, we'll get a full brief from Rick when we get there. They need us to do the descent sequence Francois and Pierre cocked up. No climbing required. Piece of piss.'

'But not an ordinary abseil,' I said.

'No,' he said, with a smile. He gunned the engine and

115

we accelerated past a convoy of sleepy camper vans before taking a tight turn towards the base of the cable car.

The car park was a hive of activity as we pulled in. A runner came out to take a cone off Doug's reserved space and Ruth ran up, clipboard in hand as soon as we climbed out. This time it was me she was after.

'Mr Darwen, we need to get you over to costumes to get you measured up.'

'Bit late for that, isn't it?' Doug called over.

'We'll try Francois' outfit, hopefully it will fit. I'm sure we can make some adjustments, there are no close-ups.' She tugged me by the arm and walked me over to one of the wagons.

I hadn't considered we would need to dress the part. The clothes didn't fit and bore little resemblance to what I would have been wearing those decades earlier. Still, who was going to notice details like that? I thought of Doug, with his home-made gear, our down jackets and facial hair. Ruth was standing in the corner of the wagon looking anxiously from her watch to the window and back again.

I waddled over to her, the trousers pulling uncomfortably into my crotch. 'Do I look okay?'

She appraised me quickly. 'You'll do. We'd better go.'

'Doug said I'd get a briefing?'

'Did he?' she sighed. 'Of course, yes…' She glanced at her watch again. 'Follow me.'

We stepped out and crossed the car park to the wagon where I'd encountered the flouncing French climbers a few days earlier. It was a mess inside, pieces of Doug Swanson kit and rope lying all over a table. Doug was there, fiddling with a rack of gear.

'Mr Swanson, Mr Darwen would like a brief on the scene.'

Doug looked up. 'Sorry, Craig. Just a minute.'

116

'Mr Swan—'

'Doug.'

'Sorry, Doug. The chopper's due in less than two hours and the director is very keen to have you on set.'

I interrupted. 'Doug, can you explain exactly what we are doing, *before* we get up there? I don't want to make a fool of myself. And can I fit out a harness?'

He looked from me to Ruth and held up his hand. 'Sorry, Craig. Yes of course. We'll be out in ten.'

'But Mr Swan—'

'Ten.'

Ruth knew when to accept defeat and with a tut backed out, removing her walkie-talkie as she went.

Doug tossed me a climbing harness. 'That should fit. Right...' He grabbed a piece of paper and a pen and cleared some space on the table. 'We're recreating a pitch of the rescue—'

'I know that, shouldn't we practise this first, at the climbing centre?'

'There's no time. We have to grab the weather window. You've no idea what this is costing. Look—' he sketched out a cliff and then drew a circle on top. Then two people hanging from the circle. It wasn't art. 'You and I will abseil down the cliff, it's a hundred metres.'

'A hundred metres? What sort of rope?' That was no ordinary pitch, a standard rope length was more typically sixty metres and when fallen on, they stretched to absorb the load. A hundred metre rope would stretch a lot.

'Yes, it's static, but it's okay as we'll be protected by a backup line. They'll take that rope out of the film somehow. We may need to shoot this a few times. We need a big single pitch for the filming, Sarah said.'

I didn't much like the sound of it. Static rope was used for lowering and lifting loads, not for climbing on. If you fell on it, it could slice you in half as the rope didn't absorb the energy. I understood the logic though, it was okay for an abseil and with the backup protecting us, the abseiling rope was more for show than for anything else. Just then a question occurred to me, 'What did we have on us—?'

'Back then?'

'Yes.'

He paused for a while and looked up at the roof, then back at the table. 'We had a couple of sixty-metre lengths. I doubled them up for the descent.'

I thought back to the weather, the cold and wind. Someone over me, Doug, talking, trying to rouse me, snow and wind, cold wind. Handling those ropes in that cold, with a patient. He had saved my life—that had been some rope-work, and now we were going to fake it.

'How are we tying together? To be honest I never did understand how you got us down.'

Doug grimaced. 'It has to be realistic. You're going to be doing nothing, just lying there in front of me. But don't worry, this isn't the real thing, the backup will be doing the work, we're just pretending. We'll be clipped together with our belay point above us, I'll handle the ropes. You keep out of the way. It's all top-notch gear.'

'But how are we tied in, Doug, just explain what we're doing?'

Doug spun around to face me. 'I'll use a couple of slings to extend each of our harnesses to a belay device in front of both of us. You will be lying on top of me effectively, and I'll control our ascent with a prusik. I'll use my legs to keep you well off the wall.' Using a prusik, meant using a small rope, wrapped into a slidable hitch around the main abseil rope. The person abseiling would use his hand to push the knot down below the belay device to safely control the descent. If the knot was let go of, it

118

would lock tight and stop the descent. Such a simple system must have saved the lives of countless climbers over the decades.

'So, I'm standing with my back to your chest?' I turned around and backed into him. 'Like this?'

He put his left arm around my chest. 'That's right, I'll guide you with this arm, and belay with the other. You don't need to do much other than keep your feet to the wall.'

'But I was unconscious?'

'Not, today, just act dumb and stop the wall from coming out and hitting us. C'mon, we need to go.'

I recalled my IFMGA training in tandem abseils, decades earlier. Doug's description sounded about right, though it wouldn't have got him very far in an exam.

That was as much of an explanation as I was going to get. Doug grabbed his gear and pushed past me, out into the car park. Ruth tutted, again, as we dropped down the steps and said, 'Follow me,' before setting off at a brisk pace in the direction of the cable car. I struggled to keep up with them as I was afraid my trousers would either split or collapse around my knees, despite the harness, which in turn was threatening to remove any residual chance I might make of starting a family.

Doug and Ruth waited for me by the gondolas as they slipped empty through the lift station. Impatience was plastered across her face and she glanced at her watch every thirty seconds as though the mere act could speed us along. Finally, we stepped into one, the news of which she announced into her walkie-talkie as though the Queen had just arrived. She took a seat and began to make notes on her clipboard whilst Doug turned his back on me and commenced a loud phone conversation about some sort of product delivery schedule. I took the opportunity to try to adjust my clothing to make it more bearable. I was feeling about as comfortable as a teenager wearing his dad's hand-me-down suit to a party. The quality was there, but nothing fitted properly and I felt like an idiot. Once I had pushed and pulled as much as I could, I gave up and tried to visualise how this harness was going to work. Doug had been attempting to sound assured with his explanation but I wasn't convinced. What he was suggesting relied on me being conscious and I hadn't been. It made little sense. I had to trust this scene had been thought through and to get through the day. It was a one-off, I should enjoy the experience.

All too soon though the view of the valley was replaced by the concrete of the cable car station. We had arrived.

A young, nervous looking lad, with a name badge that said 'Adam' was waiting for us. Doug marched straight past him but I held back.

'Can I help with anything, Mr Darwen?'

'I was wondering what exactly happened before, you know, so we don't have a repeat?' I glanced around as I asked him, but no one else was in ear shot. 'The thing is, Doug, I mean Mr Swanson, didn't have time to tell me. Bit of a rush.'

'C'mon, Craig!' Doug had turned around and was waving at me from up the path. I started after him with Adam in tow.

'I'm sorry, I'm not sure, Mr Darwen—'

'Craig.'

'Yes,' he flushed, 'there was a problem with the tandem abseil, I don't think the climbers understood Mr Swanson's system. Don't worry, we had a health and safety review, it's all fixed now.'

His answer hadn't reassured me, but I could see further questions were pointless. We caught up Doug, and Adam led us out through the tourist zone. As we descended a steep slope, he explained he was a keen climber himself and would be helping us get set up. I wondered if he had helped the previous incumbents of the shoot, but said nothing, their fall had surely not been his fault. We soon arrived at the sheet of rock that would be masquerading as Fitz Roy. It bore no resemblance.

'Well, it's rock I suppose,' I said, looking up to the film crew above us who were playing with the backup belay and return winch and then down, over the edge at the long, vertical drop towards the all-too-pretty valley floor. 'Don't worry, once post-production has been on it, this will look like Everest,' Doug said.

'Wrong continent,' I said, 'Patagonia will do.'

Adam handed him a collection of slings and tackle and started to connect them into Doug's harness, but Doug waved him away, saying he would be fine. Adam crossed over to me and clipped a long sling into my karabiner then stood back and nervously watched Doug fiddling with the arrangement, clearly desperate to intervene. It was soon evident the arrangement wasn't working as Doug had planned.

He cursed. 'No, bloody hell. Should have practised. Thought it would come flooding back.' He reached into his pocket and took out a hip flask, which he took a deep slug from.

'Not sure the answer's in there,' I said. Even with thirty people around us and probably no end of safety backup, I didn't fancy being slung to a drunk climber.

Doug scowled at me then went back to playing with his gear. Suddenly I felt a damp cloth on my forehead. I turned around to find makeup being applied by a young woman.

'Blood,' she said. 'A bit rough, but it will do from a

distance.' She carried on dabbing. 'Okay, that'll do.'

Adam returned with radios which he secreted in our jackets before clipping earpieces on to each of us. My ear filled with the chatter of Sarah and Rick.

Adam said, 'You don't need to touch them, the mics will activate when you speak—try now.'

'Hi—' I muttered.

'Doug, you ready?' It was Rick. 'We need to get going, chopper's due in fifteen.'

Doug looked at me. 'God, you're a sight.' But he was white himself and his hand was shaking.

'Let Adam help.'

Doug nodded, the boy stepped forward and expertly arranged us. Doug was at the back with me in front of him. We both had slings attached to a descender above us through which the rope ran down past Doug's hip, where the prusik that allowed Doug to control the descent rate was located. In addition, a safety rope from the hoist was clipped into my harness. Once we were set up Adam helped us back up to the edge, Doug pulled the rope tight and the hoist wound in. He placed his feet on the edge on either side of mine and leaned back. His breathing was rapid. I pressed back against him, ready.

'It's just an abseil,' I said.

'Yep. Just an abseil.' He didn't sound convinced.

'Camera roll.'

'Camera rolling.'

'Slate.'

'And…Action!'

I just had to hang there, hang there and be lowered down. The close-up shots had been done, so anyone could have done that surely, but they wanted me, because what could be more realistic than the victim himself?

Now we were off, descending down the rock face to

122

the thunder of a distant chopper. We were very much on-camera. My view was of the wall passing a bit too close to my face. In my ear I could hear Doug panting away as we slowly jerked downwards.

'Shit, sorry, Craig,' he said, as the rope slipped and I collided with the rock-face.

'Thought you knew how to do this.' I was trussed up like a turkey with about as many options to move. I had to use the same gear as Francois who weighed considerably less than me. I stupidly hadn't adjusted the harness sufficiently to accommodate my middle-aged spread, and the straps were burrowing into my legs, killing the circulation. I wondered why they hadn't used a manikin.

A familiar voice came through into my earpiece. 'Okay Doug, re-start your rap. Craig, remember, you're unconscious. Keep those legs still.'

'Shit.'

'What's up?'

'Bloody prusik.'

'Doug, get lowering, you're on camera,' the voice said.

'Why can't she do it, she's no bloody idea,' Doug said as we jerked downwards a metre.

'Relax,' I said, 'backup's got us, just feed it out.'

'Keeps sticking.'

I couldn't see the tangle of karabiners and slings above me from my almost horizontal position, but then neither would the chopper, whose rotor beats echoed off the cliff-face.

'Doug, you need to let it out faster,' the earpiece said. 'It's supposed to be an emergency.'

'Bloody hell. Shitty things jammed.' Another two metres in one jerk. What the hell was Rick playing at?

'Why can't you release the prusik and let the backup do

the work?' I asked.

'It's not active.'

We dropped and spun again.

'What?' I yelled.

'Sarah wanted it authentic. Sorry, mate. Not much further now.'

'When were you planning to tell me?' Again, my body slammed against the wall.

'Shit, sorry. Guys, this isn't working. Need Rick to control this.'

There was no reply. Rick? Can you hear us?'

'What's going on?' I shouted.

'Blinking comms have packed up.'

'Just get us down, feel like my leg's about to be amputated. How much further? Don't bullshit me.'

'Ten metres.'

'Get on with it.'

'It's not vertical enough. I can't keep you off the wall without you walking it. Mind your head!'

I pulled my head back just in time, but my helmet clipped the granite. 'Craig, you're supposed to be unconscious,' Sarah's voice came through again. So the communications channel was working at least one way.

'I will be in a minute,' I shouted. 'This is a fucking palaver.'

'Lie back, or they'll have us doing this again, only ten left—bugger.'

We jerked to a halt. 'What's up?'

'Another obstruction, hang on.' I felt us pushed out into space, a rapid jerk down and then a hard impact as we hit the wall. Doug swore.

'Don't know how I stayed unconscious through all this!' I said.

'It wasn't…like…this,' he said, drop, drop, drop.

124

'Well, I guessed that as I'm still alive!'

A minute later we hit the ground, hard in my case as I had no feet to absorb the impact. 'Thank God for that,' Doug said. 'Let's get you out of this get-up.'

He reached up to start undoing the slings but was interrupted by a voice in our ears. 'We need to run it again. Doug, can you walk it? Dropping the winch now.'

'Seriously?' I said just before the Karabiner at the end of the steel cable flashed by, narrowly missing my head.

I sat up and looked at Doug. He was red-faced and panting. 'Need a break,' he said into his mic.

'Five minutes, chopper's in the air. Rest on the winch.'

'Shit. Okay, just get on with it.' He clipped us in. 'Pull us up.'

Before I could argue the point, Doug was walking us up the face under the power of the hoist, high above. His breathing was laboured.

The ascent was almost as bad, slow enough to seem interminable, fast enough to require me to fend off oncoming boulders with my arms as my body swung back and forth across Doug's legs. By the time we reached the shelf where we started, Doug was clearly exhausted and I felt bruised on the inside and the out. Two of the support crew grabbed us as we reached the top and I had my make-up reapplied. Sarah and Rick had made themselves scarce.

'Those boys ready to go again?' Rick's voice said.

Doug had grabbed a bottle of water from one of the crew and was downing it. He shot me a look.

'One more time?'

'One more go will do it, Doug. Just try to make it a bit slicker.'

Doug spat on the ground. 'One more time then we're done. You'll have to use what you've got.' Before he got an answer, he tied me in again, and nodded to the crew

125

who ran back to the hide. 'Ready?' he asked.

I tightened up my helmet, as though that would help. 'Let's go.'

The second descent was faster than the first. I held every muscle tense, ready for an impact, but Doug steered us away from the obstacles, as though he had gained in competence already. But when we were halfway down, we suddenly stopped.

'Bugger.'

'What's up?' I asked.

'You alright?' my earpiece hissed.

Doug was panting hard behind me and clearly fiddling with something. 'I need you to take the down rope.'

'What?!' I asked. 'For fuck's sake, Doug. Ask them for help.'

'Take the strain.'

'Tie the bloody thing off!'

'Boys you got us?' Doug asked. Even from my limited viewpoint I could see the backup rope was very slack. No one replied. 'Bloody comms out again. Try yours.'

'Rick, can you hear me? Anyone?'

There was no answer.

'What's up?' I asked, attempting to sit up.

'Lie down, they'll make us shoot it again!' Doug hissed.

'Not if you're about to kill us both.'

'Don't be so bloody dramatic. I've got it, just need to unsnag the bottom karabiner. Fucking prusik's jammed.'

I then understood. The little prusik hitch had become tangled in the belay device.

'Doug, you need to tie off on your thigh and sort it out.' Surely he knew that.

'Guys, we need you to take the slack here,' Doug said, ignoring my comment.

'What's going on, Doug? Get moving again.' Sarah's

voice was loud in my ear.

'They can't hear us,' I said. 'You need my help.'

'Wait.' Doug dropped his upper arm. 'God, I'm knackered. They'll figure it out soon enough.'

'Keep the bloody rope locked off. I don't trust those idiots up there an inch. C'mon, Doug, let me help you. We can do this again tomorrow.' I started to pull my arms out of the sleeping bag.

'We're not doing it again,' he said. 'Ah, it's coming.'

At that moment we plummeted. My body spun out of control and my legs crashed hard into the wall. I ripped my arms out of the bag and grabbed hopelessly for the rope which was whistling past my face. As suddenly as the free fall had started, with a hard jerk on the rope, we were static once more, hanging from the backup rope. I felt as though I had been cut in two.

'You guys okay?'

'Get us down,' I shouted. 'Get us down… Doug?'

But Doug was silent. I tried to sit up, but my back and neck were on fire. We slowly started to be lowered down by the hoist, which presumably had arrested my fall. 'Doug?'

He didn't reply.

A minute later we were down. I ripped myself out of the collection of slings and harnesses to stand on my own feet. My back was agony but I was relieved to feel there was no permanent damage. Doug's face was ashen and his hands shook as he raised the flask to his lips. 'I'll have some of that,' I said and grabbed it off him. The whisky burnt my throat. I heard Doug mumbling to himself as he attempted to untangle himself from his gear. He looked every bit the novice who had decided it wasn't for him. 'Doug, you okay?' I said, placing my hand on his shoulder. 'Don't worry about it,' a pain shot up my back and I

127

dropped my arm with a curse. 'They were pushing us too hard.'

But Doug stared at me as though seeing me for the first time. 'It wasn't like that.'

'What wasn't?'

He grabbed my shoulders. 'I'm sorry, Craig. It was an accident. Not like that. I tried—'

'Heh, guys. You nailed it! Nice job.'

I turned around. Sarah was jogging towards us with one of the technicians and Piotr holding a small camera.

Doug grabbed my arm. 'Craig. Don't say anything.'

'About the fact we nearly died you mean?' But I didn't get a reply as Sarah had reached us.

'Awesome, awesome, awesome. We saw the preview shots from the chopper. Really dramatic.'

I watched Doug feign a smile. 'Not quite as planned, but glad it looked good.'

'More than good, Douggie. Rick loves it.'

'I think I hurt my back,' I said, and with that lay down on the mountainside, as the drizzle cooled my face.

CHAPTER ELEVEN

I made it down the mountain, just. A river of pain ran across my lower back and into my groin. I was offered assistance by some of the crew, but I wanted to return to my room, take some ibuprofen and lie down on a hard surface. It wasn't the first time I had put my back out, though the last had been a decade before. I would ask the hotel if they knew an osteopath or chiropractor as well, the longer I left it, the worse it would get.

Doug appeared unharmed, physically at least, however he was utterly subdued. His head hung low and he walked as though in a trance, ignoring the plaudits of the crew. I was not sure what the problem was. It had been nasty, but we had walked away, surely it was nothing compared to the accident itself. Perhaps, like me, shadows from the past were playing through his mind, but for him it had taken the shock of the fall to release them. Sarah had clearly picked up on his mood also and had vanished back up the hill on the pretext of helping to pack up.

We descended together in the cable car, me standing and stretching my arms to the ceiling as best I could, Doug sitting glumly staring down at the approaching valley floor. We didn't speak until I had gingerly climbed into the Range Rover.

'Your place or mine?' Doug said without a trace of humour on his face.

'Mine, just drop me. I have a back to fix. I couldn't bear any polite company.'

Doug paused, then said. 'Me neither, to be honest.'

We remained silent as the grey tarmac spun under our wheels. It was clouding over again, at least we had had some luck with the weather.

'I guess I'm nearly done then?'

Doug said, 'Hmmm.'

'I suppose there is the talking heads to go over again, but filming?'

'There's still Patagonia.' Doug's hands tightened on the wheel as he mentioned the place.

'Do you really need me there? Thought it was just landscapes.'

'Oh don't be so bloody silly, Craig! Of course we need you there. You have to see this out! Yeah? Like me. We both have to see this out…That thing, I said on the hill…'

Doug had said a lot of things on the hill, many of them unrepeatable. But I knew what he was referring to. He glanced over to me then fixed his eyes back on the road. 'Yeah, well, it was a shock, and a bit weird. It was like we were back there.'

'You were scared.'

'Yeah, of course I was bloody scared. Those idiots almost killed us.'

It wasn't just those idiots, but I decided not to mention Doug's inability to remember how to abseil rescue.

'Why didn't you insist on the safety rope tension? I don't understand. I mean, Sarah's a climber she should—'

He swung the car hard into my street and my back jolted. 'Ah, slow down.'

'Oh, sorry. Forgot about your back. You should get it seen to.'

'Don't worry, I intend to.'

He pulled up in front of my chalet. 'I'll have words with Sarah, believe me.' He took a look at me and frowned. 'Sure you don't want to come back to stay up at *Valois*? You're looking really rough. I know a good sports physio—'

'I'm sure, I'd be bad company anyway. I'll drive up in

130

the morning.'

'Have the day off, sort out your back. I'll let you know what the schedule is. I'll get the door—'

He stepped around the car and opened the door for me. 'Need a hand?'

'I'm fine.' I stepped out carefully onto the pavement and slowly uncurled myself, my back having totally locked up on the short journey. But something was bothering me almost as much as that pain. I turned to him. 'You said it wasn't like that?'

'What?'

'What did you mean?'

He crossed his arms and leaned back against the car. 'You read the book?'

'What was it really like?'

He turned his head and looked away, up towards the site of our earlier adventure. He then smiled for the first time that day. 'I'll give you a call. Take it easy.' With that he climbed back into the car and drove off.

The preponderance of extreme sports opportunity around Chamonix means it is well catered for with medical practitioners. I found an Australian locum, Carl, who described himself as from the 'snap 'em and crack 'em school'. It was just what I needed. His brutal attacks on my body were accompanied by a hilarious monologue rant on the problems of the town ranging from petty corruption to bins not being emptied. It was a strange anaesthetic, but it worked. From entering his practice walking like an old man who been caught short, I left, if not like a mountaineer, at least looking my ragged age. He booked me in for an appointment for the following Tuesday, one I intended to keep. I needed my back in shape for the long drive home. Nothing was worse for it than hours slumped in a car.

I wondered about the abseil and the accident. Doug had been useless; I couldn't believe he had taken such a chance with our safety or that he had grown so rusty. Sure, it was far from a simple task, but when it had counted all those years ago, he had done ten perhaps twenty such abseils in freezing rain, low light and high winds. In an Antarctic storm. And now, he seemed barely capable of tying a knot. I wouldn't be climbing with him again.

I went back to the hotel to relax. The clouds had cleared and the sun was illuminating the spire of St Gerome's. I looked up at the peak, wondering if there were any climbers looking back down on the town, as I had so many years before. It had been fun back then, we felt immortal, as though accidents were a thing that happened to others, and whilst I was in the Alps, that had been true. It was nearly lunchtime so I decided to stop in at one of the brasseries on Rue Denis. As I was entering though, my phone rang. It was Sarah.

'Craig, I'm choked to hear about your back. I had no idea you had been hurt like that. You waltzed off that mountain like Superman. How are ya?'

I told her about Carl and how I would feel a lot better after a day's rest. I didn't believe the interest she feigned in my back for a minute, but I wasn't in a mood for an argument.

'We were all hoping you could come for dinner tonight? Doug and I have to drive up to head office for a couple of days and we thought a get-together would be nice. We can catch up on what's left to shoot and you can see the footage we got yesterday.'

Where was Linda in all of this, after all surely it was her house and she who should be doing the inviting? I tried to think of a convenient excuse not to go, but after having verbally signed-off my back problem, my primary means of escape had been blocked. So that evening I found myself sitting next to Sarah on Doug's sofa, whilst she enthusiastically showed me the footage of our fall on her iPad. Even I had to concede it looked fairly dramatic, though it hardly felt worth it. She went to great pains to acknowledge this, with fulsome apologies about the lapse with the backup rope. If I'd never seen her in action, I would have lapped up every smooth word. As it was, I played along, wondering where this chat was leading.

She was wearing a low-cut little black number with her blonde hair crackling against the ebony of the dress. As I watched the iPad in her hands, I could see Doug struggling to keep his eyes off her, seemingly oblivious to the increasingly rapid steps of Linda entering and leaving with drinks and snacks.

A couple of girls, whom I recognised from the catering staff, had been borrowed to help cook and serve our dinner. However, this didn't prevent Linda ostensibly checking the feast they were preparing. Doug asked her to sit and join us in the lounge once, but she made her excuses and the offer wasn't repeated. Linda didn't seem keen to participate and I could guess a few reasons why. She hadn't attempted to match the artillery of Sarah's outfit, but had instead donned designer jeans and a simple blouse. To me she looked much the classier. But I couldn't catch her eye.

Doug, who was not as dapper as usual, seemed distracted, not only by Sarah's curves, but by some greater issue. Eventually Linda called us through to the dining room and we took our places, Linda and Doug sat on one side of the table, Sarah and I on the other. If Doug's input into the dinner table conversation was minimal, Linda was almost mute and it fell to Sarah and me to fill the void.

She quizzed me about my time in Chamonix before the accident and how the town had changed, whilst she regaled us with anecdotes from the US and Canadian climbing scene. I noticed both Linda and Doug were quietly consuming the majority of the wine on the table, with the first bottle not making it to the main course. The food was excellent, as was the drink, and the combination of that and Sarah's easy conversation had me almost not noticing the silence from the other two.

When the trouble finally arrived, it was I who unwittingly lit the fuse. We had finished our desserts, a light, berry-mousse of some sort, and Doug had started on the port after he and Linda had polished off a bottle of dessert wine between them. The conversation had lulled, with even Sarah struggling to lift the atmosphere. I was calculating when I could politely make my excuses and leave.

After a particularly long pause, I opted for small talk. 'So, Doug, got anything exciting planned in Zurich?' Doug looked up quickly. 'Just a board meeting. Progress report, nothing exciting. Travel Lodge then home. You know the sort of thing.' He glanced across at Linda as he said this but her eyes appeared fixed on a spot on the far wall.

I had no idea what was controversial about this, but before I could ask another question, Linda chimed in, 'A progress meeting that requires marketing input.'

'Oh yes?' I ventured on, not seeing the danger.

'Yes, he needs his marketing manager there.' She picked up her wine glass and took a large gulp.

Sarah pushed her chair back and said, 'Linda—'

'Linda, we talked about this,' Doug interrupted. 'It's a bloody board meeting, of course I need Sarah there.'

'Sarah's on the board now?'

'They want to discuss the film. We need to make a

report.'

'And you need your, "marketing manager",' Linda made quotation marks in the air, 'there with you.'

At that Sarah's seat shot back and she marched from the room. I pushed my seat back also, but Linda grabbed my arm. 'No, you stay. You need to hear this.' The glasses rattled as the front door slammed shut.

'You're pissed. Go to bed,' Doug said, his face purple.

Linda threw her remaining wine into his face. 'I know about your pathetic little affair and I've had enough.' She stood up. 'Go to fucking Zurich with her. Just don't come back here!' By this point her eyes were streaming. 'Good night, Craig.'

Doug didn't look at her as she left the room, but sat staring into his glass, port dripping off his nose onto the table cloth, like a bruised and bloody boxer. I too was frozen to my chair. Why it was unexpected I wasn't sure. Linda must have seen or heard something since our cafe talk that had confirmed her fears. Doug wasn't simply being strung along; it was much more. And I had probably been summoned just as a peacekeeper for the evening. A plan that had spectacularly backfired.

'Well. That's that then,' Doug said. He flopped his napkin onto the table, poured himself a large glass of wine then downed it.

'For God's sake, Doug, aren't you going after her?'

'Linda?'

'Of course sodding Linda!'

He answered my question by starting to pour some more port.

I yanked his glass away. 'That isn't the solution.' He continued to pour the port onto the table, as though not noticing the absence of the vessel. I took the bottle from him. 'You going to go to Zurich?'

135

'Damn right I'm going. Shouldn't you be asking if I'm sleeping with her?'

I didn't answer that. 'What about Linda? Your marriage?'

Doug sighed. 'Oh, Craig, she'll come round. This isn't our first hiccup. You've never been married, you wouldn't understand.'

'Thanks.'

'Sorry, man, but come on. Sometimes I envy you.' A hoarse laugh escaped my throat, but he continued, 'No, really, I do. Don't worry about us. There's always been a bit of fire under her mumsy exterior. Part of the attraction.'

'You're are a heartless bastard, Doug. I can't believe—'

'What? That she married me instead of you? Maybe she would have if you hadn't been such a complete fuck-up.'

I jumped up and flung my napkin down. 'You're unbelievable. I'll finish your shitty film and then I hope we never meet again.'

'God, you having your period too?'

The next thing I knew I had dived across the table and planted my fist into his smug, drunken face. It was the first time I had hit anyone since I was at school. Doug's chair crashed backwards and he sprawled onto the carpet. Once the punch had been thrown, I had no idea what to do. I stood over him, shaking with rage and fear. Doug seemed more surprised than anything. He rolled slowly onto his front and stood up.

He rubbed his cheek, then a broad smile cracked his face. 'Well, Craig. I had no idea you had that in you. I suppose I deserved it. Perhaps more from Linda than you, but I'll take it, on her behalf.' He held out his hand. I reached and pulled him up.

136

'You don't deserve her.'

'No, I probably don't. Maybe I did once.'

And maybe he had. I certainly didn't then and I didn't now.

'What you going to do?'

Doug sighed. 'Well, I'm off to Zurich before the cock crows. You can stay and comfort my wife, or you can piss off down to your dingy hotel. I really don't care. You just need to finish the film and then, sure, you don't need to see me again. Except perhaps at the premiere…'

'Good night, Doug.' I turned heel and staggered down to the guest room, the adrenalin and alcohol rattling around my system. I had consumed far too much booze to drive back to the hotel. I would stay the night and then tomorrow I was leaving. I had been wrong about the money; no amount was worth this.

I awoke to a throat that felt like paint stripper had been liberally poured down it and with a sore head to match. It was still early and dark outside, but my bladder called. However, I realised it had been the sound of a running engine that had awoken me. From the bathroom I heard the front door close and the sound of gravel crunching as Doug's car set off to Zurich.

I flopped back onto my bed and tried to go back to sleep, but it was impossible. Every time I shut my eyes, I felt the room spinning and a nauseous feeling building inside. By eight o'clock I had been sick. I was like a student, a teenager. Arguing, getting drunk, fighting with my friends. Bloody ridiculous. Should I sneak out the house once again, or talk to Linda? What would I say? That I still had feelings for her? That, if truth be told, I had never replaced her? It was pathetic. At least I was no longer envious of Doug. He had money, but his life was no better than mine. At least no one hated me.

No, I had to have it out with her. Doug had gone, it was just the two of us. I showered, which took the edge off the hangover, then crept upstairs as though at any moment Linda might jump out at me. But the lounge was empty and there was no sign of the dogs. It seemed I had the house to myself. I fixed myself a bowl of cereal and some coffee and then went to the lounge to wait. All around me pictures of a triumphant Doug stared down, on top of mountains, on a beach with Linda, signing a book for some Hollywood actor. Linda's mark on the room was much more subtle; some family portraits in small frames on a sideboard, novels on a bookcase, but not much else. Perhaps her room was elsewhere. Before I knew it, I was wandering the house, looking in every room, trying to lift a lid on the enigma of their relationship.

Away from the perfect reception rooms, the house was a mess. Doug and Linda's room was upstairs. The top floor was given over to a huge master bedroom suite, the size of my entire flat. Despite the array of mirrored wall cupboards, the oak floor was scattered with clothes. Other than a bathroom there was only one other room with a single bed in that had been slept in. No doubt it was Doug's bolt-hole, as it was decorated with his discarded clothes from the night before. How he had negotiated fetching his travel-things I could only guess. Then I got a real surprise. In the corner was a solitary wooden cot. I sat down on the bed and stared at it. Above the cot was framed a faded, embroidered ABC with different animals playfully adorning each of the letters. Someone had put a lot of care into making it. I spotted a small, silver photo frame on the adjacent window sill and picked it up. I blew the dust away to reveal a tiny picture of Linda, her face heavily flushed, hair unkempt, lying in a hospital bed holding a little baby. She was looking up at the camera, a tired smile on her lips.

'Hello.'

I almost dropped the picture, but managed to carefully replace it before turning around. Linda framed the doorway, her hair dripping wet, her trousers muddy; she was never more lovely.

'I'm...I'm sorry. I didn't mean to—'

'Explore?'

'Sorry, I thought you were out?'

She smiled. 'So, you thought you would go through our underwear drawer?'

I felt myself redden. 'No, I don't know. I just wondered where you were and—'

'Oh relax, Craig. After last night, I don't think I have any more secrets I care about keeping. You've seen the picture. Meningitis, before you ask.'

I put my hand on the cot. 'I didn't realise. I'm sorry.'

'The cot's old, a family heirloom. I thought I would need it again once, a long time ago.' She walked in and sat down on the bed. 'In the end I didn't, and that was that.'

'Oh, I see.' Though I didn't, but then this was none of my business.

'You would have been a good dad.'

'No I wouldn't,' I said quickly.

'I think you would.' She stood up. 'I need to freshen up, don't know about you but I think I had a bit too much to drink last night.'

'We all did.'

As she walked to the en suite bathroom she turned and said, 'Doug skulked in with a bit of a shiner this morning—was that you?' I said nothing. 'Well if it was, I won't ask what it was about, but well done anyway. Should

139

have done it myself years ago.'

'Why—'

'Let's talk later. How about we go out for lunch? It's probably about time we caught up properly now Universal Studios has left the building.'

Instead of turning right out of her drive towards civilisation, Linda swung her Range Rover left up the winding mountain road. Her hounds were in the back, their tails wagging excitedly in anticipation of an interesting walk.

'What's up here? Thought it was just mountain?' I asked.

'Ah, that's where you're almost right, but not quite.'

The road was a narrow concrete service road that twisted its scar through the wilderness until ending in a large car park set above a huge, white concrete dam. At one end of the car park lay a restaurant with a balcony offering a stunning vista. We jumped out the car and Linda opened the boot to release the dogs.

'Nice place for lunch.'

'Oh, no. We're not eating here,' she said. 'We're eating up there.' She pointed north towards a hanging valley where another dam was visible. The dogs had already set off on what was clearly a well-loved route. We descended from the car park onto the top of the dam and crossed it. It seemed new, almost pristine as though it were swept daily. The lake it retained was huge. Signs posted along it told us about how such dams were saving the environment; there were apparently hundreds like this one and the one above. The environment, nature, tamed by man and twisted to serve him.

The service road continued all the way up to the second dam but I was glad when the dogs took a path off it, leading us into an environment much more reminiscent of Snowdonia: narrow, rocky paths, damp cliffs, moss and lichen. For a while the concrete was out of sight, the dogs were charging ahead and we were in the shadow of a peak. It almost felt like we were back home. We made small talk about the hounds and about Lottie, about the scenery and life in Switzerland. Village life in Finhaut was much like home with its annual cycle of ceremonies, twitching curtains and local politics. Some of the issues were the same; refuse collection and housing, others were different; noise and obsessive tidiness, but Linda and Doug had fitted in well. A bit of his money thrown in the right places had helped as had their willingness to become part of the community.

We arrived an hour later at the second dam and with it the chalet-style restaurant that was our destination. It was constructed of dark wood at the top of the link road. The decking outside was empty, but would no doubt be full of chairs in midsummer. The hounds bounded up the steps and pawed the door, which was duly thrown open by a moustachioed, grey-haired man. A large white, rug of a mongrel ran out past him to greet us.

'Linda, Linda, why have you left it so long?' He kissed her on both cheeks and pumped my hand, with a wink in my direction.

'Meet Luc, the custodian of my favourite escape.'

Inside the room was like a scout hut, made of modern, varnished pine, with exposed cross beams and pictures showing the construction of the dams. The windows were surprisingly small, hinting at the need to keep the room snug against the elements. It was much smaller than the lower restaurant and was virtually empty but was far from the sort of generic tourist magnet found in Chamonix.

The appeal was obvious. I wondered if it was a place Linda normally came to alone and if not, with what company?

On one side of the room chairs had been stacked up on tables. Luc saw me looking at them. 'Ah, you have caught us on the last day of the season. We are closing tonight.'

We took a balcony seat which gave an uninterrupted view across to the lower reservoir and dam. Linda rattled away to the owner in fluent French. They laughed at some joke and then he left us alone.

I picked up the menu.

'I recommend the rosti, it's divine,' Linda said, without even glancing at it.

'Okay, rosti it is, whatever that is.' I put the menu card down.

'So, about last night…I'm sorry if I embarrassed you.'

Embarrassment had been low down on my list of emotions the previous evening, but I chose not to say that. 'To be honest, Linda, I think we had all had a bit too much to drink.'

At that point Luc came back with a bottle of Chablis and water. Linda ordered for us both, and once we were alone, continued as though we had never been interrupted. 'No, well yes, you're right, but I owe you an explanation.'

'I was a bit confused by it all, and…' I showed her my bruised knuckles.

She smiled. 'Yes, that. Well thanks, if that was for me. Not that I want to encourage people to hit my husband.'

'What was it you said about marketing? I didn't follow.'

Linda sat back in her chair and looked into the vista beyond. 'Well, in vino veritas and all that.' She took a sip of her Chablis. 'Sarah Hughes isn't who you think she is. Well, who I suppose you think she is.'

142

'She told me she was an upcoming film producer, something like that.'

'Well, that's how she's styled herself, but didn't you wonder how a girl in her mid-twenties could suddenly be making a multi-million-pound movie?'

'I suppose she raised the money from a studio or something?'

'Oh no, that comes later. No, no. This is Doug's money. Our money. That's what's being poured away on choppers, makeup artists, trailers.'

'I knew he was investing but assumed that was only a fraction. He isn't anything to do with films?'

'That's right, he isn't. Let me start at the beginning. A couple of years ago, this pretty Canadian arrives at SummitSeeker's offices, asking for an internship in the marketing department. She has a film studios major and a masters in marketing having unsurprisingly failed to crack Hollywood in however many weeks she spent there. Her references were excellent and with her climbing background and North American outlook, the marketing department snapped her up, after all she was cheap. It quickly turned out she wasn't just any marketing girl, she had a particular interest in Doug's story, and had an idea for a film, to boot. Apparently, she strode into his office one day complete with a film storyboard and some bits of a script and sold it to him.

'Well initially he didn't do anything about it, though he told me about it. I didn't take it seriously at the time, but over the next few months her name cropped up—Sarah this and Sarah that, but only in regard to marketing, the film wasn't mentioned.'

She sipped her wine and gave me a look as though waiting for a prompt.

'So, what happened?'

'Doug came home one evening, he had been over in Zurich most of the week. I could tell as soon as he walked in something exciting had happened. He pitched me the whole film idea, told me it would boost the company enormously, that the board was willing to fund it. I was happy for him; it had been years since I had seen him so animated and alive. I had no idea at the time of the true cost. I realised the film appealed to a middle-aged man's vanity and put his name out in front of a new generation of climbers who had never heard of him, but knew the brand. He had worked hard to create SummitSeeker and I believed too he deserved to be in the limelight again. Next thing I know, the head of marketing has left in a strop of some sort. Jealousy, I assumed.'

'When did you meet her?'

She looked me in the eye. 'Oh that's easy to remember. I had heard about the wonderful Sarah Hughes of course, but it was at their Christmas do, a year ago. She wasn't what I was expecting.'

'What was that?'

'Oh you know, fawning, I suppose. Some gorgeous young creature sucking up to Doug. I had seen plenty of those over the years. But she wasn't like that then. She almost seemed uninterested in him at that do. She had a boyfriend, some Swiss banker type, don't know what happened to him...Well, she was perfectly charming to me. Wanted to know all about our family. Or lack of it.'

'I see.'

'No, you probably don't.' She waved her hand as though batting a question away. 'By this point the film preparations had started. She pitched it to me—it seemed convincing. Looking back, I suppose she wanted to ensure there was no opposition at home. Sensible really. Sorry, do you mind if I smoke?'

I was surprised, but nodded. 'Course not.'

'My dirty little secret.' She lit a cigarette and blew the smoke high into the air. I glanced over her shoulder to the bar. 'Oh, Luc doesn't mind, he's a darling and the place is empty.'

'So, the film?'

'Yes, well she told me she'd been in contact with a studio and they wanted to make it. They had seen the success of *Touching the Void* and *Everest*; there was an appetite for heroic rescues and disasters it seemed. She didn't mention the budget or the financing, or anything much about her involvement. I suppose I fell for it all, like Doug already had.'

'What do you mean?'

'The finance. There was no studio. The whole thing is a vanity project, Craig. She persuaded Doug they would win the Palme d'Or or something, a distributor would pick it up and he would earn millions. Didn't need a greedy studio paying for it. The budgets would be kept down, the crew minimal, the filming tight. She knew all about it. She had connections…' She stubbed out the half-smoked cigarette. 'She lied. You've seen it all, haven't you. Nothing burns cash faster than a film. That's one thing I've learnt.'

'How on earth did he pay for it?'

'You won't believe it. I didn't and he sure as hell didn't tell me. He sold most of his shares. He's just a minority shareholder now. It was the deal he struck with the board to persuade them to agree to putting the money in. That and his spiel about the chance to boost their brand and market their gear. He raised a bit from some friends in Zurich too, there's no shortage of cash there if you know where to look.'

At that point our lunch arrived, a steaming dish of roast potatoes, cheese and bacon. Luc laid the two dishes

145

reverently in front of us, topped up our wine glasses, then with a 'Bon appetit,' strode away.

'And the affair?'

She snorted. 'That? Well, no idea, though I've had my suspicions for a while. You've seen how he looks at her?'

'But maybe that's all it is, some infatuation? She's—'

'Beautiful. Yes, I know. You men are so pathetic, so easily manipulated.'

'I—'

'You're here aren't you, Craig? What are you doing in Chamonix? Weren't you happy in your life in Wales? Do you want to tell the world about how you fell off a cliff? How you needed rescuing? Is that really what you want, Craig?'

'I needed the money, Linda. We don't all have mountain villas.'

'None of us will soon at the rate Doug's spending the money.'

'Is it as bad as that?'

She sighed. 'I don't know. I really don't know.'

'Why have you stayed with him?' the question blurted out of me like air escaping from a balloon. But it was a question I had wanted to ask from the moment I had seen Sarah climb into the car next to him.

'You mean besides his millions?' She removed another cigarette from the packet and lit up.

'Yes, besides that.'

'You really think me that shallow? You think I care about the money?' She blew smoke into the air. 'I suppose I did once, I wrapped it around me like a blanket. After Ben…' Tears welled in her eyes. I didn't need to ask who Ben was, I had seen his crib earlier.

'I still love the bastard, despite it all. That's why, Craig. I love him and I'm not going to let that bitch take that

146

away, even if her folly strips every last penny.'

I felt crushed, only at that point did I realise fully what I had hoped for from this meeting, this lunch together. Doug had even encouraged us almost. How thoroughly stupid I was. Now Linda was looking at me, a dawning recognition crossing her face.

'Oh. Craig. I'm sorry...I—Oh, God.' She stubbed out the cigarette.

'What?' I asked.

'I didn't mean to lead you on, not after all these years. I thought—'

'I can't believe I let him take you,' it was all flooding out now. 'I can't believe I let him steal you from me—'

'Steal me? Steal me? He didn't steal me, Craig! It was my decision. I chose Doug.' She jabbed her thumb into her chest then pointed at me. 'You never came back from that peak. It was as though he came back with himself plus half of you in him and you had just half a man left behind. Have you ever found that other half, Craig? Have you?'

I lifted my glass and knocked back the remaining wine. On placing the glass back, I saw her expression softening like a mother seeing tears forming in her child's eyes. She reached out across the table and took my hand. 'Craig, darling, don't you remember where we were at when I came to stay with you in Chamonix?' Her voice was gentle, soothing. I remembered that tone from all those years before, from her final stay in Chamonix.

'What do you mean?'

'Craig, we were over before I ever met Doug. We were just friends, don't you remember? My visit to Chamonix was—'

'To finish it.'

'There wasn't anything to finish! We had already split up—don't you remember? Isn't that why you left for

France? I wanted us to be friends, like we were before we went out. I thought that's what you wanted too…We weren't made for each other, Craig. I'm sorry.'

I stood up slowly. 'Excuse me.' I walked outside onto the terrace. The sun was now out fully from behind the clouds, the peaks were bright, beautiful. She was right, half of me had been left behind on that accursed mountain.

I stood out on that balcony looking at the mountains; the stark grey buttresses, the deep blue reservoirs, the road winding down to the dam, the civilisation. An accident here could cost you your life but help was never far away. A flick of a mobile phone and the helicopter would come, rotors beating across the valley; expensive, yes, but timely. When we had been in Patagonia, two decades before, there were no phones and no help. We had had to deal with what happened alone and we had. I had survived but something inside was still eating away at me, stopping me getting back to the person I had been. Linda was right. Perhaps I had to go back there and re-live it to finally move on.

My phone buzzed; it was Sue.

'Craig?'

'Hi, Sue. How are—'

'I'm really sorry, Craig. I think you need to come back.'

Her tone was grave and I felt my skin go to ice. 'What's up, is Lottie okay?'

'Lottie's fine.'

I sighed with relief, but Sue continued, 'No, it's the shop…. There's been a fire.'

CHAPTER TWELVE

It was a blackened ruin.

I had driven up through France over night until exhaustion forced me to sleep for a few hours in a lay-by. The Calais ferry and a greasy breakfast gave a bit more respite, but when I'd driven down the metal ramps into Dover docks, I'd still had a long, grim journey ahead of me. My back had seized to such a degree I could barely stand up straight, but I needed to return.

After Sue's call Linda and I had driven back down the valley in virtual silence. I'd contemplated leaving my car and flying back, but that would have necessitated a return, something I didn't want to do. I'd only had bad luck since Sarah had first pitched the film to me. I needed to break free of that cycle. I'd packed and after a long hug in the hall climbed into the Fiesta.

As I drove away, I'd looked in the rear-view mirror. Linda was framed against the opulence of her home, *Valois,* one hand raised in farewell, the dogs circling her legs.

I finally arrived back in Llanberis in the dying light of the late afternoon. The sun which had accompanied me through France had disappeared behind thick cloud somewhere around Birmingham and now a light drizzle fell upon my windscreen wipers.

Sue had warned me to go to her house first, but nothing could stop me passing by the shop. I drove through the centre of the village and out to my former home. I parked in the car park and walked around to the front.

I thought I was mentally prepared; I had rehearsed this moment in my mind, pictured the devastation, the rubble.

In some ways my mental image may have been painted in more dramatic colours than what lay before me, but no imaginings could soften the impact of the reality.

On the top floor, the windows had been blown out, or perhaps knocked in by the pressure of water. I could see little but the black slime coating the walls behind, where once had been my bedroom. The downstairs was no better. Chipboard had been nailed across the windows in a pointless attempt at security after the event. The door itself had been knocked away leaving only an apathetic show of police tape to prevent entry.

I stepped forward and with one rip was into the building. Immediately I was hit by the stench of sodden ash. Under my feet was a sea of charred mush; melted plastic, burnt cardboard, shrivelled rope, tarnished metal. The fire had clearly been intense, destroying everything flammable in its path.

I looked up the dark stairwell to my flat. Was that all gone too? That was the only bit that mattered. I clambered over the broken stands towards the stairwell.

'I wouldn't, Mr Darwen.'

I spun round. A police officer stood on the other side of the tape illuminated by a flashing blue light. I recognised him as one of my customers, Sergeant Alan Baxter, who also volunteered for the mountain rescue. He had once tried to persuade me to join, a 'man with my experience' and all that. I had declined, perhaps a little too forcibly.

'Alan.'

'You shouldn't be in there, Mr Darwen. Very dangerous. You need to follow me to the station please.'

Alan was hardly a friend, but when had I become 'Mr Darwen' instead of 'Craig' to him? I didn't argue, and after one look back up the stairs, left the shop and returned to my car. I followed Alan through the few streets of the village to the police station, a grey, pebble-dashed house I had only visited on a couple of occasions in relation to shoplifting incidents. Even then, I had never been beyond the front desk. Alan unlocked the front door, turned on the lights and summoned me through to a small, beige room at the back. It contained a Formica table with two plastic chairs on either side and a black recording device bolted to the wall above the table. The only decor was an analogue clock and a tea stain running down the wall by the door.

The details of the fire were simple. An anonymous 999 call had been received shortly after one o'clock two nights before. By the time the fire engines had arrived, the shop was virtually destroyed. It had taken a couple of hours to get it under control and it had not been deemed safe to enter until the following afternoon. The formal investigation was underway but initial signs were a large amount of 'accelerant' had been poured through the letter box by 'persons unknown'. He explained my legal responsibilities and the general insurance process, which sounded horribly long-winded.

He then sat back and said, 'Do you have any enemies, Mr Darwen? People you owe money to perhaps? Customers you insulted?'

I laughed.

'Is that funny?'

'No, yes, I owe some money. But not the sort who would torch my shop. Businesses, that's all. It's outdoor equipment, not drugs.'

'This is potentially a serious crime. Not just property destroyed, people could have been killed. You could have been killed. Any idea who might have done this?'

'No. The Sons of Glyndwr?' The name of the historic attempt at Welsh terrorism had come to me. It was an idiotic suggestion.

Alan leant back in his chair, crossed his arms and stared down his long nose at me. 'Is that a serious suggestion? If I may say so, Mr Darwen, you don't seem very upset.'

I had been upset, really upset, but now I was just exhausted. 'I'm sorry, I had a long journey home. It's all been a bit of a shock but I didn't own much and the dog's safe.'

'There'll be an investigation, you know that? Arson's a serious crime. Insurance companies don't like it. They'll expect us to be very thorough.'

'I hope you will be.'

'Wouldn't want it happening again, would we, Mr Darwen?' Alan lifted an eyebrow.

I'd had enough. 'Look, I could really do with going home—I mean to my shop manager. She's offered to put me up.'

'Ms Walsh. Yes, I met her yesterday; she was in the process of contacting the insurers—needed our say-so as it were…Is that where you'll be staying for the next few days? In case we need to talk again? Rather, when we need to talk again?'

'I suppose so.' I hadn't considered what I would do longer term. Sue wouldn't want me knocking around for more than that, surely?

We stood and Alan showed me out of the interview room and through to the front door. We were the only ones left in the small police station; he would be locking up for the night.

'Um, what happens next? When will I be able to get my stuff back? If anything's left, that is?'

He leaned against the door frame. 'There are a few

items, I believe, but they are inaccessible at the moment to the likes of you and I. Safety, see? We will be in touch...But please don't go anywhere, will you? Not without telling us first.'

I stood and left, unsure of whether his parting remarks were an order or a threat.

It was past eleven when I arrived at Sue's house. She lived in a pebble-dashed grey semi, on the outskirts of the village. Most lights in the cul-de-sac were already out, but hers burned bright. I was expected.

As I approached the door, I heard familiar barking from within. I could hear Lottie's tail beating out a fast rhythm on the wall even before I could ring the bell. Sue opened it and gave me a hug without saying a word, which was handy as Lottie was ready to knock me over.

'It's good to see you, Craig. I'm so sorry about the shop. But we're both excited to have you back, aren't we, Lottie?'

Lottie jumped up to lick my face.

We went to the back room. After all these years of working with Sue, I had never been beyond her front door, even when dropping Lottie's things off before my departure. Family portraits adorned the spotless surfaces, her sons at various ages, her parents and brothers and sisters. The furniture was modern and tasteful, none of the chintz I had somehow expected. The pride of place was a picture of Sue ice-climbing, a big grin on her face as she pulled up on an axe. I realised I'd never made the effort to get to know her, to discover what her interests were, that she had ice-climbed even.

I put the case of all my worldly possessions down and took a seat at the kitchen table. The excitement had already faded for Lottie and she found her way to her basket in the corner, a rag doll in her mouth. A kettle rattled and clicked off; perhaps Sue had had a premonition of my exact arrival time? I didn't think so.

Sue put a cup of tea in front of me. 'So you saw the shop then?'

'You knew?'

'Bryn told me you'd parked up and Alan had nabbed you.'

'The sarge; yes, he gave me a right grilling. Like he had had the place staked out.'

'Most exciting thing to happen around here for a while. The fire crew were particularly enthusiastic about it.'

'Once the place was wrecked no doubt. They think I had a hand in it. Well, Alan does anyway.'

Sue took my hand. 'Don't worry about stupid Alan, he always was a bit of a dunce; sat at the back of the class picking his nose from what I remember.'

'Old school mate then? Didn't realise you were acquainted.'

'At school together, yes; mate, no…And come on, of course he knows me—' she squeezed my hand, 'this is Llanberis, not Liverpool for goodness's sake! He's been in the shop enough times. This is his moment, chance to be the big man in the village like on one of those cop shows.'

She paused and then raised my chin so I was no longer staring into my empty cup but into her hazel eyes. She held my gaze for a moment and her hand fell away before saying, 'C'mon, you'll bounce back, what with Hollywood calling and everything? Don't need to worry about little old Llanberis now do you?'

My expression told her otherwise and she pulled back. 'It not working out then, Craig? You sounded fine on the phone.'

'I've had more fun.' I told her much; about Doug and

154

Sarah, the green screen interrogation, Linda and Doug, even my pathetic punch. But I couldn't tell her about the nightmares or explain about what Linda had said about part of me missing in Patagonia. I couldn't tell her this was true.

'There's one other thing.'

'What's that, sounded enough to me?' Sue said.

'It's like there's someone has it in for me, for Doug, for the film.'

Sue frowned. 'Go on.'

'Look.' I fumbled through my holdall and pulled out my copy of the book. I handed it over to her.

'Doug's book. Yes, I've got a copy too.'

'Open it.'

Sue opened it and I saw her expression change. She frowned deeply then looked at me but said nothing, passing the book back.

'Well? What the hell's all that about? Who would write that? Why?'

Sue appeared confused. 'What are you talking about, Craig?'

'The Liar word! Thick red pen!'

'Craig, love. That's your handwriting.' She said it in a calm, matter of fact voice leaving no room for dispute.

I opened the book up, shaking my head. 'Liar!' I stared at the word for a minute. 'Really?' But it was true. I couldn't argue it was my writing, perhaps written decades before. 'I don't remember—'

'You must be wrecked after your journey, I'll show you your room.' Sue said.

'Thanks, I think I need some sleep,' I said grateful to her for changing the subject.

I felt a lick on my cheek. Lottie was standing on the chair, kissing me in her own inimitable style.

155

The following days were a litany of phone calls; hold music and ignorant agents, the same security details listed over and over again. Options laid out before me, decisions to make, assessors, adjusters, buildings insurance, contractors, demolition…There was a whole ABC and by the end of the week I had almost reached Z. It was going to be months before I received any insurance money, so it was a relief to be able to pay in Doug's cheque; I had to start paying my way. In the streets I met a mixture of sympathy and suspicion, as though the village had divided itself into two camps. I felt a claustrophobia I had not experienced for many years. It was a great relief when I happened to run into my climbing club mate, Sean, in the Spar.

'You sound like a man who needs to get out and do some climbing,' he said once I had given the standard update.

'You know what, I think you might be right,' I said.

He slapped me on the back. 'Come on, let's give you something more to worry about than being homeless.'

Sean's medicine was bouldering, climbing alone and unaided. The thin mat he threw down at the base of the Cromlech Boulders wouldn't fool anyone into feeling safe as they felt the igneous rock under their fingers. But if you wanted safety, you wouldn't go bouldering; you weren't responsible for anyone else and no one was responsible for you. No belaying, complicated rigging or ridiculous winches. We stood at the base of one of the huge rocks, looking up at the routes. Faint chalk marks littered the face, marking successful and problematic ascents. A couple of youngsters, shirts off, chalk bags swinging, were making light work of it further along.

'What d'ya fancy?' Sean asked. 'Plenty of problems here

to get your head around. Sure you know most of them.'

'You should be asking what I'm capable of.'

'I know what you're capable of, Craig. Not sure you do though.' He tossed me a battered guide book. 'Pick a problem, I'm starting on something easy.' With that he was climbing, his fifty-year-old frame moving swiftly skywards, hands gripping invisible holds, feet brushing the surface. He was at the top. 'C'mon, get on with it!'

I dropped the book and began my first boulder. My muscles were like sponge, my fingers soon screamed for mercy and I kept it simple, very simple, but within a few minutes I was sitting on top of a boulder next to Sean, breathing hard. 'Bloody hell.'

Sean slapped me on the back, almost knocking me over the edge. 'You, boyo, need to do another.'

So began the most intense climbing experience I'd had since the Andes. I could barely move after an hour and I was left lying on a grassy bank staring into the darkening sky to the sound of Sean swearing as he laboured up his last problems.

We walked back down to the car together. 'Same again tomorrow?' He asked.

I nodded.

Three days later, the fire department finished their assessment. It would never be safe to go up there; I would only see the remains once a wrecking ball had visited the property.

That morning, Sue had left early in a suit; a job interview perhaps though she had been too kind to say so. Not long after the front door had clicked shut, the bell rang. A flatbed truck was sitting outside with a single pallet lashed to the back; the surviving contents of my house. It was my metal filing cabinet, charred but intact. I left it in the front garden, not wanting to ruin her carpets, and opened the drawers one by one. The top was full of the hideous bills I had hoped had gone up but had somehow survived the inferno. Then there were bank and tax records, the lacklustre history of my life in business. But in the bottom a few personal items had survived, including photo albums dating back to my time at university and beyond. I lifted these out carefully and took them inside, leaving the rain to fall on the rest.

I leafed through the pictures slowly. Had I ever looked that young? And my friends too, most of whom I'd forgotten existed. What were they all doing now? With Facebook, I could probably find out, if it really mattered…

And there was Linda, stunning in a summer ball dress; our graduation bash. I walked over and made myself a cuppa. Those pictures were hard to bear.

I finished the albums. There was little after my return from Patagonia. I had returned to England broken in spirit as well as body. I had stayed with my parents for a few weeks until we had grown fed up with each other and then gone back to my university town, Bangor. The shop assistant post had been advertised in the job centre. I was lucky, selling mountain gear was one thing I was good at, my degree counting for tuppence. The shop had been independent back then, as the ruins of it were now, and I had become the trusted right-hand man of Joe Spencer, the proprietor. We got on well, both single, neither of us being big talkers and with common outdoor interests. He understood my reluctance to return to the rock faces having suffered an injury himself in his early twenties, however he introduced me to the local climbing fraternity who proved reliable patrons of the shop over the following decades.

The days after he passed away suddenly from a stroke whilst striding the hills above the shop were both terrible and surprising. He had left me the business in his will. It was in good shape, unencumbered with debt and with a loyal customer base. All I had to do was to keep doing the same thing. Little did we understand that around that time Tim Berners-Lee was inventing something called the World Wide Web in a cave in Geneva. And Tim had no idea what that would do to businesses like mine.

As I put the last album down, I noticed a bulge in the negatives pockets at the back. Rooting around I found an envelope containing a few un-filed photos. The writing was in Spanish. I slowly lifted the lid, feeling as though an icicle were hanging above me, ready to crash down.

It was a collection of pictures from our trip someone had processed in Argentina. I pulled them out gingerly. They were in perfect condition. The first picture was from Calafate, I guessed, Fitz Roy was a small silhouette on the horizon, a detail lost to those who didn't know what they were looking for. There were then some pictures taken from the road on the way down there; broody clouds hanging over the peaks, wide, flat pampas, a llama, a long, straight dirt track.

Then came the pictures from the hostel. I froze. The picture was of Doug and me, but with another two people. We had arms around each other's shoulders, great beaming faces. We were friends. Doug, Craig, Bob and Cassie.

I moved on to the next image. Bob, Doug and Cassie with a map in front of them, gear strewn everywhere across the lodge's dining room. Beer bottles were lined up along the table. This was a planning meeting.

I found my legs lifting me, taking me away and out

through the front door. Soon I was in the Queen's Arms with a pint in front of me. I sipped it slowly at a table away from the regulars. There were glances in my direction but no one joined me. They were probably thinking I was drowning my sorrows about the shop.

They were wrong. This pint was all about the events of two decades before.

The landlord encouraged me to leave at nine. Bill was an old mate and was doing me a favour. I knew that even in the state I was in.

I staggered down the road back to Sue's and crashed in through the front door.

'Oh, for God's sake! You bloody fool.' Kind hands guided me up to the spare room. 'I was afraid you'd react like this, he shouldn't have told me really, young Bryn...He said they hadn't managed to get hold of you.'

'What are you talking about?' I was beginning to feel queasy. Tomorrow would bring a monster hangover but for now I wanted water and sleep.

Sue stepped back and eyed me quizzically. 'Well, the bank of course. You know, Bryn at Lloyds.'

'What about the bank?'

'Well about....' Even through my drunken eyes, I saw her expression change, a realisation dawning, 'Oh, Craig. I'm sorry.'

'What?'

'The cheque bounced.'

My hangover was every bit as bad as I deserved. I woke up disgusted with myself and what I'd become; a drunk living in the spare room of an increasingly long-suffering ex-employee. I wondered if she'd got that job. God knows she deserved it.

I staggered downstairs at close to eleven am, glad to find the house deserted. A least Sue didn't have to lay eyes on my wreckage.

The photos were still lying on the table. I hadn't made it to the bottom of the pile, and though I was half-tempted to throw them in the bin, I resisted the urge and instead replaced them in the envelope. I'd more immediate things to worry about. The past was the past; I'd had enough of it for one year.

Yes, I had a much bigger problem to deal with— Bloody Doug. I should have known his cheque was a dud. Everything about him was beginning to smell fake; his marriage, his business, the film, probably his sodding tan. My shame began to be replaced by a righteous anger. Here was I, skint, having spent a chunk of my savings wasting time on a stupid, lying, vanity project. One that didn't even have the decency to honour the commitment to one of the people it was trampling all over.

I read through the SummitSeeker contract again, this time with my eyes open to the weasel words it contained. A bit of searching on the internet revealed the ugly truth of how hard gaining a distributor contract was, making the promise of the other half of the money about as worthless as the cheque.

I picked up my mobile and dialled Doug's number. It rang and rang. I waited for the voicemail wondering what to say. I was angry, upset, hungover; should I give him both barrels, implore him to cough up or threaten him?

The ringing stopped, replaced by breathing. 'Yes?' It was Linda. I paused, unsure of what, if anything, to say. 'Who is this?'

I put the phone down. Had they patched it up? The mysteries of married life were an enigma to me. I sat down, breathed in and re-dialled.

161

'Yes, hello?'

'Linda, it's me.'

There was silence at the other end of the phone and then the faint sound, slow at first, but then louder, sobbing.

'Linda? Are you…okay?'

For a while she said nothing and I wondered if she was still there, but then she spoke. 'If it's Doug you're after, he's gone. Not left me with a lot.'

'Gone where?'

There was a loud sigh. 'Oh, I don't know…I should have seen it. It's been going on for years.'

'You mean with Sarah? I thought…Well, he only met her recently…'

She laughed mirthlessly. 'Oh, no. Some other woman, regular payments, probably rent on some little love-nest somewhere. Found it in the bank account; he always was one for filing all his statements away neatly. Wasn't much else to find in there.'

'In where?'

'We're basically bankrupt, not that he seems to care, not now he has his little lover. He will when she moves on.'

'I'm sorry.'

'Are you?' It seemed a genuine question, rather than a rebuke.

'I am. Really.' I sat down at the table. 'Why don't you tell me about it? We can share our troubles.'

Linda recounted what had happened almost a week earlier. Doug and Sarah had returned from Zurich. Doug was steaming drunk and in a foul mood and Sarah had stayed out in the car. He had announced the company had pulled the plug on the film due to the debts it was racking up and had fired him. He was leaving with Sarah to complete it in South America. He had left with a single suitcase of clothes vowing he 'would show them' with barely any acknowledgement of Linda's presence. He hadn't been in contact since, but she had seen the money going out of the bank account for a flight and from a cash point in Buenos Aires.

'...That's when I noticed the payment. I hadn't looked at the statements for a long time, complacency I suppose; about money, the marriage, the business...I feel so stupid...At least he's far away. Don't have to put up with more of his nonsense.'

'How bad is it?'

'The money or our marriage? Both dead, I think. He's been paying out to some woman for decades, right back to when we were first together! Can you believe it? All that time!'

I thought back. Doug hadn't had a girlfriend when I knew him, not before Linda. Back then he hadn't seemed the womanising type at all.

My mind had drifted but I realised she was still speaking, '...found a letter from some lawyers listing their annual fees and payments made to this woman. I didn't understand what it was about, so I phoned them. He's had this little scheme going since 1992! Two years *after* we started going out. I can only think it's a love child, he was a cheat even back then. Payments for some little Douglas bastard running around the USA.'

Two years after they started going out. Yes, they got together on Doug's triumphal return from Patagonia. Barely a day later.

'Who is she?' I asked for want of something to say.

'Does it really matter?' There was a rustling sound at the other end of the line. 'I only have initials...Here it is, a Mrs Borresen. That's all I have, that and account details for a US bank, branch in South Dakota of all places. That's

163

as far as my detective work got. I'm not sure I want to know the rest.'

It made little sense to me but then how well had I really known Doug? It was more than possible he'd had an American girlfriend at university, though he had made no mention of it I could remember, but then it was all a very long time ago.

Linda picked up on my silence. 'Is it someone you know? I'd love to meet her! I'm sure we'd get along famously...Craig?'

'No, just wracking my brains, that's all. It could be someone he met after we returned. I didn't see a lot of Doug after all.' I had started to be a bit irritated by the conversation. I hadn't phoned up to hear more of Doug's sins. She may think she was poor, but whatever she meant by that, it was surely no match for my position.

I said, 'I'm sure there's a simple explanation.'

There was silence on the end of the line, then she said, 'I'm not sure why you're defending him, Craig? Why did you call exactly?'

'There's been a problem with the payment.'

'What payment?'

'For the bloody film work! Doug gave me a cheque—'

She cut in, her tone shifting from aggrieved wife to prim schoolmistress. 'I don't think I can help you there. You'll have to talk to Doug—'

'But you just answered his phone! How the hell can I do that!'

'I'm sorry, Craig, but it isn't my problem. You could email him, not that he has replied to mine—'

'Give me his address...Please.' I tried to keep my voice level and calm. 'I can see you're upset, I'm sorry to be a bother.'

'Oh, God...Try DougSwanson264@gmail.com, that's

his private one. The SummitSeeker one is probably a waste of time; I certainly haven't bothered. Sorry, I have to go.'

'Good—'

But the line was already dead. She hadn't asked me a thing about the shop, the fire, where I was living, not about Lottie, nothing.

For a while I sat on the sofa and stared at the wall. I thought back to the Linda I had known, had loved, at university. Linda, Linda…

I started to smile. I could feel something inside me being cured. I summoned Lottie and donned my coat and boots. Outside lay that rarest jewel, a beautiful, crisp November day. Tiny cumulus cast shadows raced east along the valley across hillsides that glowed red with the autumn bracken. We were soon out of the village on the shore of Llyn Peris and were then climbing Elidir Fawr, one of the high peaks that surround the lake. Lottie darted ahead, splashing in and out of her favourite streams, circling and bossing me, shepherding me upwards. With every step my head cleared and a sense of purpose embedded itself, one I had not felt for many years.

That evening, I was a considerably less shameful prospect than that morning. The house was tidy and I was dressed, sober and on the internet. I had sent a short email to Doug, telling him about the bounced cheque and asking him to contact me. It seemed a long shot given what Linda had said, but I had nothing to lose. I then started to see if I could locate his mysterious beneficiary. It seemed to me there was something significant about the payments he was making, but I couldn't put my finger on what exactly.

Borressen was an unusual Danish surname it seemed, at least in South Dakota. I found a single Borressen, a Mr

A Borressen on a US phone number reference site who lived in a village called Cresbard. There was a phone lying across the table from me.

'Going somewhere?' I turned around. She had entered the lounge silently and was peering over my shoulder at the map of the USA on the screen. She was in a business suit, the new job I supposed. I still hadn't asked her about that.

'Oh, sorry, I hope you don't mind…' I said, suddenly deeply aware I was using her computer, in her house, living off her.

'Oh no, of course not.' She waved her hand at the laptop. 'What you looking at?'

I told her everything; about Doug and his philandering, the collapse of the film, the mysterious payments.

'And why do you care about who this woman is?'

'I've no idea,' I said. 'Can you help me?'

She smiled and rubbed her hands together. 'Why not? There's a challenge. Let me get changed and I'll give you a hand.'

'New job…?' My words trailed off as she left the lounge.

Ten minutes later she was back in the room. I had done some more searching but found no other Borressens.

'Well, looks like you need to phone him up. See if he has a wife. Better not mention though she has a sugar daddy paying her money from the other side of the Atlantic.' She checked her watch. 'Probably lunchtime over there.'

'I was wondering if you…'

'Oh, Craig, you're so pathetic!' She grabbed the phone and looked at the screen. A moment later the handset was pressed to her ear. 'Hi, hello…Is Mrs Borressen there?'

There was a pause and Sue nodded. 'Oh, I see. Oh, no,

166

no I'm not selling anything, is she back later?...I see...No, a friend, I'll call back. Oh, well, thanks. Very kind. Good bye.' She hung up.

'And?' I said.

Sue shrugged. Well, there's a Mrs Borressen there, but she's not back until the weekend. Thought I was trying to sell insurance. I got her name though.'

'Yes?'

'Cassie.'

I had only ever known one Cassie. A woman who had saved my life two decades earlier. I had absolutely no doubt Cassie Borressen was formerly known as Cassie Green, widow of Bob Green.

Sue had clearly seen the expression on my face when she told me the name, but it had meant nothing to her. I reminded her about Doug's book, and after a rummage upstairs, she produced a dusty copy.

We turned to the chapter where Cassie figured, or rather the two. She was mentioned on only a few pages. The brief description of our time in the Hostal Laguna Sucia and the mention of her finding him in the cave. Doug thanked Cassie in the book, of course, but the implication was he would have sorted himself out if needed. But then he implied maybe I had needed her help as well as his. I couldn't argue with that.

'...and he's being sending her money ever since,' I said.

'Since when?'

'I'm not sure. Linda said a couple of years later, when the book was published.'

We stayed up late talking it over. I finally found out Sue had indeed taken a finance assistant job in Bangor. She hadn't told me to spare my feelings, but I was delighted for her. We got a takeout and stayed up talking over her big plans to study accountancy, she had already found evening classes. At least my financial failure and the shop's destruction had done someone some good.

Sue turned in ahead of me, but before I went upstairs, I checked the email account. To my great surprise, Doug had replied.

Hi Craig,

Great to hear from you! I can't tell you how sorry I am about the cheque. I had no idea SummitSeeker was going to pull the funding. They have a contract with you, they need to honour it and I'll make sure they do when I get back.

But listen, the film isn't dead. Sarah has explained about films made guerrilla style, things like The Blair Witch Project, shot with a single handy-cam. The technology has moved up hugely since then and we have what we need with us. Piotr came out and if we shoot a few scenes down here, we're done. She'll edit with Piotr and then they can hit the film festival circuits.

Come and join us, Craig! I'll make sure you get your money and with SummitSeeker disowning us, we can split the profits between us. You won't regret it!

As way of an apology I've transferred £2k into a transfer account for you to pay for your flights and expenses. You'll get the withdrawal details in another email.

Please come, I'll have a beer waiting for you in El Chalten.

Cheers,
Doug

The film isn't dead! I almost threw the laptop across the room. I couldn't believe his gall, that he would mess me around like this, leave me on the brink of bankruptcy and then invite me down to carry on with this vanity project. He was unbelievable. Even his offer of money...it grated on me I couldn't afford to tell him where he could shove it. As for all the nonsense about 'guerrilla style' film-making, wow, that girl could persuade Doug of anything.

I stood up and went to pour myself a whisky, but then held back. Alcohol had not served me well of late. Instead, I wandered over to the coffee table where the envelope of photos lay, and shuffled through them again. The pictures of Patagonia weren't art, but looking at them took me straight back to that time. I couldn't deny part of me wanted to see Fitz Roy again, if only to rekindle my memory and to separate my dreams from the physical reality. Perhaps that would stop my nightmares? I had nothing much left tying me to Llanberis; just a burnt-out shop and some friends. As I lay down on my pillow, I closed my eyes and pictured the scenes again. That planning meeting that had turned into a fierce argument and then the frosty atmosphere between us until we split up. We had really let Bob and Cassie down. I had never even thanked her for saving my life. As I lay there my feelings of guilt intensified. I wanted to get her side of the story and to tell her about the film, on the off-chance it was actually produced. There was also the question of why Doug was paying her—could she be blackmailing him somehow? I could try phoning or emailing her, but my instinct was driving me hard in a different, more radical direction.

I was awoken the next morning by my phone buzzing on the bedside table. It showed an unfamiliar, local number.

169

'Mr Darwen?' It was Sergeant Baxter's nasal tones.

'Hi, Alan, is there any news?'

'We would like you to come down to the station. We have some new information pertinent to the investigation of the uncontrolled incendiary incident.'

'You mean the fire?'

'Yes, that's what I said. Two pm, please.'

I felt a shiver of ice pass through me. 'Why?'

'We can discuss that in detail when you come in. However, we now have confirmation of arson as being the cause of the fire. You understand, Mr Darwen, we need to understand more about your movements.'

'For God's sake, find out who did it! They've taken my livelihood.' This was ridiculous, lazy policing. I breathed deeply to maintain my composure. 'Surely you can find a real suspect, rather than someone who was hundreds of miles away at the time?'

'Yes, that was very convenient for you.'

I hung up. The idea of another session with that jumped-up little prig filled me with a mixture of fear and fury. I felt like going down there immediately and smashing him in the face, I'd had recent practice. However, I was sober enough to know the folly of such a move. And who had attacked my shop? I had run it trouble-free, other than the odd bit of pilfering, for twenty years. Why now?

I marched round to the little police station in a rage, hoping every step would calm me down. Sergeant Baxter let me through to the interview room in the back and sat me down. I wasn't offered tea. He made a great show of setting up their interview recorder. It probably hadn't been used for a year.

'We have some new information, a witness. A

caucasian male, matching your description, was seen running across the field at the back of your shop, at approximately 11.30pm on the night of the incendiary incident.'

'Who saw him?'

'I'm afraid that information is not for disclosure at the moment. We wouldn't want any intimidation.'

I shot out of my seat. 'This is bloody ridiculous; I was in France for God's sake!'

'Sit down, Mr Darwen.'

I breathed in deeply and retook my seat. I clasped my hands together and closed my eyes for a moment, then said, 'Look, Al—Sergeant Baxter,' Alan nodded, 'I was in the south of France, I have witnesses who can attest to that fact, I had my passport coming into the UK. You really need to pursue a different line of inquiry here. Please?'

Alan nodded, then said, 'Can we talk a bit about your finances? We have seen your full bank accounts now. Not pretty reading.'

'No…' I paused, 'I accept that, it's been a difficult few years…but it's no crime to have a few debts. I was in France to make some money to pay them off. I intended to square them all and to carry on.'

'Ah yes, the bounced cheque.'

I could have screamed, but somehow I managed to hold onto the last shreds of my composure. 'Yes, the cheque. It's a mistake, I have a contract and I've been assured by the owner of the company that the cheque will be honoured. Anyway, I really don't see what the purpose of this is. I was away, my house and shop have been destroyed, I just want to get back on with my life.'

'And for that a little insurance pay-out would help…'

I locked eyes with him. He was smirking, the self-

171

righteous little brat.

'Yes, I do require the insurance to pay out.'

'And for that, you need to be eliminated from our enquiries.'

'I suppose so.'

'So a bit of co-operation from you would help in that process. Do you agree, Mr Darwen?'

'Yes. Look, I am co-operating, it's just I know nothing.'

'Nothing?'

The word hung in the air, but I didn't reply.

He slowly tapped his pencil on the table and pursed his lips. 'How...unfortunate.' He made some notes in his notebook. 'Well, Mr Darwen, if you do recall anything, you know where we are. In the meantime though, please don't go anywhere.'

I stayed seated. 'What do you mean?'

'We wouldn't want you using your passport again, would we? Not with our investigations at such a delicate stage.'

He looked up from his notebook with a thin smile. I felt the plastic on either edge of my chair flex as I gripped it hard, pulling it upwards as though it could lift me out of the room.

And then I relaxed. His final comment had confirmed for me what I would do. He remained, silent, spinning his pencil through his fingers.

'Is that it?' I asked after a minute of silence.

He closed his notebook. 'Yes, you can go. Interview terminated, 1432.'

He had no idea just how far I would soon be going.

CHAPTER THIRTEEN

When I stepped into Alba travel in Llanberis and asked about a flight to Aberdeen, the young girl, Lizzie, started to type the location into her PC before I had had a chance to finish.

'That would be sixty-four pounds, but to be honest it would be cheaper to book online,' she said, her voice hushed, glancing towards the back room where no doubt her fearsome manager lurked.

'Sorry, you didn't hear what I said. Aberdeen, South Dakota, it's in America.'

'America?' she raised an eyebrow, as though I had mentioned the most bizarre of destinations. She started to tap at her keyboard. 'Hmmm.'

'I'll be wanting to go on to Patagonia from there.'

'Patagonia…?' She looked at the brochure racks for inspiration

'Argentina.'

'Right…' Her gaze returned to her screen and she typed. 'And when would you like to go to… Aberdeen?'

'Tomorrow ideally.'

It wasn't a short appointment.

I left the shop with a maxed-out credit card. I had just about afforded the return fare, but Doug would need to pick up my bills in Patagonia, that was for sure. Once Lizzie had grasped my plans, she had become quite animated. It was the most unusual trip she said anyone had booked from there since a girl from her class had taken up relief work in Africa, mind you even she had planned to come straight home. The flights were not complex, but Lizzie worked hard to get me a good deal using a combination of air passes and tourist discounts to piece it all together.

'Send me a postcard,' she had said.

'Where from?' I asked.

She looked out onto the high street for a moment, then turned back to face me. 'Anywhere.'

As I packed each item into my small suitcase, I was gripped with a feeling of immense trepidation. Would the trip be one-way or return? And if it was a return trip, what version of me would be coming back? The sergeant wouldn't be impressed, but I wasn't going to let his petty suspicions dictate my life. I would face the music another day, for now I had an important question to answer. I descended the stairs to find Sue waiting for me in the kitchen with Lottie, who wagged her tail expectantly. I bent down to kiss the dog and she licked my face with her moist, meaty breath.

'Sorry, Lottie, no walk from me today. I'm sure Auntie Sue will take good care of you.'

'Of course, Lottie and I have grown very close, haven't we?' Lottie's tail started wagging even faster. I ruffled her head and turned to the door.

'What about me?'

I turned to Sue and we embraced quickly. She grasped my arm. 'I don't know what you're up to, but take care of yourself. Not sure I've ever harboured a criminal before.'

'I'm not a criminal,' I said.

'Even if you were, I don't care.' She put her finger to her lips. 'Mum's the word.'

'Stop it.'

'At least let me run you to Bangor?'

I smiled. 'I wouldn't say no.' It wasn't as though I had another plan. 'I'm not sure how I'll repay all this.'

'Lottie's doing that for you.' Lottie jumped into the

back seat of the car and we set off. I sunk down into my seat and donned a baseball cap, half expecting a police car to swoop up at any moment. Sue didn't comment on my pathetic attempt at disguise and we wound our way past my beloved mountains up to the coast.

Another hug, another face lick later and I was on my way to Heathrow.

At the time of the last census, Cresbard, South Dakota had a population of thirty-four families, a mere one hundred and four adults, living in sixty-one households scattered around a handful of streets. It boasted a hotel, which was going to be useful, but there was no chance my arrival could go unnoticed. I hadn't made any attempt to make contact hoping the element of surprise may yield more honesty. Of course, it could also yield disappointment. Perhaps she would be away on holiday, maybe long moved house, maybe dead even. I shivered at that thought.

I collected my hire car at Aberdeen's small, neat airport avoiding the slew of extra taxes Lizzie had warned me about. I was frazzled after two days of travel and sleep only in seats. I had been surrounded by people, in trains, planes, in the confines of London and New York's urban sprawl and then in the sweaty airport at Minneapolis. So, it was wonderful to breathe fresh air and to escape into the limitless flat plain. No twisty narrow roads here, but a simple highway south and then one west. One hour and I was rolling through the alien landscape into the dusty village.

My plan was simple, if full of potential pitfalls. I would find a motel, smarten myself up, and then turn up at her door. The plan didn't extend beyond that, so much depended on what happened. For some reason Doug had been paying money to Cassie since our accident. That Doug was grateful for her assistance I could understand, but to pay out money like that, it made no sense. And there was no love child, Cassie had been in the early stages of wedded bliss when we met, and pregnant more to the point. I could see only three explanations; gratitude, guilt or blackmail.

I crossed the 'City limit'. By now my stomach was turning with nerves, she could refuse to see me, I could be chased off a farm by a shotgun-wielding republican, she may not even be here…

The first problem was the motel; there wasn't one. I drove through the village and out into the endless fields on the other side. Nothing. The second issue was that I'd lost my hastily drawn sketch map of where their house was in the village and my mobile phone had no signal.

I had passed a gas station on my way in, sitting forlornly on the city limit and decided that in a place this small they were sure to know where she lived. It turned out to be more than a gas station, but the local store supplying everything from processed ham to guns. A bell rang above the door as I entered and an obese man garbed in checked shirt and baseball cap appeared behind a counter. He grunted a greeting and eyed me with suspicion. I feigned interest in some ancient beef-jerky, which I dropped on the counter. He picked it up, glanced at the back and grunted again. 'Bit old, that one,' and tossed it into a nearby bin. He leaned over the counter and pointed at the rack it had come from. 'Try the back.'

I did as he suggested and found a more recently dated pack that was of as little real interest to me. I smiled, thanked him and my mouth took over before my brain had considered the best tactic. 'Do you know Cassie

Green?' The man's eyes narrowed slightly, but he said nothing.

'I'm trying to find her house, you see...I used to know her, she was a climber. Like me.'

The man scowled at that. 'A what?'

'A climber, mountain climber.' I found my hand making the shape of a Himalayan skyline.

At last, the man grinned. 'A climber. In Dakota. Think you're in the wrong state, mister.'

'Cassie Borressen, she was Cassie Green?'

'A climber, you say...' His lips cracked with a wide smile. 'She ain't no climber. She a farmer. Lives up by St Augustine's church,' he nodded his head westwards, 'with Tom and the boys.'

'Thanks, I'll pay her a call.'

'Ain't no climber, sir.' He grinned again. 'Thad'll be three dollars fifty.'

'Pardon?' I didn't realise the information would cost me, then I saw him pointing at the limp packet of jerky I was still holding.

'Oh, sorry.' I fumbled through the dollar bills I had, trying to identify a suitably small one, but fifty was the lowest.

He grunted and rang it into the till. 'Have a nice day, sir. Look for the white fence.'

As the door closed behind me, I could hear him chuckling, but I ignored him. This was Cassie Green, I knew it. I pulled off the forecourt and headed west in search of a church. I found the white clapboard building a mile outside of the village and sure enough next to it was a neat white picket fence, with a long, straight gravel drive cutting perpendicular through it into the fields. In the distance sat a large farmhouse, shimmering in the late afternoon heat. I pulled off the tarmac and headed up

177

there.

The farmhouse was grey painted clapboard set over two stories. It was huge, as wide as a town hall with apparent space for five families. Just how many 'boys' were there? It appeared well cared for, clearly the corn farming was working out well, but as I stepped out of my car and looked around, I wondered how a young woman so in love with the mountains could have found happiness amongst these monotone plains. Other than a light breeze running through the trees and the ticking of the cooling engine, the farmyard was utterly silent. I wondered if the family were all out at work, after all it was the middle of the morning and I was unexpected.

I stepped up onto the shaded veranda and rapped on the grand front door. No sound of approaching footsteps answered and after trying once more, I walked around to the back of the house beyond which a large barn and miles of fields lay.

'Hi?' A young man had appeared on the veranda behind me carrying a box of groceries. He was over six foot with a muscular build and a deep tan gained from working outside. His eyes squinted. 'You from DF Agro?'

'Sorry?' I asked, 'No, um, I'm here to see Mrs Borressen.'

He seemed a tad confused. 'Cassie? Oh. She expecting you?'

'No,' I confessed, 'I was just passing through.' Why I said that, I had no idea, but he seemed to accept this and stepped back into the house. I heard him call, 'Mom, some guy's here to see you…No, no idea.'

I couldn't make out the reply, but a minute later I heard footsteps and a woman stepped out, rubbing her hands on a tea towel. 'Can I help you?'

I took off my sunglasses and looked upon the woman

who had ultimately saved my life twenty-five years before. I was hugely relieved to see it was indeed her, Cassie Green, now apparently Cassie Borressen. Her face was heavily tanned with deep laughter lines playing around her blue eyes. Her thick brown hair was pulled back into a ponytail much as it had been when I had last seen her in Argentina. Perhaps she had put on a bit of weight, like we all had, but she had aged well under the Dakota skies. 'Sorry, sir, do I know you?' She tipped her head slightly and her eyes narrowed, a small flicker of recognition crossing her face.

'Cassie, I'm Craig. Craig Darwen.'

She frowned and stepped back, then her jaw dropped and she put her hands to her mouth. 'Craig? Well I never, Craig Darwen!' She rushed forwards and embraced me. 'Craig Darwen, how the hell are you? What brings you to these parts? Surely you haven't come all the way out here to see me?'

'Well, I have really. It's…it's a long story.'

She clasped my hands and stepped back to look at me. 'Well, you'd better come in and tell us all. Craig Darwen, well I never.'

Whilst my visit to Cassie had been impulsive, probably the most impulsive thing I had done in two decades, I had had many hours to consider how I would approach meeting her. Would she remember me? Would she hate me for what happened? However, these worries disappeared the minute we were reunited; her reaction was not that of someone with a grudge, not unless she was a master actor. The payments though remained a mystery, one I needed an answer to. To that end I had concocted a thin cover story for my visit; I would tell her about the film and say I had been sent to see if she was interested in being interviewed in it. As I had reflected on the previous

179

weeks on my flight over, I realised, that neither Sarah nor Doug had mentioned Cassie being in the film even though she had played a key part in the story. That was odd given Doug clearly knew something of her whereabouts.

Cassie invited me to sit out on a set of easy chairs on the rear veranda, looking over their land. 'Would you like some tea, Craig?'

I said yes and she appeared minutes later with a glass jug of clear brown liquid, packed with ice cubes and some pastries. 'Hope you like iced tea, Craig,' she said as she poured me a long glass. It was sweet and not exactly what I was expecting, but I drank it down all the same. 'So, I'm sure you weren't just passing through. I'm intrigued—how did you find me and, well, why? Not that it isn't great to see you an' all.'

'Well, yes, you're right, of course I'm out here to see you. Did you hear about the film?' Cassie's blank expression answered that question.

'Sorry, I thought…' I continued. I told her about Sarah and how she was working for Doug to make a film of *The Empty Rope*. At the mention of that Cassie's smile faltered and she crossed her arms as I continued. I steered clear of any personal comment about Doug or Sarah or their relationship, making out the film was in its early stages, which it was. Very early but probably final stages.

'So, Doug didn't contact you?'

'I haven't heard from nor seen that man since when? 1990? Since I last saw you in fact.' Her voice took on a note of ice that had been very much absent up to that point. She must have registered the surprise in my face. 'Why would I? You both left me high and dry searching for my Bob. I was there a month trying to get the Argies to put out a search and they did eventually, but we found nothing. I was pregnant and my papa came out there to
180

help and eventually brought me home. I think if he hadn't, I might still be there. Like Bob.'

I understood what she meant. 'I'm sorry, I—'

'Oh, I don't blame you, Craig. Jeez, you were in a state when I last saw you, barely conscious. I'm just glad you made it. Doug mind…Well, I think he could have done more. After all, I helped him out a little too, not that you'd know it from his book. In fact, there were a few things I didn't care much for in there. Here…' She leaned over and refilled my glass before I could protest.

'So, you've never seen him since, nor heard from him?'

'No, like I said, I thought he would come back but he never did and once I got home, I tried to put it all behind me. No body to bury even. The search didn't last down there and I had to rebuild my life; I'd lost my Bob but I had a baby on the way. When the book came out and was such a hit, well some journalist found me and asked me about it. It was the first I knew of it. I went out and bought a copy. A load of bull if you ask me. Doug the hero, Bob and I made out to be naive. You—'

I raised my eyebrows and she paused and put her glass down. 'Well darling, you didn't come out so great, did you? Causing the accident that he saved you from an' all?'

'It wasn't like that.'

'Well, I'm sure that's true, but that's what he said. Will this film just be more of the same? That's what you've got to ask yourself, mister. Mind you, as you're here, I guess you're in?'

She didn't realise how far. 'I was thinking seriously about it, yes.'

'Well then, you need to tell the truth, set the record straight.'

'I don't remember a lot.'

She answered with a 'Hmmmm' to that statement then

sat back in her chair and considered me. 'So how about you, Craig? What ya doin' these days?'

I told her about the shop in Wales, about Lottie, there wasn't much else to say.

'Sounds mighty restful. You didn't fancy more climbing then? I heard you were pretty good.'

'Who from?'

'Oh, some climbing buddies back in Utah knew your name from the Alpine scene. Seems you had a bit of a reputation back then. Doug, not so much.'

I decided to change tack. 'How did you cope after you got back? Financially?'

'Financially? My papa was good to me, Mom had passed away. My aunt too. Beccy, that's my girl, was born and we lived with Pa for a year before I got back on my feet. I got my job back teaching in elementary school, started to live again. I never forgot about Bob, I had Beccy growing up every day to remind me. She has his eyes, not that I see much of them these days.' She looked away towards the fields.

I leaned forward and took another sip of the cool tea. 'She's not around here?'

'Oh no, she had no interest in moving up to boring Dakota. She's a grown woman now with her own job. No, I met my husband, Tom, whilst on holiday when she was a teenager. They didn't hit it off, she always was strong willed, but, Lord, when she was fifteen, she was unbearable, a real bitch. She was a straight A-grade student, real bright but she kind'a fell in with the wrong crowd. I had high hopes for that girl, she was all I had, and I was gettin' worried.

'Tom used to come down to stay for the weekend when he could, but the farm didn't allow him away much. I flew up here, but the distance was killing us. Yeah, well, after one particularly shitty day at the school I decided to make the move. I wanted Beccy to come, begged her, but by then she was sixteen and had some trailer-trash boyfriend. She moved in with him and that was the last I saw of her for a few years. She's doin' alright now...' She sighed. 'I got a room made up for her in case she ever decides to call...Maybe she will one day.' She looked back at me. 'You got no woman then, Craig? No kids tucked away anywhere?'

My face must have answered the question and she continued, 'Well it's not for everyone. More pain than love when it's all added up for many folks. Sounds like your dog's a lot simpler.' Her smile returned. 'You'll be staying for supper, I hope? I'll get a room ready for you.' I made a feeble attempt to protest but she was having none of it and within minutes my small bag was out of the car and I was installed in her lounge.

Her husband, Tom, was out on the farm for most of the day along with two of his sons who still worked for him, despite having left home and married themselves. There were four boys in total, I had met the youngest, Joel, who was nineteen and keen to do anything but corn farming, anywhere but Dakota. But he was a nice enough lad, and pretty interested to hear about life in Britain. He was heading off to play in a gig with a local band that evening so didn't stick around. Tom arrived at the house in the late afternoon. I had expected a giant in a Stetson, but he was small and wiry with an intelligent, deeply lined face. He went off to change then came down, offered me a beer and invited me back out onto the veranda for some 'man talk'. Cassie laughed at this idea but let us go. I still was no further with understanding the mystery of Doug's payments to Cassie and was at a bit of a loss as to how to find out without a direct approach.

We sat back down in the easy chair and Tom took out a packet of cigarettes, offering me one. 'D'ya mind? Bad habit, I know. Cassie don't approve.'

He made small talk asking about my journey and a little about the film, but after the conversation petered out, he took a look around, leaned forwards and said, 'Craig, you seem a nice guy and I can see Cassie is right pleased you showed up, but, well, we're pretty settled here now. Hasn't always been the case.'

'I see.'

'Well, Craig, man to man, you're not here to cause trouble, are you? I don't want Cassie getting upset after all this time. I'm sure Bob was a great guy but he's been a bit of a tough act to follow.' He nodded towards me. 'You get my drift?'

'No, honestly, that's the last thing I want. It was just to see if—'

'But you were there, right? Tell me, what was he like?' He glanced over his shoulder again, 'Cassie doesn't like to talk about him, says it was the past and I've never gotten to meet anyone who knew him.'

I was a bit taken aback; I was certainly no expert having been acquainted for only a few weeks, many years earlier. 'He seemed like a decent guy, and an excellent climber. I'm sorry I didn't really get to know him that well. They were a young married couple, happy, with a baby on the way. He was determined to climb Fitz Roy though, that was for sure.'

'I know Cassie still thinks about him, even now. Her daughter, Rebecca, she…' He tailed off and looked away. 'Well, we never hit it off. I was never going to be as great as her pa, the legend. He was a valedictorian—did you know that? Top of his class at some fancy school.

Destined for great things apparently, that's what they say. Real golden couple they were. Mr perfect, not some simple farmer...' He lifted his beer as though raising a toast. 'That's what little Rebecca says, so it must be true.' He seemed to have forgotten I was even there as he stared out into the darkening sky.

'I'm sorry. I didn't really know him. He seemed—'

Tom's head jerked slightly as though waking from a daydream. 'No, shit, I'm sorry. Shouldn't speak of the dead like that. It's just I love my Cassie and I'm sure Bob was a fine man; she wouldn't have married him if he weren't. We've had a few bust-ups thanks to that girl, so the Bob subject, it ain't on the table right now. I think Cassie and Rebecca would sure like to know what happened to him though. I suppose it would be good to lay that ghost to rest. But then I'm not sure if I want all that shit stirred up again.' He took a deep pull on his beer. 'You know, they never found him, or if they did, Cassie don't know. That storm you were caught in, I guess it finished him off.'

'I don't remember a lot, but yes, the storm came in very quickly and it was bloody fierce. Doug had a tough time bringing me down through it.'

'I think you both did, but I know Cassie ain't no fan of that book, won't even let me read it. I made a solemn promise.' He winked at me. 'I don't think she liked being portrayed as the doting, obedient wife waiting around whilst the men did the tough stuff even less that some guy got rich on the back of it.'

'Oh, she was every bit as tough as us, we knew that,' I said, and it was true. I suddenly had a flashback, as vivid as if it were from a day before; Cassie pouring tea into me in a blizzard, helping me walk, a long walk, across ice...

'You okay, Craig?' Tom brought me back to the present.

185

'Just thinking back.'

'Yeah…Her Rebecca, that's who should be in your film. Made a real job of researching ol' Bob. Proper little expert, when she ain't stoned or drunk.'

'Where is she now?'

'No idea, haven't seen her for years. Like I said, we didn't hit it off. I know Cassie hears from her occasionally. I can tell by her mood.'

At that moment Cassie stuck her head out and called, 'Okay, boys, man talking over, come 'n get it.'

She had whipped up a delicious Mexican chicken dish with a sizable kick in it, which we washed down with beers. The conversation steered clear of Doug and film. I could see she didn't like discussing her past much with Tom and he was happy with the arrangement. So, I was glad when he stated that he was turning in early as he had to be up at dawn, leaving us to talk over old times.

After he had gone upstairs, Cassie said, 'I've got something to show you,' and she disappeared off into another room, to re-emerge with a large, red album. We moved to the sofa and she started to leaf through pictures of her looking even younger than when we had met. 'Life before Tom, I call this album. Fancy a nightcap?' She stood up and started pouring herself a Bourbon. I declined, still remembering the events of a few nights earlier.

Soon enough we came to her first honeymoon and some stunning shots from South America, including her at high altitude and climbing. 'You see, I could climb too,' she said, at one of her dangling from a rock wall. 'That was the last climb I did, an easy thing near to La Paz. Found out I was expecting later that day. Thought the puking was dodgy street food. I was wrong. Now where are you…' She flicked through a few more pages and there we were, an almost identical picture to the one Doug had put up as a slide all those weeks before. Three men with overlong hair and beards, standing in the Argentine sun, ready to go and conquer Fitz Roy. Our grins that were in the previous photo though were replaced with what I interpreted as determination. I stared at it; there was something wrong but I couldn't figure out what.

'What's up?'

'Oh, nothing...Just memories. Is that the last one you have of Bob?'

Cassie sighed. 'No, a couple of others.' She turned the next page and there was one of him walking away, and then as a red dot on the white background.

'Sorry, can I see that?' I asked.

I took the book from her and stared at the image. 'That's Bob?'

'Of course. Why?'

'I thought he had a green jacket?'

Cassie took the album back from me and flicked the pages back and forth. 'Err, no, honey. This one was green—' she pointed at a photo of him in an earlier part of their trip, sat in the back of a truck, shades on, smiling, wearing a green down jacket. 'His coat was red. I remember it well; I bought it for him. Look—' she turned back to our group shot and tapped the page. Sure enough, that was the difference. We were fully kitted up, coats and rucksacks on. Doug and I had blue coats, Bob's was red. I flopped back in my chair.

She peered at me quizzically. 'Why does it matter?'

I wasn't about to tell her about the dreams I had had. 'No, nothing...memory playing tricks on me. The years. Can I have a copy—you know, the one of the three of us?'

'Well, I guess,' she said. 'I could scan it in and get you a print?'

187

'Could you? That would be great,' I said and Cassie pulled it out of the sleeve and went off again to another room. Whilst she was gone, I flicked forward through the album. Cassie had been a keen, excellent photographer and had used the time waiting for Bob to return, to capture the beauty of the shifting light in the valleys. The glaciers with their blues and greys, the granite towers at once in the bright, moist sunlight and then shrouded in black cloud. I recognised the Supercanaleta and searched for any tiny dots that could be us climbing the mountain. Over on the wall was a beautiful landscape shot of Fitz Roy. I walked over to it, wondering when it had been taken, before or after the events?

'Here you go—' Cassie had come back in and was standing behind me. She handed me a copy. 'That's where I found you.'

I turned around. 'Where?'

She pointed to an indistinct spot below 'La Brecha' the lower shoulder that sat south of the towering peak. I frowned, then tapped the photo. 'Here?'

'Yes, it was about there, at the base of the Francesca, it was where I was expecting Bob to come down from. I was worried sick, I knew he was a good climber, but the storm was vicious, even down on the glacier. When it abated, I spent the next day scouring the rock face with my binoculars. That's when I saw you.'

'Are you sure?' I said, 'it's just—'

'I know. Doug's rescue. Well, he didn't come down the way he said, did he? I think he got disorientated in the storm. I can see he had to leave you; you must have been half-dead. I found him stumbling down the Torre glacier. He was acting crazy, babbling on about the storm, about having to leave you. I had you in the tent by then, warming up. Doug went the next day to get help and the Argies flew you out. You were a lucky guy.'

'You didn't find him in the cave? That's what he said.'

'I know what he said, but no way I was climbing that far up the glacier by myself, not in that shitty weather. He also said he'd left you in a bivvie bag; that was total bullshit too. I don't know why he wrote those things; not sure I care.'

It was a mystery to me too. 'You saved my life, Cassie. I don't think I ever thanked you.'

'No, you didn't. I never heard from either of you again until now, just that bullshit book.'

I retreated to the sofa and flopped into it. 'God, I was such an idiot. I went to pieces after that. I was completely self-absorbed. I'm so sorry, Cassie. You lost your husband—'

'And you two did shit all to help. Yep, that's right, but don't beat yourself up about it. Like I said, you were in no fit state. Believe me, I scraped you up.'

'What happened…I mean from your viewpoint? I never asked.'

'Ya mean after we left you?'

'Yes.'

She frowned, leaned forward and took a sip of her Bourbon.

'It's okay…I shouldn't have…' I mumbled.

Cassie waved my objection. 'We didn't part on the best of terms, did we?'

'I don't remember.'

She sat back into the soft foam and appraised me. 'Look, see, Craig. I think you do. Perhaps that's why you're here. Do you really want to talk about it? It was a long time ago. We were young.'

'Tell me, I can't remember a lot.'

'Okay, buddy, if you say so…So, what do you recall?

How about our little stay together at the hostel?'

I was a bit surprised by the question but answered nonetheless, glad of the opportunity to talk it over with someone uninterested in self-promotion. 'I remember it getting a bit boring. We played a lot of cards, didn't we? Had some walks around the lake. The owner…Marco and Rosa, was it? They were pretty friendly. Not so sure about the food…'

'What about us, Craig, Bob and me?'

'Well…You seemed a great couple, very much in love, fun—'

'C'mon! What about the big fight we had? Let's cut to the chase here—Don't tell me you've forgotten?'

I hadn't. It had taken me to the pub and through a few too many pints only a few days earlier. The planning meeting, the argument. Bad blood.

My face told her as much and she cocked her head to get me to go on. 'Well, yes. I remember. I'm sorry—'

'For God's sake, Craig. Stop apologising. So y'all wanted to do the same route, go the same way. You and Doug didn't like the idea and persuaded, let's call it that, us, or rather my husband, Bob, to go up a different way. Let's say it all now; that decision maybe cost him his life…Maybe it didn't though, we'll never know. He was a big boy, it was his decision too, wasn't no one going to tell him what to do.'

'I think that was part of the problem. With all of us, that is.'

'Too many egos in one room. You guys and your testosterone,' she said.

'Exactly. I'm sorry,' she pulled a face at me, 'I mean I do regret it, that argument. We had been getting along so well. I thought we would be a good team.'

'It was Doug, wasn't it?'

'What? Who started it you mean? I can't remember—
honestly. It would be easy to pin it on him, he's thousands
of miles away, but no, I think it was me too. We were
trying to create a tiny piece of climbing history. We didn't
want anyone else coming along. We'd never climbed with
Bob, thought he might slow us down, cause an accident,'
I grimaced at making this statement, 'I'm ashamed to say
it, but it's true. We were wrong.'

'Yes, you were. But let me tell you what happened next.
We made up a bit, Bob said he wanted to solo and off we
all went. But it was tense and when our paths split there
were no hugs or kisses.'

I thought back to my recollection of our journey from
the hostel to Fitz Roy. We had walked briefly as one
group, but in reality, as two pairs, separated by an
argument only two nights before. That had been
fearsome, not helped by overly heavy drinking on Doug's
part. Had I been willing to risk her husband's safety for
the sake of creating a trivial new route? Were we really so
selfish back then? I knew she spoke the truth, as had Doug
when he talked about how we got lost. But he had lied by
omission.

She continued, 'I camped out below the East face of
Fitz Roy by Laguna Sucia, I won't forget that lake or that
sight, I spent long enough searching for him after. Bob
kissed me then set off. I watched him through binoculars.
He was fast, smooth. He was burning up that rock. Then
the storm came…' She turned away and raised her hand
to her face. 'Look at me, still hurts bad…I never saw him
again. I waited there for two days, even where I was the
weather was truly shit—it was everything: rain, snow, hail
and wind. Lots of it. When it finally died off, I had to do
something. I left my tent with a note and hiked around the
south, following the path you guys had taken. I figured

maybe if it were sheltered on the west, he may choose to come down that. I had no idea where the weather had come in from, it seemed to blow in from every direction. Every now and then I'd scan what I could see with my binoculars. The clouds were covering the tops and weren't lifting much, but I could see the lower slopes a little. Well, that's when I saw you, in the south. You were collapsed in the snow, a half-dead lump. I thought you were a small boulder at first, but the colour wasn't right. You weren't movin' though, might as well have been a rock. There was no sign of anyone else about.'

'Was I conscious?'

'Sort of, barely, I don't know. I gave you a bit of a slappin' and that woke you up. After that you could walk, but you had a hell of a wound on your head. You were very cold, but you were able to stagger back to my tent right enough. I left you there in a sleeping bag, gave you hot tea, did what I could then got right back out there. Of course, I asked if you had seen Bob, probably more than once, but you were mumbling all sorts of rubbish and saying sorry a lot—hell that hasn't changed!' She smiled and it was a relief.

'Thank you,' I said.

'No problem. But don't expect me to do it again.'

'No danger of that around here!' Was it coincidence she had ended up in one of the flattest places in the world?

'Yeah, well after you were tucked up in a bag, I went back out into the weather. This time I tracked all the way around the south face until I saw a figure coming down. How I ran. But it was Doug. He was pretty out of it too and messed up—blood all over his face and shaking constantly. I remember that, it wasn't like a shiver, more like some sort of fit. Just a constant shake. He couldn't make eye contact; said he'd had to leave you. He was mighty relieved when I told him I'd found you and you were safe. Perked right up.'

'So, he wasn't asleep? Exhausted?'

'You mean like in his book?'

I grimaced, 'I suppose so.'

'Yeah, well no it wasn't like that. I mean, that guy wasn't about to climb any peaks or anything, but he was a hell of lot better than you—didn't have half his brain hanging out.'

I sat back and looked across at the picture on the wall. Why had Doug lied about that? Had he not remembered properly? Maybe he'd been ashamed of leaving me and taking shelter, but then moving a dead weight through the snow was no easy task. Was it a lie, or a small embellishment? I felt Cassie's eye boring into me.

'Ya wondering why Doug lied, aren't you?'

'Yes.'

'Hell, I wondered the same thing when I read the book, but back then it didn't matter much. I was mad he'd hardly mentioned Bob. The details about him didn't matter.'

'Did…did you contact him? I mean after the book came out?'

'I've never passed a word with him, no. And I don't want to now. I mean, I ain't mad like that no more, he didn't kill Bob, that storm did. He tried to help me find him too, up to a point, though he was more interested in getting you out of there. He was your friend, that was for sure. The book brought it all back. I had hoped to see some kind words, maybe a dedication to his memory. All we got was a couple of lines and a load of factual errors. I chucked the book in the trash and that was that—until now.

'Aw, sorry. Didn't want to get all down on you. Not after all these years.' She crossed the room to a bookshelf

193

and picked out an album.

'I had some happier times later, look.' She sat back down next to me and flicked through pictures until she found one of her holding a baby. Then there was a christening, some school photos, a nativity. 'She was a lovely little girl. She was everything I had. She didn't look a bit like me, if I hadn't been present at the birth, I would have wondered who she was! But she was Bob's that was clear, all that mattered.'

'Did Bob leave you any money?' I asked.

She shot me a sideways glance, 'You seem awfully interested in my finances, Craig.'

My face grew hot. 'I'm sorry, it's just…'

'Yeah, you're feeling guilty, I know. Well, a little guilt don't hurt. To answer your question though, seems he had some sort of trust fund, started paying out a year later for some reason, maybe that's when he was declared dead— no corpse you see. It helped a lot, particularly before I went back to work. Didn't realise Bob had had that sort of foresight, but he always was a secretive one.'

But I knew different, and it wasn't a secret I would be sharing. My trip out there had been misguided. From thinking Cassie was running some long-distance hate campaign, I now knew she was an innocent. A recipient of Doug's donations, perhaps set up in a fit of guilt, but now damaging his already weak marriage.

Cassie turned over a few more pages in the album to show me a classic school portrait shot of a beautiful teenage girl, with deep blue eyes and a golden plait hanging over her shoulder. 'That's her now, gorgeous ain't she, my Beccy.'

I felt the room spinning around me. I knew this girl, but not as Rebecca Green.

It was a photo of Sarah.

CHAPTER FOURTEEN

'You okay, Craig?' Cassie put her hand on my arm. 'You look like you've seen a ghost.'

I sat back unsure of what to say. There wasn't a short cut. 'I know Rebecca.'

Cassie frowned and smiled. 'You know Beccy? What d'ya mean?'

'Well, I know this person—' I jabbed the picture,'—but she isn't called Rebecca. This is Sarah. The one I was telling you about.'

Cassie stood up. 'What are you saying, Craig, you had a bit too much to drink? Don't fool me around here.' Her voice trembled and tears appeared in her eyes. 'Don't be upsetting me, mister. Not about Beccy…'

'I'm sorry, Cassie, really sorry. But Rebecca. Well, she's working for Doug.' How could I sweeten this? 'She's doing well for herself. Making a film for him.'

'What the hell! Ya saying she's calling herself Sarah? That's her middle name, she always hated it! Why the hell would she do that? Why wouldn't she call me? Three years! Three fuckin' years! How do I know this isn't all some bullshit? You'd better not be lying, Craig, or you're out on the street. Don't mind if I tell Tom to give you a good hiding first.' She was shouting and I feared Tom might charge down the stairs at any moment with a shotgun.

Then I had an idea. 'Get the SummitSeeker website up, she might be on there.'

Cassie strode out of the room and I followed. In a small office was an old PC which she turned on. It seemed to take a lifetime to boot in which time she said nothing, but sat staring at the screen, lips tightly pursed. Eventually she pulled up the SummitSeeker website and went to the about us page. There was Doug with lots of blather about his climbing heritage, his books, his commitment to excellence and of course, a picture of him, big handsome grin, mountains in the background. A man of action. As for the rest of the team there was nothing. 'Google her name and SummitSeeker.' Again, there were no obvious hits. 'How about award ceremonies?'

That was when we had a lucky break. A group shot from the Outdoor Expo show in Amsterdam, Doug in black tie, holding some sort of trophy surrounded by a grinning team, amongst them in a dazzling full length dinner dress, Rebecca Sarah Green.

Cassie stared then zoomed in until Sarah's face filled the screen. She said nothing before slowly standing up and walking out. 'I'm goin' to bed.'

I was left alone, to retreat upstairs to my room and contemplate what this meant.

I found Cassie early in the morning cooking bacon and pancakes. Tom was already out and Joel was nowhere to be seen. She smiled when I went into the kitchen. 'Hope you're feeling hungry. Make yourself at home and I'll bring it through.'

I had not slept much, trying to work out what to do next. I had a ticket to Patagonia and was desperate to get there to have it out with Sarah. I wanted to reveal who she was to Doug, having connected the dots, but I was sure Cassie could add to that tally.

Sure enough, breakfast arrived minutes later and she joined me across the kitchen table. 'I think we need to trade a bit of information, Craig,' she said.

I nodded. 'I've told you most of what I know about Sarah, sorry, Rebecca.'

'I'm sure there's more.' She smiled. 'Let me tell you about her first, then we'll see.'

She sipped her coffee then fixed me with her gaze. 'So, Beccy, she was a pretty normal child, did well at elementary, lots of friends, good grades, asked about her pa, but seemed at peace with his absence. She had friends whose dads had left home; it wasn't uncommon to be a single parent. Not sure there were any other widows though, not of my age.

'Anyway, all was fine until she came across that book. I told you I trashed it. Well, maybe that wasn't quite true. I'd buried it on a shelf in a spare room. I was a big reader back then, mostly crappy novels and chick lit. Anyhow, they ended up lining the spare room and Rebecca started to pick them out when she got to an age where adult novels began to have a draw. She didn't know about Doug's book, her narrative about her pa was about her pa, not about two other guys there at the same time. I don't know why I had never told her but it was a mistake, like not telling an adopted kid they're adopted, I suppose.

'Anyhow, one day she comes flying into the lounge when I'm sat there watching some TV. She's raging, waving the book in the air, calling me a liar, worse. She could cuss real good by that age. I stood up, tried to calm her down, get something coherent from her. My reaction to seeing the book confirmed in her head my guilt in not telling her the truth about Bob. But I had, I just hadn't told her he was also a bit-part player in someone else's story.

'She calmed down eventually after much tears, pouting and door slamming. We by then were up in her bedroom, me on her beanbag, her with little legs dangling over the edge of her bunk bed. I got out what had upset her so much, that there was a published account of his last days, albeit a short one, that there were other people on the mountain when he had disappeared, people who might know what happened to him. I told her what had happened again, but this time involving you and Doug. I told her everything, didn't discuss my views on the book, I realise they were coloured by my grief. After that the book stayed in her room and I thought that was the end of it.'

She paused and turned the mug in front of her staring into the brown liquid.

'What happened then?'

'Nothing...For at least two years, but a distance had appeared between us. She became withdrawn, spent a lot of time on her laptop with her door shut. I put it down to early teenage behaviour. I didn't like it, but hell, I hadn't been an angel myself. My mom told me not to worry. Then she took up climbing, the first positive thing she had done since the discovery. Started to hang out at the climbing wall, spend her money on gear. I went down and watched her a few times—she was exceptional.'

'Like you?'

'Oh, Craig, I'd fallen out of love with the sport after Bob died. I never wanted to go back, but I could see how positive it was for Rebecca. She needed a focus, something to put her energies into. Boy, did she focus on it! That girl, when she gets the bit between her teeth, jeez, she started getting obsessive, spending every day down there, then asking to go on days out to Pima Canyon, the nearest outdoor cliffs. I wasn't totally happy, particularly as she was still a young girl, but was surrounded by a lot of horny young men and she was an early developer, if you get me.'

I did, I had seen her. I could also see how the temperament Cassie described fitted the woman I knew. The drive to push the film through, the manipulation of those around her.

'Her grades started to suffer at school. I tried to talk to

her about it but by then she was fifteen and I was shut out. I had started dating Tom, mostly online, but she knew and she hated it. Tom was patient, bless him, I thought I would lose him because of her, but he stuck with it. We tried everything, but she went out more and more and saw less and less of us. By then she was screwing some of those boys down at the wall, I was sure of that, and she'd started smoking weed. It became intolerable. You got to understand, Craig. She was pure A-grade, she could have had anything back then, been anything she wanted to be. I thought she would get into a great school, maybe even Ivy League, but she was dropping like a stone. I had to get her away from that scene. I thought Dakota was the answer...' She looked back into her mug as though into a crystal ball, seeking a past that had never happened.

'But she didn't come?'

'No. When she turned sixteen, she moved in with some guy called Troy. I met him once, didn't like what I saw, but I'd seen a lot worse. At least he told me he would care for her, it was better than nothing...It was the last time I saw her before I moved up here. God, I should have done a lot more to stop her, but she was stubborn and I'd lost control.'

I was stunned. 'She's never been here?'

'Doubt she could find it on a map. Plain refused to come. There's always been a room waiting for her...'

I put my head in my hands and tried to reconcile this Rebecca of eight years ago with the Rebecca I knew now. I knew a beautiful young woman who was poised and controlled, a graduate apparently who had climbed a small corporate ladder rapidly. Obsessive, yes, but not the drug taking waster Cassie was describing. I had a big question that needed answering.

'What's she up to, Cassie? What's she doing in France?'

Cassie ran her hand through her hair and breathed a long sigh. 'Well, I don't know, I could take a guess…' She looked up at me, 'I think you could too, Craig.'

'But tell me a little more. Since you moved here, Tom said you've been in touch. Is that true?'

'Yeah, it's true. I didn't hear anything for a while, got really worried about her, then the next thing I hear, she's calling me from Banff; has moved up there with a new climbing boyfriend. I flew up and visited her. She was studying, had straightened herself out, but wouldn't come here. We had a bit of a fight over that and that's the last time I actually saw her. Just been the odd call and email since then. Last time we spoke she said she would come and stay when the time was right, whatever that meant. She told me about her job as an instructor and a marketing course she was doing. She said she was working on a big project and would visit when it was done. She said she was going to make me proud of her, make things right. Until you showed up, I thought she was still in Canada.'

I couldn't believe Cassie had not managed to track her to Europe, but I could see she felt the same.

'You've not seen her since when?'

'Over three years… I had to protect myself, Craig. I know it seems crazy but too much stuff has happened. I've got a good life here. I need to protect it. I know she'll come back one day, when she's ready. There's not a day goes by and I don't think about her. Over to you, Craig. Tell me everything about her now. Any pics on you?'

I told her everything, from the first moment in the shop, through to her departure with Doug. This time I didn't gloss over the details, the relationship with Doug, nothing. Cassie remained impassive as I spoke, perhaps she had heard so much worse before. When I got to the end, I said, 'She's out to get Doug, isn't she?'

'I'm not sure. She's out to find out about Bob.'

'What's Doug got to do with that? Why this bloody film?'

Cassie frowned. 'Yeah, that's the bit I don't get either. Yes, Doug's account sucks a bit, but it's basically what I remember too, just a bit sanitised. Bob went off on his own, he was a big boy. Doug may be puffed-up, conceited asshole, but he ain't responsible for Bob's death any more than you or I are. Can't say I understand it.

'Tell me Craig, what about Doug's wife, Lynsey you said—'

'Linda.'

'Yeah, what's her take on all this?'

I had taken care not to say too much about Linda, but somehow Cassie had picked something up. 'She knows something's been going on. With the money too—she's not happy. To be honest, Cassie, she's part of the reason I'm here.'

At that Cassie raised her eyebrows. Then she slowly nodded, 'Ah, I see. Craig, I think you missed something out in your story?'

'Linda's an ex. That's all. I…I thought there was still something there, but I was wrong.' I felt the heat rise under my skin.

'Pffft, you don't owe her shit, mister! You telling me your gal ran off with that asshole after the accident? Honestly?'

'Well, it wasn't quite like that—'

'Sounds like it was just like that! I bet she's regretting it now.' She looked across at me and tipped her head. 'Sorry, Craig, that was unfair. It's none of my business…' She paused inviting me to fill the void with a confession.

'It's history, I'd rather not talk about it. Look, there is one more thing I haven't told you. Why I came.'

201

Cassie leaned back and crossed her arms. 'Go on.'

'So, Linda found something, a money trail that led to you. Doug's been paying you money, Cassie, since a year after the accident.'

'What money? What are you talking about? He hasn't paid me a bean.'

'The trust fund you spoke about?'

I watched as she digested this. Tears welled in her eyes. 'That, that was Bob's money. It was a lawyer who told me…'

'I'm sorry. Maybe it was, but…Linda saw the bank statements, Cassie. With your name as the recipient. Maybe it's some other account?'

She stood and left leaving me with my bacon and pancakes, now cold on the plate. I had known this was the difficult bit, but I was committed now. It all had to come out. There had been too many secrets and it hadn't done any of us any good. I looked out onto the swaying corn fields. It was another lovely day in flat Dakota, but it was time to move on to some mountains.

Cassie didn't return for ten minutes and I had no interest in tracking her down. When she finally came back, she had a sheaf of papers. She sat opposite me again and fixed my gaze. 'Did you see how much he paid out?'

'No, she just said he'd been paying out monthly since 1992.'

'Did you think I was blackmailing him? Is that why you came here?'

'No, not really. I don't know, didn't know. But yes, that's why I came out. I needed to know.'

'And now?' She raised an eyebrow, challenging me.

'No, of course not. I think maybe he felt sorry for you. Guilty we survived. He hadn't written the book then; I don't think it was a money thing.'

202

'Why couldn't he have just phoned, like a normal person. I thought he didn't give one. Oh, Craig, what are we going to do?'

'I'm going to go and find the truth, that's what.'

CHAPTER FIFTEEN

I had forgotten just how arid Argentina is. I gazed through the plane window at the semi-desert slipping below the fuselage. The flight had taken us firstly across the sea and then along the chain of the Andes over the jungles of Columbia, the high volcanic peaks of Peru and now the folded golden earths of Northern Argentina. Nine hours of dozing, trashy movies and bland airline fodder. I felt utterly detached from the landscape outside; we could have been skimming another planet.

I stank, and probably looked a complete mess. I had not changed for three days. Did airport hours count the same as those strapped into a plane seat? Were they as tiring? I was taking the trip of a lifetime, but without the pleasure and excitement usually associated with one. The lady sat next to me of course was too polite to comment, but I had seen her nose twitch as she took her seat in Lima. She was an elegantly dressed Argentinian businesswoman in her late forties, perhaps returning from a successful deal, selling or buying? She had slipped an eye mask on soon after take-off. We wouldn't be conversing.

Lizzie's planning in that little travel shop in Llanberis had paid off, all the flights had linked effortlessly and the longest stretch, from Miami to Lima, had given me a long sleep. But I was desperate for a bed. I needed to recover my strength before the final long trip south to confront the two.

Despite days of travel and combined hours to contemplate the encounter, I was as clueless as to my approach with Doug as I had been with Cassie in Dakota. What I was clearer on though were my objectives; to unmask Sarah, to get her to explain herself and to get the truth out of Doug.

But that wasn't all. There was something else, something nagging in the back of my mind; a reason to return to Fitz Roy beyond simply straightening out the chaos that had rocked my life. It was there, a message from the past, through dreams, through photos, through conversation. I looked back out at Argentina. Buenos Aires was approaching and so was an emerging truth.

The sun had long gone down when I rolled finally into El Chalten. I stepped down from the bus and picked up my rucksack. Five flights, fifteen thousand kilometres, a bus ride and now I was at last using my preferred means of transport, my feet.

The town had changed beyond all recognition; in fact, there had been virtually no town there last time I had been in Patagonia. El Chalten grew up in the 1990s with the rise of the trekking industry, the same industry that had been paying my bills for the past three decades. It didn't consist of much, a dozen streets in one of the only flat pieces of land in the district, hemmed in by the contours of hills and cliffs. The buildings were mostly low-rise; bungalows or a couple of storeys, nothing obviously worthy of Doug. I was exhausted and felt the pressing need to sleep before I found him, to clean myself up and plan what I was going to say.

I walked down through the town until I found what looked like a clean hostel but was low rent enough to match the remaining cash I had on me. My mobile was dead and the guide books said my credit cards wouldn't work here, even if the machines recognised them, which in itself seemed unlikely.

'Buenos noches?' A young woman greeted me from a reception desk.

'Sorry, English? Do you have a room?'

'Of course.' She smiled. 'You here to trek?'

'Something like that.'

She pushed over the inevitable police form to fill in. 'Thirty dollars a night, in advance.'

'Just one night please.' That, hopefully, would be enough.

It didn't matter my room turned out to be tiny and damp, the windows were uncovered and the toilet down the corridor stank. I slept as soundly that night as I had for weeks. I woke up in a state of complete disorientation. It was only when I looked through the grimy window I realised where I was. It was time to find Doug, and Sarah.

My plan was to visit the tourist information, assuming I could find one, then work my way down the accommodation list, from most expensive to cheapest, until I found them. However, when I stepped out into the street and looked up at the hillside, I had a revelation. I knew where Doug would have headed, it was obvious, it was just a matter of locating it. I wandered the streets, some metalled, some dusty and gravelled. Outside of the centre, the town was a building site with smart wooden villas interspersed with ugly concrete, discarded caravans and rusting cars. When I came to the north edge, I found it, Hostel Laguna Sucia. The name hadn't changed, however the hostel had, almost beyond recognition. The modest farm house was now a boutique hotel, a small piece of opulence in this humble town.

'You bastard!'

A half-clad Doug was hanging out of a first-floor window, a huge grin spread across his face. I couldn't help but smile back at him. Finally, I had arrived.

'Stay there, I'll be right down.' He disappeared from view, to appear at the front door moments later, and then

206

I was embraced in a bear hug. 'Craig, I'm so glad you came.' He couldn't wipe the smile off his face as he dragged me through the reception into the dining room.

Whilst the inside was smart, every fine detail thought of, it was unquestionably the same house we had stayed in years before. More memories flooded back, of card games, shared meals, laughter over bottles of weak local lager, empanadas and stew, the wind whistling under the door and rain beating down noisily on the thin windows. We made our way into the lounge which was empty but for us. Doug poured out a couple of coffees and we reclined into a deep sofa.

'Do you remember it? Marco and Rosa sold out, live up north now in the sun apparently, but sounds like they did alright...' He continued to ramble, casting his arms this way and that as he pointed out landmarks outside and changes to the building inside. 'I'll make sure you get a room here. When did you arrive?—'

'Where's Sarah?' I asked, breaking his flow.

His smile faltered. 'Oh, she's out at Fitz Roy already, wanted to get in there and start getting background shots. Lots of work to do.'

'Piotr?'

'Yes, she's with him.' I saw something flash across his face, but his composure quickly returned. 'He's filming. Grand job. We'll have this in the can in no time. Meanwhile, there's a holiday to have here.' He must have caught my grimace. 'Oh, come-on, Craigy-boy, I know it wasn't all plain sailing back in Chamonix, but let's forget about that. Sarah says she's got great footage, with what we get out here we'll have a top-class movie, no problem. They'll be lining up for it.'

'You sure about that?'

Doug frowned. 'Spit it out, man. Something's bugging

207

you. No point travelling ten thousand klicks to keep it on your chest.'

'Fifteen thousand.'

Doug frowned again at this, but didn't question my maths. 'Go on.'

Despite all of my time to prepare for this moment, I still didn't know what to say. 'Well, it's about Sarah.' He nodded at me, willing me to go on. 'She isn't who she says she is. Not Sarah, I mean. She's actually Rebecca. Rebecca Green, Bob's daughter.'

For a moment Doug said nothing, but then his head dropped and he slowly raised his hands to his face covering it.

'I'm sorry to break the news this way. But I've no idea what she's up to with both of us, she's messing us about, Doug, I don't trust her, that abseil—'

Doug's hand palm flew out, *Stop!* He looked back at me with a reddened face. 'Craig, I'm sorry—'

'Well yes—'

'Hear me out. I know about Rebecca.'

'You know?' I shot out of my seat as though stung by a wasp. 'What do you mean?'

'Sit down, man. Just listen for God's sake.'

I did as he requested, feeling my hands shake. This was not a bit what I had expected.

'She told me…A few months ago, nothing more. Believe me, I was as surprised as you must have been. Poor girl, she'd been worried sick about me finding out, but with our, um, relationship developing, felt I should know everything.'

I put my head into my hands which slid down over my ears. I didn't want to listen; so infantile, so utterly ludicrous. I had flown thousands of miles for this? What was I thinking?

208

I sat back and folded my arms. Why hadn't I expected this? Everything else had been a lie, why not this?

'I can see you're sceptical, man. God, I should have told you earlier.'

'You didn't tell me. I can't fucking believe it.'

'No, no, I'm sorry. I'll tell you everything, honestly.' He stood up and started to pace the room.

'No, no,' I felt my legs rising beneath me, propelling me to the door, 'I've heard enough. Good-bye.' I set off down the road, no idea where to, just away from that place, that idiot.

'Craig, come back, don't be ridiculous. I can explain!' He was bawling down the street. I heard his running steps then he grabbed my shoulder and spun me around. I pushed him away and turned to set off.

'Look, I'm sorry. I know what we've done is wrong. I should have told you. But I can explain. Sarah had a rough time growing up, no dad, no grave even. Fell in with some of the wrong people. A good mother, but perhaps not the best stepdad by all accounts.' I stared upwards; I couldn't meet his eyes. I held my tongue at this point, he still hadn't asked how I knew but I let him continue. 'Anyway, climbing saved her, she got a job as an instructor, worked her way through a college degree. Really worked hard...'

What a saint.

'She saw our internships programme in the *Climber* magazine around the time she graduated, hopped on a plane and landed the job. I never met her until the Christmas party, nothing to do with me her getting the job.'

'And her name change? What was that about? Where were your checks? Visas?'

'Ah, yes. A bit simpler than you'd imagine. She got married when she was eighteen, some awful guy she'd run

209

off with when she was sixteen. It didn't last, of course, she escaped and took up the course, but she kept the name— Sarah's her middle name—wanted to stop her mother tracking her down, that and the odious stepdad.' He paused with his back to me, looking out down the valley at the mountain vista. The clouds had noticeably lifted from the morning. It was going to be a beautiful day.

I didn't believe a word of it. I had a lot of questions. 'What triggered her confession?'

He turned around. 'Hardly a confession, man. More of an opening up, a yielding. Love, simple as that.'

'Do you love her?'

He didn't hesitate. 'Yes, I'm sorry, but I think I do. I'll see Linda right; I know you still feel for her and this is all terrible. I never meant to hurt her, but you know, our marriage was dead years ago. I'm doing her a favour really, releasing her; perhaps she can find someone who will treat her better. A soulmate.' He nodded towards me, but refrained from the patronising wink his statement deserved.

'But you haven't told her?'

'She knows we're in love. Pretty much kicked me out. I messed up. Too much drink. I'm on the wagon now, won't happen again. You know, Craig, this film is going to be a success, we'll all make a lot of money out of it, you'll see. It'll change your life.'

I looked around me. We were still on planet earth, in an anonymous street in South America. This conversation was actually happening. Where to start? 'So, you honestly believe Bob's daughter, who lived halfway across the world, just happened to see a low paid job in a foreign country which coincidentally was run by a man who was one of the last people to see her father alive and whose mother has been receiving payments from you?' I checked

210

his face for a reaction. Yes, the mask dropped, a flicker of surprise running across it as though he had just received a small electric shock, then it returned; Doug the composed salesman. 'By the way, Linda knows about that. Not that you probably care. I can't believe someone so smart could fall for such a stupid pack of lies.'

He stood before me, head hanging like a naughty schoolboy caught smoking down the bike sheds. A car beeped its horn, breaking the moment. We were standing in the middle of a street, in a small town in Argentina talking about relationships from another continent.

'We need a beer.' He didn't wait for an answer but went straight through the doors of an adjacent bar. I followed him. For once he was right about something. He called, 'Dos cervezas,' and held up two fingers to the barman to doubly confirm the order. We sat at a small table by the window.

Doug continued, 'Right, seems like I've even more explaining to do. You're wondering why I've been bunging money to Cassie? Of course you are…Guilt, mate. Pure and simple. I was gutted about Bob. You were out of it, probably don't remember a lot about it,' he looked out of the window. A coach full of trekkers had arrived and was unloading its cargo onto the dusty street outside. 'I made a packet with that book. Didn't expect to, but I got lucky, it launched my brand. Two years later I was standing in a showroom in Switzerland in front of my first BMW and it dawned on me, like a revelation, a visitation…do you know what I mean, man. Has it happened to you?' He put his beer down slowly and looked at me. I said nothing. I wanted to hear this, the whole truth if that's what it was.

'No, you haven't, have you? It was weird, like he was there. It was like I received a message to take care of his widow—'

211

'Oh, for God's sake, spare me the mysticism. I get it, you felt guilty, wanted to share the profits. Embarrassed maybe…She thought it was a trust fund from Bob—is that what you intended?'

He glanced outside again. The coach had moved off. 'I don't know, didn't think about it. Just wanted to share it out.'

We sat silent after that for a while, sipping our beers, watching life pass by outside. It was Doug who eventually broke the deadlock. He muttered, 'I guess you've talked to her then?'

'Who?'

'Cassie of course. Can't see how else—'

'I did more than that. I've been to see her. You'll be pleased to know she's well and her husband is a great guy. Your bullshit story was just about credible, if a bit of a stretch, except I know the bit about him isn't true. I'm trying to work out if you actually believe it or are just trying to convince me for some reason.'

He slowly drew on his beer, emptying it. 'Okay, mate. I've taken the bollocking, that's enough. Bottom line, I love her, she loves me.' He held up his palm. 'You don't have to believe me but that's how it is. You're pissed off; I get it—of course you are, but now you've got a simple decision. You're here, you've worked it all out, so are you coming climbing with me or are you going to fly away home? Mate, I know I'm a shit, but I need you.' He sat back in his seat and folded his arms.

It was all so simple. He was like a teenager, cheap engagement ring on, leaving home for a new, easier, life. How utterly different the reality was. I contemplated one last attempt to change his mind, but what if this latest revelation was true? After all nothing he had said contradicted what Cassie had told me. Perhaps about the stepdad. He hadn't struck me as remotely odious, but then Sarah had been a kid when he had arrived, it was natural for her to dislike him and she had been associating with the wrong types by her own confession. Yes, there was nothing that directly contradicted him. Nothing except for my intuition that it was a pack of lies. For the moment though, I was defeated. I could have just returned home from the USA.

'Why aren't you with her now?'

'Someone had to wait for you, didn't they?' He smiled.

I breathed in and looked away, to the mountains. Linda had been right; I needed to do this for myself, not for Doug or her or even Cassie for that matter. There was no marriage to save, no truth to reveal. I was there with one reason only left, to sort out my own demons.

I finished my drink, placed the glass on the table and locked eyes with him. For all the bravado I could see uncertainty flicking across his face. I said, 'Just don't balls-up the climbing,' and walked out of the bar, Doug in my wake.

Doug insisted I take a room at the Laguna Sucia and within an hour we were walking over together back to my lodgings to gather my belongings. The clouds had evaporated to reveal mountain tops glistening in newly discovered sunshine. Now I had unburdened myself, I relaxed. I had no more secrets and I doubted Doug had any either. I was grumpy of course, but I also began to feel a thrill I had not experienced for decades. The mountains were calling to my old body to return and to climb. It was a fantasy, like the film, like Doug's romance, but I let it run; at least I could go back and revisit and see what I had once been almost capable of. My problems of dealing with Doug and Sarah had not been solved. I was back to being their lackey, attempting to pay off my debts through their uncertain patronage, but for a moment I decided to put that to one side and to make the most of the privilege of being in one of the most beautiful places on earth.

My room in my new lodgings proved to be a huge step up from where I had been staying and it was a relief when Doug handed over his credit card details to cover the cost. However, I had not asked what the plan was at that point.

'Don't get too comfortable, Craig. Tomorrow we ship out. You can help me get some more of the gear together this afternoon.'

'What gear?' I asked.

He grinned at me. 'Climbing tackle of course! I could only bring a limited amount with me, but no worries, I haven't been idle. There's one of you here.'

'Of me?'

'A climbers' shop.'

It wasn't anything like my shop of course, for starters it wasn't burnt out and secondly it wasn't a shop. Instead, Doug led me to what looked like someone's garage. A couple of mangy dogs lay in the dust outside, collecting the intermittent sunshine. We were warmly greeted by a tall, thin Argentinian, with a mop of curly brown hair hanging loose about his shoulders.

'Vincente!' Doug pumped the man's hand.

'You brought him then,' Vincente said, nodding towards me with a grin. 'The famous Craig Darwen.'

'Not sure I'm famous,' I said.

'Oh, you are around here,' Doug said, 'We both are. Put the place on the map.'

I mumbled it was probably Francisco Moreno who had done that but Doug's new friend opened the garage doors

214

and beckoned us inside. The daylight fell upon wooden shelves heavy with an ordered mixture of old and new tackle, bundles of rope, rucksacks and waterproofs.

'Where on earth does all this come from?' I asked.

'An Aladdin's cave of climbing gear. Years of bartered kit disposed of by climbing teams. The guy's a bit of a magpie,' Doug explained whilst Vincente disappeared into the adjoining guest house. 'He runs a guest house as well as easy climbing tours, nothing serious, just glacier walks and the like and a bit of low-level stuff, gives the tourists a few war stories to take home with them.'

Vincente reappeared holding a sheaf of papers. 'Okay, I have your lists; so, rope, three racks; you okay with Petzl, don't have any SummitSeeker…?' He continued to pull out boxes and bags and rummage through putting together a set of gear that would have put an Eiger expedition to shame. '…Ice tools, screws…'

'Doug, why do we need all this kit? I thought we were just visiting the scene?'

'We are.' Doug had started to carefully inspect the tackle, rejecting the occasional quick-draw and nut, tossing them aside as though discarding old newspapers. His focus seemed to be as much about avoiding my eyes as anything to do with the quality of the metalwork and slings.

'You're not seriously suggesting we're climbing it again?'

He carried on flicking through the equipment as though he had not heard my question.

'Doug? We're not up to it. You do realise that?'

He stopped and looked up at me. 'Don't panic, man. Just a bit at the bottom for the film, no crux moves or anything. Nothing we can't handle. Got to cross the glacier too.' He resumed his checks. Vincente had finished ticking his list off. 'Our man here is going to help us haul the stuff to our base camp and we'll take it from there.' Doug was now filling three large rucksacks.

'You need any clothes?' Vincente asked.

I shook my head, but Doug answered for me, 'Craig needs boots, crampons and I'm guessing…'

And so it went on. An hour later we emerged dressed to tackle anything the Andes could throw at us. Vincente and a mate would help us carry all the gear out to the others the next morning.

As we turned in that night, the sky was cloudless with only a light breeze apparent in the town's few trees.

The paths through to Fitz Roy had changed almost as much as the town. Where I had remembered us getting lost on poorly marked tracks, now we were on well-beaten paths following another group. Our packs were heavy, though were considerably lighter than they would have been but for the help of Vincente and a Kiwi called Tama. Vincente was very chatty, asking many questions about our previous experience, which Doug handled with his customary charm. Tama was much quieter, a habitual traveller who was passing through and living off casual work. The path led up out of the town then climbed steeply through woods before we emerged into the open ground after an hour. Cerro Torre, the only peak in the area that made Fitz Roy look simple, glistened as an exposed needle ahead of us. It was a challenge that had lain beyond us two decades before, a mountain mired in controversy over the use of a compressor drill in the first ascent to add bolts to the mountain. Mountaineering had an unwritten set of ethical rules which would probably be forever argued over.

Our route took us west, along the edge of a roaring Rio

Fitz Roy. To the north of us the walls of Mount Fitz Roy loomed, hiding its peak from view. The path wound in and out of woodland but was uniformly well marked. We passed a couple of tours returning from the viewpoints, a mixture of old and young trekkers, a population to whom this area would have been almost inaccessible at the start of the 1990s. They were on their way back to the security of El Chalten after a leisurely lunch. Finally, after about three hours and a final steep climb, we reached the shores of the grey lake, the end point for day trippers. Stopping was not for us, it was late afternoon and our objective was the far shore. Sarah and Piotr had set up camp there, short of the glacier, whilst they shot film of the surrounding area. Shadows from the peaks to the west were now etching their way across the water; within a couple of hours the whole valley would be in darkness. I could make out the tiny orange dome that was a tent perched at the far end of the lake. I felt my pulse quicken and our stride lengthen. As we neared, we could see steam rising from a stove and a figure waving at us.

'There they are!' Doug said. 'I hope they've got a brew on.'

The walk around the lake seemed to take an eternity, as there was little in the way of a path and at places boulders had tumbled almost to the water's edge forcing awkward climbs to avoid getting our feet wet. Beyond the lake the glacier stood tall, rising up towards the base of the cliffs where an attempt on the summit would be launched from.

I caught Vincente looking up at the sky. 'I can't believe this weather. You guys need to make the most of it. Must be the longest window we've had in a few seasons.'

'It was all cloudy when I arrived,' I said.

'That was normal—good to normal. Weather here changes every day, every hour. Sorry, you know that. This

217

is as good as it gets. Maybe a bit too warm.' He looked up at the sheer cliffs to our right, and as if to emphasise his point, a small rock ricocheted onto the path only metres from where we were standing.

'We'll be okay in a moment. Always a bit lively here.'

'We're not climbing you know, not really,' I said, half to myself, half to Vincente.

He smiled. 'A lot of gear for someone who isn't climbing.'

The path broke out from between two large boulders and we were on top of the campsite. Sarah stood drinking from a thermos mug whilst another figure stooped over a tripod, a lens focused on our arrival; I should have expected that. Sarah beamed when she saw me. 'Doug, you brought him! I never thought you'd come.'

'He wouldn't miss it for the world,' Doug said, embracing her, before dropping his pack.

She stepped over and kissed my cheek. 'Thanks, Craig. We can make a great movie here, you know that, right?'

I looked into her eyes. Sarah, Rebecca, whoever she was, what was she planning?

Piotr stepped forward and we shook hands. 'Good to see you again, Craig.' His words though lacked any enthusiasm and I caught his sideward glance towards Doug, who was helping Vincente and Tama arrange the gear.

Vincente said, 'I'm sorry but Tama and I have to leave immediately, we need to get onto the main path before dark.' That was three hours away. At least with their packs shed they would be able to move much faster. Doug thanked them profusely for their help and confirmed that he wanted them back in three days.

'Can we radio back sooner?' I asked.

'There's no radio contact here,' Vincente said, 'we are in the shadow of Fitz Roy. Don't worry, we'll return whatever the weather. If you need longer, we can come back another time.'

Doug really must have opened his cheque book. With that we said our goodbyes and watched them disappear into the lakeside boulder field.

Once they were out of sight, Doug said, 'Sarah, can I have a word?' He glanced at me—I knew what the contents of this conversation would be. 'Just a bit of housekeeping.'

'Sure, honey.'

'We'll get the tents up,' I said, going over to where we had dropped our sacks. It was then I saw Piotr had raised a camera and started to film again.

'Don't mind him,' Sarah said, seeing my surprise, 'he's going to be shooting everything, in fact we all are, then we can decide what's usable at the end.' She tapped a little camera she was wearing on her jacket. 'GoPros. I've got enough for us all and we'll all need to wear clip-mics. Don't want to miss a word!'

I didn't much like it, but I nodded my head and we got to work erecting two more tents, one for Doug and me, or more likely Piotr and me, to sleep in, and one for storing gear. Doug and Sarah set off walking around the lake, hand in hand, but were soon out of earshot. I tried to strike up conversation with Piotr, 'What've you been up to?'

He grunted. 'Background shots, scenery. There's been a lot of cloud.'

'You been up on the glacier?'

'We were waiting…'

'For me?'

'For Doug. Didn't think you'd come.' He said the

219

words with the tone of a disappointed finality. I had come. Plans would have to change.

'You've known Sarah long?' I asked. Piotr's head jerked up from the tent peg he was pushing in.

'A few years.' I saw a slight blush on his cheeks.

'Oh, d'you work at SummitSeeker? I thought you were part of the film crew.'

'A bit of both.' His head dropped again and he carried on with the guy ropes. I could see as far as he was concerned the conversation was over. We finished off pitching the tents and then I sat down on the dirt and admired the view across the lake. Sarah and Doug were not long in returning. If she had been perturbed by the knowledge that I knew her past, there was no sign of it at first. But when she walked over to give me a brief hug, I saw her eyes were clouded by tears. 'I'm sorry, Craig. I should've been more honest—with both of you. Thanks for your understanding. But my daddy is somewhere here…On this big lump of rock and ice, and well, I want to commemorate that. I'm shooting this movie in his name.' She looked over at Doug, who nodded. 'Doug understands that. It's kind'a emotional for me, I didn't want to talk about it. I'm sorry.'

'Yes, well…' What could I say to that?

'No more secrets. We're a team, fuck the money men—we'll make a great movie and prove them all fools! Yeah?' She stood waiting for my consent, my approval, like a schoolteacher before a football match.

'What's the plan?'

Doug stepped in at that point. 'We've got a window, Craig. You know how it is down here. We can't afford to waste any time.'

'We need shots on the wall, to film a few pitches, enough to appear like you mean business. We got a lucky break with the weather—let's use it,' Sarah added.

'We'll go at first light. We'll move up the glacier tomorrow and set up camp there near the foot of Supercanaleta, then we can film the next day.'

'Film what exactly? Come on, Doug, I thought we were here to do some interviews in front of Fitz Roy. You know we're not up to climbing it. It's ridiculous!'

Doug laughed, enraging me further. I flung down the peg I was holding. 'What's so funny? Don't you value your life? Wasn't once enough? What are you trying to prove?' Out of the corner of my eye I caught Piotr filming again. I spun around. 'Put that bloody thing down for once! This isn't some sort of game, Sarah, Rebecca.' I checked for her reaction to her real name, but she remained impassive, as though waiting for my petulant outburst to run its course.

Doug put his arm around my shoulder. 'I'm sorry, man, don't worry, it's nothing like that. We need to climb the first few pitches—you know, the easy ones before we hit the couloir. We can do some climbing shots then, side on, fake it a little. That's it. Nothing vertical.'

'I swear, Doug. If you place one piece of gear there, I'm off.'

Doug squeezed my shoulder. 'Think the man needs convincing, Sarah. Can you show him some of what we've got so far?'

'Why not?' Sarah went into her tent and after a moment emerged with an iPad. After a moment of fiddling with it, she handed it over to me. A video was playing, a movie trailer of sorts, a camera sweeping across an alpine landscape, Doug's talking head and then shots of us plummeting, taken as though the camera was sitting on our shoulder. I stood watching it, transfixed. It was truly cinematic in a way I hadn't expected.

'Good, isn't it?' Doug said, 'and that's just a
221

fraction…A teaser this good lady's put together for the festivals and studios. They'll be queuing up.'

'We need some of the real zone, Craig,' Sarah added. 'You two, back together on the rock. We need to weave the narrative together, get the audience on the edge of their seats.'

I looked up at the glacier, at Fitz Roy beyond. The rock was being painted red by the dying sun. I felt the rush, I needed to go up there; I couldn't explain it, but it was a simple fact. 'Okay, what time do I need to set the alarm for?'

We spent the next hour getting the kit set up and making tea, a boil-in-the-bag chicken-something. It surprisingly tasted delicious. Sarah gave us all our GoPro cameras and explained how they worked. She wanted us to capture as much as possible. Perhaps a few minutes would be used, but it was enough to cap off the film. Piotr moved his kit out of Sarah's tent into mine and then we all sat around until it was dark and the temperature had become uncomfortable. We could have done with a big, roaring camp fire, but with only ice and water around, that wasn't an option. I watched Sarah and Doug together. They seemed relaxed, though the same wasn't true for Piotr, who was withdrawn and avoiding eye contact with us all. He only seemed happy behind the camera.

By nine-thirty we were tucked up in our sleeping bags, ready for the off. Piotr lay with his back to me, flicking through film clips on his tablet. He had said very little and didn't offer me a view of anything, though I glimpsed shots of the scenery around us. The fragments I saw looked professional and I said as much, but only received a grunt in return and an almost imperceptible angling of the screen away from me. I could see we weren't set to be lifelong buddies after this and I didn't like the idea of

222

climbing with someone with whom I had so little understanding. After fifteen minutes, he unzipped his bag and crawled to the tent door.

'You okay?' I asked.

'Need a leak.' With that his warmth was replaced by a blast of cold air as he stepped out. Before I had had a chance to consider what I was doing, I zipped the tent door and grabbed the tablet to take a look at the film clips. If he was going to be childish about showing them, I could be childish too.

I wasn't familiar with his tablet, but pressing the button on the side turned it on and immediately opened up an app, Filmstudio Pro IV, which listed thumbnail pictures in a menu down the side, each with a title and date caption. Some were immediately familiar—our fall in the Alps, my head in a talking-heads pose, the same for Doug plus lots of scenery, the most recent being dated that day. However, amongst the familiar, expected collection were lots of other clips. There were many from Doug's chalet, as though taken from hidden cameras—strange angles, some black and white, some with wide lenses. I flicked up through the list. The titles were odd as well. There were 'Torres morning' and 'Ascent 1' to '5', but there were also 'boardroom chaos' and 'Doug drunk 1' to '7' neatly grouped together. Then I saw a long lens shot of me and Linda in the meadow above the house. What on earth was all this about?

I heard the outer tent zip reopen and I tossed the tablet back to where it had been and lay down. Piotr crawled back in and I turned out my lamp. I lay on the hard roll-mat, my eyes closed, listening to Piotr's breathing and the low moan of the wind outside. I had arrived knowing Sarah was a manipulative liar, but the situation was even worse. She and Piotr had some greater plot to discredit

223

Doug, I couldn't see any other explanation. Here I was though, about to embark on God-knows-what expedition supposedly to complete a film that surely had a different agenda. I had to tell Doug, didn't I? Did I owe him that? He wouldn't believe me anyway, not without Piotr's iPad, which was safely tucked away now.

My head was spinning with these questions. I had two basic choices. Have it out with them first thing, or press on and keep silent for the moment.

There was one other factor. As I lay on the ground, I felt more surely than ever before I had to go on, to return to the scene of the accident, to find the truth about what happened. All I had was the knowledge Doug's account didn't match Cassie's and my limited recall of being rescued.

Sod Doug, sod Sarah and Piotr. I needed to go on; it was my turn to control the situation, to use them to get to the Supercanaleta.

With that conclusion I fell into a fitful sleep, but it only seemed like moments later when I was awoken by a beam of light and my shoulders being shaken. It was Piotr's head torch dazzling me, reflecting my breath's tiny icicles.

'C'mon, time to go.'

CHAPTER SIXTEEN

I sat up and climbed out of the tent. It was 7am and already light, not that the sun was visible. The wind had picked up and we were enveloped in a freezing, low cloud that swirled through our camp, up the valley and into the glaciers above. This was more like typical Patagonia, but at least it wasn't snowing or raining.

Doug and Sarah were already packing away their tent.

'C'mon, lazy bones, let's get up that glacier!' Doug grinned and handed me a mug of tea. 'There's some porridge for you.' He nodded in the direction of a steaming saucepan precariously balanced on a tiny petrol stove.

'Piotr?'

'I've eaten,' Piotr mumbled. He stepped past me and started to collapse the tent.

Just how long had the rest of them been up? I went over and helped myself to some of the gruel, but I wasn't truly hungry. Feeling the need to get away from the others at least for moment, I wandered down to the lake shore. I dropped down onto a pebble beach and bent down to wash up. The only sounds were the low moan of the wind and the lapping of the small waves against the surrounding rocks. I swirled the pan in the water and watched blobs of grey porridge floating away into the crystal, lifeless water where it might sit for years. It was a landscape that killed the living and preserved the dead. Was Bob's body lying somewhere in these glaciers, on a century-long journey to this lake? I shuddered and turned around but our campsite had been devoured by the low cloud. A dark shape moved in the mist.

'Hello?'

'Craig?' It was Sarah's voice.

'Hi.'

Sarah's silhouette and then form emerged. She stepped down to the lakeside to stand next to me, staring out into the mist. I gave my pan an unnecessary final swirl.

'How's Mom?'

I stood up slowly, not making eye contact. 'Fine. Missing you.'

'Tom?'

'Yeah, he's okay. Seems like a decent guy. Look—'

She turned to me. 'Why did you come, Craig?'

'Doug asked me to.'

'You always do what he says? Cut the bullshit, Craig. We both know you don't believe in the film. Doug's not here. Be honest.'

For a moment I didn't know what to say. That of all people, Sarah should be asking for honesty from me seemed particularly ironic. I was in search of the truth; it was as simple as that. I had thought telling Doug about Sarah's identity would change things; it hadn't. The whole film idea was clearly a charade of some sort but I needed to go up to Fitz Roy. I hadn't come all this way to turn back, so I needed this team, whether I liked it or not.

But I wasn't keen on sharing this. 'I'm skint. There was a fire at my business.' I looked to see if there was any recognition at this, but she didn't react.

'Yeah, Doug told me. I'm sorry.'

'Doug said he'd pay me what I'm owed. What about you? I mean the film's dead, surely? Why are you doing this? Are you hoping to find your dad?'

'There's no way back, Craig. You know that.'

'You mean with the film?'

She met my eyes and seemed as though she were on the point of saying something but then changed her mind. After a beat she said, 'C'mon, we need to get movin',' and

226

she turned and disappeared back into the mist.

I followed her up to the camp. When I arrived, she was talking to Piotr.

Doug said, 'You ready, man? We're raring to go.' His voice had lost the artificial bonhomie and he banged his mittened hands together. I noticed someone had already packed my rucksack for me; they were in a rush and I didn't like it.

Sarah said, 'We're thinking it will take about five hours to get to the base of the climb, but we'll stop to film a few times on the way. Gives us plenty of time to find your cave. You okay with that?'

Did I have a choice? Doug answered for me, 'Sounds grand. Let's go.'

We set out northwards onto the glacier following compass and GPS to take us around the east side, skirting the worst of the crevasses to the west. Our eventual destination was the Sitting Man Ridge which sprung from the glacier and marked the start of the route east onto the great cliffs of Fitz Roy itself. The cloud was still low and all we could see was filthy ice, cracked and scarred beneath our feet. Initially the gradient was gentle and the route we were following should keep us away from any danger.

We stayed spaced apart joined by a loose rope in case of trouble. Sarah led followed by Piotr and then Doug, with me bringing up the rear. I was glad of the distance from the others. How could I make easy conversation? Sarah whom I didn't trust an inch, Piotr who was somehow in with her on whatever her scheme was, and Doug who at best was horribly naive and at worst complicit. I focused on the ice below my crampons, axes at the ready in case of a problem. At the lower reaches, the gradient was not steep and the ice was clear of snow, but rather a dirty grey, rutted and marked with loose moraine.

Our pace was steady and Sarah showed a keen eye for the terrain with an expertise and knowledge of the glacier that surprised me. She had clearly been over this ground before, more than once I imagined. I thought back to when Doug and I had clumsily traversed this glacier previously, following rough notes from the hostel and relying on youthful enthusiasm and good luck, something that had held out for the early part of the expedition. For sure we were much better prepared this time but I didn't feel one iota safer.

After an hour the sun momentarily broke through the mist. I stopped and looked up and there it was again, sitting like a silver coin in the sky. The rope tugged as Doug reached the limit, but he too stopped and turned with a thumbs up.

Soon the mist had lifted, hiding the peaks but revealing our target ridge, a few miles and a thousand feet above us. Below us the grey lake shimmered as the sun came and went behind the fast-moving clouds. All around us was granite. It was beautiful.

Piotr called for a stop. He climbed up past us to join Sarah and after a brief conversation set up a tripod. It would be the first of a number of walk-bys. Doug and I roped as a pair and Sarah and Piotr stayed together, filming from a few angles. Quite soon, the stop-start nature it created became irritating. Even Doug seemed less enamoured with the process than his usual self. Our pace had slowed to a crawl and our destination for the day, which was now bathed in sunlight ahead of us, didn't seem to be getting any closer. After perhaps the fifth set of walk-bys, he called back to Piotr and Sarah, 'We'll stop at the bergschrund,' and set off, almost at a jog. I had no choice but to follow at the same pace, but was mightily relieved to be free of our partners.

The bergschrund Doug had referred to, is a crevasse that lies between a glacier and the slope above. Sometimes a glacier can meld into the surrounding rock but frequently the terrain is less forgiving and a crevasse lies between high ice and the cliff face. A bergschrund can be hard to cross and requires some care and probably protection. It wasn't a place for machismo.

As the gradient of the glacier increased and we neared the ridge the pace was faster still, and I had to work even harder to keep up with Doug. The glacier became progressively steeper until we were onto forty-five-degree snow, which ran up to our knees in places. I was feeling tired, but also carried a sense of elation I was back again doing what I had loved best and which I had exiled myself from for so long. Doug was coping, but he was only gym-fit. I doubted he had seen much real rock in the intervening decades, not once his business had taken off.

I heard a shout from below. Sarah was waving up to us, they had fallen well back. Piotr appeared to be sitting down, at the full extent of the rope from Sarah. I called for Doug to stop and he dropped to the ground. I was beginning to wonder if there was a problem with Piotr, but then they started to move again, and so I continued up to join Doug. He was sitting in the snow staring out west across the valley towards glowing granite spears. With the sun now out, the temperature had rocketed and I wanted to lose a layer before I became drenched in sweat.

I flopped down next to him and took my pack off. 'Nice view.'

'Yeah, really is.' His breathing was laboured. He reached into his pocket and pulled out his slim hip flask, but I put my hand onto his wrist. 'No.' It fell from his hand onto loose rock and rolled a few feet down the slope.

Doug leaned forward making to stand up. 'What you do that for? Was just setting myself up.' His voice held no conviction.

'Leave it. On the wagon, remember?'

He turned to me. His face was pale and his lips trembled. There was something I had not seen in him before, real fear. Below us I could see the two figures close together, moving in tandem.

'What's up?'

'Just tired. Bit unfit.'

'That all?'

He held my gaze for a moment and his lips began to move, but then he seemingly thought better of it and the moment was lost. He dropped down the slope and retrieved the flask. 'Twenty-first present from Ma, can't lose it.' But at least it was returned, unopened, to his pocket.

I stowed my fleece and put my jacket back on. Below us our companions were making their slow ascent. 'Can that guy climb?'

'Piotr? Oh yeah, he's good, one of our product testers. Least of our worries. Let's go. Don't want the youngsters cramping our style.'

'Yeah, let's show them how it's done,' I replied, in mock bravado. I had no doubts about Sarah's ability. Of Piotr, I was less sure. We would soon see.

The bergschrund appeared not long after. Doug stopped ahead of me, lying belly-flat in the snow. When I reached him, he was shining his torch into the black chasm.

'How deep is it?' I asked.

'Deep enough.'

I scanned back and forth along the glacier line. At this point the slope was forty-five degrees and the gap between the glacier and snow above mostly small. Sarah and Piotr were at least five minutes behind us; we could make the call on the crossing. There were snow bridges to our left and right. 'You want to lead across it?'

Doug sat up to face me. His eyes were glazed. 'D'you think he's down there?'

I felt a wave of ice run through me. 'What do you mean?'

He shook his head slowly and looked up at the dark rock above us but said nothing more.

I thought of asking him who he meant, but I knew and he knew that I knew. I said, 'I'll lead. I'll set up a belay point on the other side.' I started moving immediately, before Doug had even had a chance to take the rope in. I wanted to get away from that place. I scrambled across the slope to one of the thick snow bridges. I grasped my ice axe and slowly crossed it. The rope was tight behind me; if I fell Doug had me. I was soon past the crevasse and onto firm ground, glad to be beyond the black scar. I started to search for a rock pillar as an anchor point, but couldn't see anything suitable. Below me was just rotten snow, ruling out the use of ice screws. I looked up to see how far the nearest rock was. It was perhaps twenty metres distant. Not ideal, but I could reach it, so long as I carried on leading. I turned to call to him to tell him my intentions but to my surprise he had already moved, risking both of us if he fell; perhaps he liked stopping there as little as I had. Sarah and Piotr had reached the point where we had stopped and I could see Piotr was pointing something towards us: we were on film, again. I swore and looked for something I could throw a sling around, but there was nothing. I quickly dug my axe into the snow to act as a 'dead man'—it was better than nothing. I called down to Doug to wait, but he seemed unable to hear me. By this point he was onto the bridge and making good progress. I cursed him, wondering whether to move up to the rock above or to stay static and braced in case he fell. I counted each step across breathing a sigh of relief as he made the upper slope.

'What the hell was that about?'

Doug gave me a blank stare.

'Why didn't you wait?'

He looked back down at the others who were now approaching the bridge. 'I couldn't wait there. Didn't want to be there with them.'

Sarah had stopped now, presumably to repeat our belayed crossing. Doug collapsed into the snow.

'Doug, what's going on?'

'I'm fine.'

'Come on—we don't need another accident on this bloody mountain!' I fiddled with my harness as though that could protect me alone. It couldn't. I needed a partner, one I could trust, one who didn't drink whisky whilst climbing a glacier. Sarah was now working up the slope towards us, her moves were as elegant as they could be for a climber wading through snow. I turned to Doug and lowered my voice. 'I need to know, are you up for this? It's not a climbing wall.'

'I said I'm fine.' His head was bowed, staring down into the valley below, or perhaps still fixed on the black icy crevasse. I sighed. We were only tens of metres from the bottom of the vertical ascent. A few pitches up it should be enough; it was surely all we were capable of as a team.

'C'mon let's tie in properly before Sarah arrives otherwise, we'll get a telling off. I think there's a pillar just up there.' I stood and clambered up the slope, Doug following. Sure enough only feet above us we ran into the first outcrop of exposed rock and tied in.

232

Sarah was soon with us. 'Jeez, you in some kind'a rush? We were hoping to get some approach shots, so much for that!' She dropped her sack to the ground and turned to watch Piotr. 'You boys okay? Ready for the climb?'

I ignored the question. 'How's Piotr doing?'

'Oh, he's fine. He's just catching as much as he can on film. We both are.' She tapped the side of her GoPro. 'Hope you guys are going to turn yours on soon?'

Doug grunted and Sarah shot me a glance, eyebrow raised—is he okay? I looked back down the slope. 'Think he's ready.'

Sure enough Piotr was waving up at us. Sarah tied in, sat down next to me and pulled the rope through. Once she was ready, she waved back down. Piotr started to ascend towards the bridge. After Sarah, his movements appeared laboured. I wasn't intending to let him belay me.

'You two climbed together a lot?' I asked.

'Some,' Sarah muttered. 'God, he's being slow today.' She turned to me. 'Relax, he's up to it, he's just seconding a few pitches. He can handle it. His head's in movie-mode.'

'Well don't mind us, don't want to get cold—Doug you ready?' He nodded to me but kept silent. 'We'll wait on the ridge.'

'No wait,' Sarah said. 'We've got to get filming now or we'll have nothing. Doug?'

Doug grunted in some sort of assent.

'Come on,' Sarah said, pulling Piotr's rope tight. I saw him jerk slightly; she was in danger of pulling him over. I said nothing but her tension made me uneasy.

Piotr finally arrived five minutes later.

'Did you catch the crossing?' Sarah asked Piotr. 'Are you ready?' She grabbed his shoulder and peered into his eyes.

233

Piotr appeared exhausted, and we hadn't even started to climb, but he nodded and pulled out an energy bar. 'I'm fine. Got some good shots.' *Of what?* I wondered. Piotr said no more but locked eye contact with me as he bit into his bar.

'So, Sarah, what's the plan?' I asked. I was feeling cold and was keen to get away from them. Doug looked wrecked and was extremely subdued, Piotr was clearly out of his depth, that just left Sarah and me fit to climb. I knew she was up to something; I just didn't know what.

'You two go on,' Sarah said. 'Wait for us on the ridge.'

I didn't need asking twice. Soon we were huffing and puffing up through the steep snow. My mind cleared of the intrigues of earlier, of Sarah and Rebecca, of Bob. Doug and I moved together, not fast nor elegant, but as a team in harmony, it was untechnical, simple grunt-work, purely muscle and balance; none of the skill the mountain proper required, but climbing nonetheless.

We didn't stop until we reached the wide ridge; Doug first, turning and exclaiming and then me, moments later, drinking in the view. It was fantastic to finally be standing on rock, rather than ice, and to be able to remove our crampons for a while. The mist had dissipated and the clouds' grand prix had lifted heavenwards. Below us kilometres of glacier rippled away into the distant lakes. Despite being in the lee of the wind, intermittent strong gusts shoved and pulled at our exposure, threatening to slide us over the edge of the ridge into the northern valley. I could see Sarah and Piotr were at least ten minutes behind us, presumably held up by the repacking of the cameras.

'We should find some shelter,' I shouted to Doug.

He frowned and looked down the ice towards the ascending figures below. He turned to me and nodded.

The start of the Supercanaleta involves a down-climb eastwards from the Sitting Man Ridge into the start of the chimney. It was in this area twenty-five years before we had found a cave to shelter in, above the bergschrund. So having walked north up onto the ridge, we would walk east along it and then move south a matter of a few hundred metres before making the climb up the western wall.

Doug and I rose east along the ridge until we found the point to descend. The main western buttresses of Fitz Roy now loomed high and impenetrable above us, swallowing up our entire vision. Somewhere, not far from here, was the cave we had spent the night in and where we intended to camp out again, assuming we could find it.

As we dropped off the ridge, I felt my pulse race and for the first time that day a real fear came over me. The drop down became steep enough to require a short abseil. I went first and immediately on reaching the bottom, spotted the dark gash in the granite that marked our cave. I waved to Doug, then clambered up the cold rock to the low entrance. Looking inside, I doubted it would take all four of us, let alone our kit as well. I dumped my bag and crawled in. It was smaller than I had recalled it to be; damp, jagged and dark. A Mars bar wrapper was pushed into a crack in the rock, an unwelcome memento of a recent expedition. I lay out on the rock, the stones digging into my soft, middle-aged flesh. I was tired. One more day with these people then what? To return, skint, to the ashen ruins of my former life? There were still unanswered questions, calling from the summit above, a summit I had never reached.

'Doug, you coming up?'

I didn't get a reply. I wasn't surprised at his reticence. On the cave roof, drops of water slowly formed along a

235

thin crack before dripping onto the floor next to me, beating out time. I closed my eyes, savouring the brief moment alone.

'Don't nod off in there! There's work to be done.' Sarah's head appeared in the mouth of the cave, blocking out what little light there had been. She shone her head-torch around the space. 'A bit cosy, but at least we can keep warm, whatever the weather does.'

She pulled herself in, next to me.

'You've been here before, haven't you?' I asked, not meeting her gaze. The question hung in the air. 'How high did you get? Did you reach the summit?'

She didn't say anything but started to crawl out of the cave. At the entrance she looked round and said, 'I want Doug to show where he left you. Film a piece there.'

The change of subject took me by surprise but before I could say anything she was a silhouette again in the mouth of the cave. I followed her out and descended carefully down to the path. The start of the gully, the Supercanaleta, was only a hundred metres away. Doug's book said I had been left up there somewhere, Cassie said otherwise.

It was mid-afternoon by the time we were all gathered at the base of the chimney. We stared up into the heights, the ice and endless rock rising into the sky. We were at the bottom of the ice shelf that rose to where the rock pitches began and the chimney closed in around you. The ascent, seen from a mile distant as a diagonal line upwards across the face, was far more complex close-up, crossing back and forth across the couloir, switching from ice to rock and back again as the conditions dictated. It was a relatively warm period of weather and even from where we were standing, we could see chunks of debris falling above us before embedding themselves in the ice or being hurtled out into space.

'Look out.' Sarah tugged at my sleeve as a small missile missed my helmet by a few feet. 'It's too late in the day to ascend further. Let's see if Douggie can remember where he left you?'

Doug and Piotr were standing ten metres below busying themselves over the camera and tripod. I wondered if Doug knew what to expect.

Sarah called down to him over the wind, 'Honey, we're going to do some recollection shots.'

Doug turned around and pulled his zip higher so only his eyes were visible. He muttered something which I couldn't catch and then turned back to cross the steep ice at the base of the chimney. Sarah beckoned me to follow and pointed to Piotr, who detached the camera from the tripod and started filming.

I hurried down the rocks and quickened my pace to catch up Doug. I felt a mixture of intrigue and horror to see how he confronted his lie. I soon caught them. Should I contradict his words or play along as I had for the last quarter century?

Doug had planted himself on the ice, perpendicular to the slope, his upper leg bent to keep his torso vertical. Below us the ice-fall dropped away thousands of feet at a forty-five-degree slope, a gradient that only steepened above until it became vertical rock, where the Supercanaleta route began. On either side of us, small chunks of ice rolled past us, ricocheting from the parallel cliff sides on their journey. I stood behind Sarah, the two of us facing Doug. I saw her turn on her GoPro, whilst over my shoulder Piotr was filming as well.

Doug looked from her to me and then said, 'God, it's strange being back. I remember some areas so clearly, as though I was here yesterday, but other things, not so

237

much.'

He turned his head upward towards the steep slope and the cameras followed his gaze.

He pointed. 'You can see the start of the climb there, probably another five hundred feet above us, this is the large chimney, the Supercanaleta as it's called, that Craig and I ascended and descended. The route criss-crosses the rocks above—'

'Where d'ya leave Craig on the way down?' Sarah shouted above the wind.

Doug gave a start. 'I thought you wanted a narrative about the route?' Confusion crossed his face. 'I'll get onto that—'

'Just point it out, sweetie, we'll get this all edited later, don't want to hang around here.' Sarah's voice had softened but still held an accusatory edge.

Doug paused for a moment. I cast my eyes back up the glacier toward the route. I could understand why Doug might have dumped me at this point; abseiling would have become very tricky once he hit the ice and to an exhausted partner, I would have been even more of a liability.

But it wasn't true. Everyone standing there on that ice knew it. Doug turned back to the ice above us. 'I think it must have been about there,' he waved his arm loosely towards the southern wall of the chimney, 'it was dark, I was not with it by then, just working like a robot...' he looked upwards again, as though searching for evidence of his descent, of his heroism. He turned to me, as though for assistance. I shrugged.

'Well, we'll see tomorrow,' Sarah said. 'Let's get set up, early start.' She turned and strode back across the ice, as though it were firm, hard concrete ground. Piotr lowered his camera and trudged in her wake, leaving Doug and me standing there. Doug still had a dazed expression.

He scanned the slope again. 'What was all that about?' he said, as much to himself as to me.

'Hole in your story.'

He shot me a glance. 'What d'you mean, man?'

'She knows your story doesn't match her mum's version of events. What really happened, Doug? Why can't you tell me? How *did* you get me down?' Across the valley from us, the granite spears were casting their long shadows, like a claw expanding to catch us.

Doug shook his head slightly, but didn't respond immediately. But then he suddenly touched my arm and said, 'Just stick with me on this and we'll both be okay.' He looked beyond me to Sarah who was calling us, and then made his way past me, slipping slightly on the ice as he did so. I saw Piotr was filming us again. *Just stick with me—* what was he on about? That's what I'd been doing for the last few months and now I was broke, up one of the world's most dangerous mountains with two apparently malevolent strangers and one old fool. I followed after him back to the cave. It was going to be a long night.

Somehow, we squeezed into the tiny space together and climbed into our bags. The air was damp and sweaty below the low roof. I tucked myself up against one wall, Sarah on the far side with Doug and Piotr in between us. There was little room to move and in the close proximity, little room for much more than small talk. Piotr fiddled with his cameras and Doug got a brew going at the mouth of the cave. Sarah outlined her view of what we would be doing in the morning; rising early then filming the first few pitches before descending. She wanted to capture our recollections and feelings. Well, that was her rationale for the plan; I had ceased to believe anything any of them said. We ate an indifferent selection of boil-in-the-bags and then, as the light faded at the mouth of the cave, turned

239

in.

I lay in the dark for what seemed like hours without dropping off. I was amazed to hear snores from the others, but the ground beneath my sleeping mat was insanely uncomfortable, regardless of how I moved, and it was cold, really cold. Outside in the darkness, the wind groaned and rocks tumbled.

I dreamt again of the mountain. I was trapped, arms pinned to my side and legs tied together. It was so cold. All around me the ground was shaking and then he appeared over me. 'Trust me, I'll get you down.' He busied himself tying me tighter and tighter. I called for him to stop. 'Trust me.' Was all he said. Then he appeared over me again, but it wasn't a man. It was Sarah. I screamed.

I was awoken by a hand on my leg, shaking me. 'You're shouting, man.'

I opened my eyes but couldn't see anything. My bag had wrapped itself tight around me like a straitjacket. 'Sorry, bad dream.'

'We'll be fine. Get some sleep.'

Somehow, I did. Doug woke me at 4am with a gentle shake. 'The others are setting up the cameras, it's time to go.'

I quickly packed my sack and left the cave. The night sky was incredible, the Milky Way's billions of stars not obscured by the slightest hint of cloud. Around us the air was also as still as could be possible in Patagonia. It was perfect.

I watched Sarah and Piotr closely as they adjusted their harnesses and gear. They both seemed slick handling the equipment which was slightly reassuring. That Sarah knew what she was doing was no surprise, but Piotr was a stranger, one whom we may end up entrusting with our lives.

We donned our heavy climbing packs, roped up loosely and climbed onto the glacier, Sarah leading followed by Doug and me, with Piotr at the rear. From here we needed to head south for a hundred metres to where the grand chimney of the western wall started, as we had done the day before. Initially our climb would be up forty-five degrees of ice before it turned into vertical rock and the chimney narrowed. This was where the Supercanaleta route could be said to really start—when the glacier walking finally ended and rock-climbing began. By setting of in the early-morning darkness we were ensuring that any ice was solid and were minimising the chance of being hit by chunks of ice or loose rocks, released as the ice melted during the day.

The glacier was sound, with light snow scattered over it in the lower parts. The straps of my rucksack dug into my shoulders and I felt the lead in my legs as we ascended. Ahead of me the light from Sarah's headtorch danced over the dirty ice. Looking round I could see Piotr's light, but he was now only a silhouette against the shimmering glacier below. Sarah was moving quickly, faster than I had expected, and the rope soon became taut between her and Doug, forcing him to call to her to slow down. This she did briefly, but the same situation was repeated again and again. I called forward for a stop and suggested we split into pairs and swapped order. Doug and I would lead off and Sarah and Piotr would follow behind. The others' faces were shadowed under their helmets, so I couldn't see what Sarah really thought of this suggestion, however she agreed. 'Just stoked about finally getting on the rock!' was her explanation. Doug was silent on the matter, but that silence was all I needed.

The approach from the cave to the start of the rock climb took an hour, much longer than I had remembered. It was a trudge through progressively steeper snow, peppered with boulders. I lead with Doug roped up behind me, the occasional pull on my harness reminding me to keep to his pace. He hadn't argued when I had suggested I go up front again, in fact with every minute he seemed less the alpha male.

It was a relief to finally hit the rock, which sprouted from the snow at first like ancient gravestones in a churchyard, ground down by the elements and time. I carried on until I knew we had to stop and set up a belay point. The chimney was upon us, now it would be real climbing. The sun was fully up, the sky blue. It was cold, but we weren't ever going to get a better day. It was a shame we would be constrained by the filming as for a moment I believed we really could make the summit this time. However, one look down at Doug told me otherwise. His face was ashen and his head bowed, like a man condemned, waiting for the gallows. There was no danger of him agreeing to such a fantastical change of plans. In any case we weren't equipped; it was a crazy idea but I allowed myself that short-lived moment, standing at the base of the wall, my head back in 1990, ready to ascend.

I took a final view of the end of the valley; it would soon be out of sight. I shivered; the temperature seemed to be falling despite the dawn. As soon as Doug arrived, I started to busy myself preparing the gear. I needed to get away from that place and to start climbing.

'You feel it too?' Doug said, his voice muffled by his buff which he had pulled up over his chin.

'What?'

He stared at me. 'You know what.'

I looked down at the other two. They were at least ten minutes behind. 'You mean the cold?'

'Stop fucking me around, Craig. Him of course. You know exactly what I bloody mean.' He whipped the hip flask out and took a pull on it before I could stop him.

'You mean Bob?'

'Of course I mean bloody Bob, who else would I mean?' He fumbled with his karabiner and clipped in.

'Take me in,' I said, ignoring his comment. The ropes went tight as Doug fed them through. 'Okay, climbing.'

'You not waiting?'

'Too bloody cold.' I set off up the gully; finally climbing again, finally on the Supercanaleta. The rock was cold under my fingers, but the holds were easy and I made quick progress. I was soon ensconced on a ledge, belaying Doug who was making competent, if slow progress. The same couldn't be said for Piotr, who Sarah appeared to be almost dragging up through the snow below us. Even from that height I could see the frustration pouring out of her every sluggish step. We were in for a telling-off when we stopped, if we stopped. They were still well off the bottom of the first climb.

Doug reached me and made himself safe. He blew on his fingers and flexed them in and out.

'Enjoying it?' I asked.

He looked at me but didn't reply.

'You carrying on?' I asked.

'What?'

'Next pitch?'

'You bloody joking?'

'Okay, I'll lead.' I stood up to start reversing the ropes so I could lead again.

'What are you doing?' he asked.

'Another pitch.'

243

'For fuck's sake, Craig! We need to wait. If you want to do something, let's top-rope them, help them to get a shift on.' He shook his head. 'Don't know what's got into you. Thought I was supposed to be the lunatic.'

He was right; it seemed to be getting colder by the minute and the sitting around wasn't helping, but us setting off independently was only going to make things even slower. I sorted the ropes out again, checked they were clear of the bottom, shouted a 'below' into the space and threw a rope out, part of me not that bothered if the end of it hit Sarah. I sat back down and got my flask out, but there was little left. I needed to wait for a tug on the rope to signal they were ready to climb. For a moment the light dimmed. I looked up to see a small, fluffy cloud race across the sun. Across the valley, I noticed a haze as though the peaks had been pulled slightly out of focus. I nudged Doug and pointed at them. 'What d'you think?'

He squinted and looked back and forth. 'It's nothing. Maybe later though. All the more reason to let them get this bloody filming over and done with. Less of the racing off.'

So, Doug was less keen about the filming than I was. That was a new development. A moment later and I felt a firm pair of tugs on the rope. I pulled it taut and returned the tug. The rope moved fast through my belay device; it was clearly Sarah climbing. I was a little surprised she hadn't sent Piotr ahead as he was obviously the weaker of the two. Sarah did indeed make short work of the first pitch and her head popped over the ledge after only ten minutes.

'Everything alright?' Doug said as I clipped her into the anchor to make her safe.

'Guys, you need to slow it. We know you're good climbers, you've proved that, we need to get some film down. Okay?'

'How's Piotr?'

'Don't worry about Piotr,' she snapped back. 'He's a good climber, but he needs time to get the shots.' Shots of our arses? I wondered.

As if in answer, she said, 'He's climbing over there.' She nodded towards high ground to the right of our gully, but off the cliff faces. 'He's going to set up the camera to get shots of the next pitches and then your raps.'

'Our abseil? You don't mean—'

'Yes, only a pitch or two. I need it on the granite.' I looked across and sure enough the small fluorescent orange figure was climbing through the snow to a point at an elevation of about halfway up our last pitch.

'Forget it,' I said, 'that's way too dangerous. I'm up for a few pitches, but tandem abseiling whilst I pretend to be unconscious...' I turned to Doug for backup, but he was just staring at the ground. 'Doug?'

Doug remained silent whilst both our sets of eyes bored into his skin, waiting for a decision in our favour. Of course, regardless of what he said, I wasn't going to participate in such madness, but I needed to hear him say it.

'Doug is going to do it, aren't you Doug?' Sarah's voice suddenly had a needle in it I hadn't heard before. She was staring at him, her eyes two hard diamonds. There was clearly something happening I was missing. She looked at me. 'Doug needs to show the world how he did it, how he performed such an...amazing feat.' The sky went dark again. A much larger cloud had now parked itself across the blue sky, behind it lay a sea of grey. The haze in the valley had thickened. Doug remained silent.

'Doug?'

His face was unlike one I had seen in him before. It

245

was the face of a man who was beaten, resigned to some fate over which he had no control. 'We need to do it.'

'We don't need to do anything.'

'Actually, Craig, I believe you do. You need to prove you both didn't make the whole thing up.' Sarah spoke her words slowly and carefully.

I looked wildly between them. 'You know we didn't make it up, your mother found us! What are you talking about?'

'Where did she find you?' Sarah let her words hang in the air. I turned to Doug but he avoided my eyes. I felt my throat dry.

Sarah held her gaze. 'One more pitch, Craig. Show us, show the world. We know you can climb. Show us you can come down again.' At that moment a small rock came hurtling down past us.

'Fuck you, Sarah.' I quickly sorted the ropes out and nodded at Doug. 'Take me in.'

Doug paused for a moment and then pulled the ropes through his belay device. He gave me a silent, sullen nod.

'Climbing.' I set off up the rock, adrenalin rushing through my arteries, my heart pounding. The granite was a blur under me, flowing away, but my eyes saw something else. The event decades before. A man in a red jacket roping me in, lowering me alone. Beard, snow, wind and cold. And then I was belaying him, my turn—

Another rock sailed past me, pulling me into the present. I looked up to see ice crystals falling. We were moving into a shooting gallery. I realised I had scaled fifteen metres without adding any protection. I quickly pulled out a nut and dropped it into a willing crack, then clipped. Calm down, Craig. Slow down. Below me I could see Piotr filming me. I felt a small thud as a stone bounced off my helmet. I needed to move. We would have to descend a different way, away from this funnel. A different way...Cassie had found me at the end of the valley, not here, not at the bottom of the Supercanaleta. Doug was a liar. But then I had always known that.

I started to climb again, my pace steadier, the protection placement more conservative. Concentrate, concentrate. Another stone ricocheted off a boulder above me and I flattened myself against the cliff as the rock disappeared over my head into the valley below. I would have to find some shelter; this was getting out of hand. Above me was a small overhang, the first challenge of the day. There was no obvious way around it and I was buggered if I was going to make it easy for the other two. In the event, it was straightforward to power over it, with large holds like handles in the rock. Higher up, at the first crux, wouldn't be so simple, but then we weren't going higher, were we? After the overhang, I moved onto a second narrow rock shelf that curved into the right wall of the gully, outside of the main fall line. I wondered if it could give us a way of escaping the dropping rocks as we descended.

I set up an anchor point and edged along the wall to take a look at the options for getting down. However, as soon as I stuck my head outside of the gully's relative shelter, my face was attacked by the needles of a thousand small shards of ice and a biting wind that burrowed right through my buff. The sky was darkening quickly and the other side of the valley was obscured by a wall of precipitation hurtling towards us. I quickly re-established myself on the ledge, set up my belay and took up the slack.

I could soon feel Doug climbing, but only one of the two ropes was moving, the other remained static. I guessed we were now climbing as a three, Doug on one rope, Sarah ascending the other. But as soon as he arrived,

247

I resolved for us both to abseil down. No way did I want her back up there with us. Her agenda was clear. We all knew what it was, we just hadn't said it out loud. Part of me desperately wanted to untie the second rope to stop her climbing on it, but years of mountain safety restrained me.

Doug climbed quickly and the rope gathered in a pile. It was a relief to see the rate of rock falls had not increased, nor had their size. Perhaps one or two small stones had struck Doug, but nothing more. He didn't fall and his progress was better than mine had been. We could still get out of there, talk some sense into Sarah and make our camp, but only if we dropped down immediately. At least the change in conditions would have stopped all talk of this tandem abseil madness...

A white helmet appeared over the ledge followed by Sarah's face, flecked with ice. She smiled malevolently at me.

'Where's Doug?'

'We thought it best I second. Quicker that way.'

Speed wasn't her motivation. She wanted to stop us running off; sidestepping our planned humiliation. 'You do realise with this weather a tandem abseil is completely impossible?' As soon as I spoke the words, I regretted them.

'It wasn't back then. Give me slack.' She pulled on her rope, grabbed a sling and started creating her own anchor at the other end of the shelf, rather than clipping in on mine.

'We need to abseil out of here before the weather forces us,' I shouted.

'Oh no, Doug needs to join us.' She jerked twice on the second rope, which presumably Doug was tied in to. 'You're going to show the world what happened.'

'That was all bollocks and you know it!' I shouted.

The second rope now went slack. Doug was climbing. I started pulling it through.

'That's not what Doug says.' She continued to look down the line. 'You don't remember anything, do you, Craig? He can give us a demonstration in a moment.' The rain had now turned to blowing ice. Piotr had disappeared from view. I could see I couldn't talk sense into her.

'What do you want from us?'

'The truth, that's all I've ever wanted.'

'And your dad?'

She froze and her head spun to face me. She hissed, 'Yes, Craig, my dad.'

The sky lit up and an explosion of thunder boomed across the valley, echoing a hundred times off the cliff walls. A small shower of stones rattled down the gully. The rope kept feeding though, Doug was almost with us. We were sheltered from the westerly wind, but outside of our protective chimney was now a wall of white, blowing hard northwards, up the valley. And I was back there again, like two decades before, teeth chattering, hands numb, wanting to descend, to escape. Finally, I was beginning to recall what had happened.

Doug's helmet appeared over the wall followed by one hand, then the other. He almost rolled onto the rock shelf. Blood was running down his face. I knelt to see him.

'Stone clipped me. I'm fine.' He sat up and wiped his face whilst I leaned over and clipped him into the anchor to make him safe.

'You okay to descend? We need to get out of here.'

Doug nodded.

'You need to do your tandem rap, Doug,' Sarah called over me. 'Remember what we agreed. Let's finish the film.'

'Just fucking ignore her. We're going down, she can do

249

what she wants. You go, I've got you.'

Doug stood up and started to fiddle with the rope gear, tying a sling into his harness. I couldn't believe it; he was actually obeying her.

'That's right, Doug, let's get this on film. Silence the doubters.' She tapped the GoPro on her helmet. 'I'm going to film you from the bottom. I'll give you a bit of time to sort yourself out, Doug. I'll let you double up your ropes, like you did before.' She pulled another rope from her rucksack then swiftly started to set herself up to abseil down on it.

Doug was fumbling, like he had in Chamonix, but without the aid of a film crew and a backup. I laid a hand on his shoulder. 'Forget it, Doug. You've nothing to prove. I understand. No one could have done that rescue.'

He ignored me, setting the belay up. It almost looked like it could work. Then he said, 'I need you to clip in to me, then we're ready.' His voice was calm.

'Doug, this is crazy, let's just abseil out of here.'

'Clip in, Craig.' He was staring down at the ropes, his hands shaking as he tried to complete the set-up.

'It's suicide. I'd be safer down-climbing and she knows it.' Across from me Sarah was ready to go, but was filming every motion. 'Doug, you can't do it!'

With that he let out an almighty scream. It flew across the rocks, the snow, the ice, all the places we had loved and now hated. 'I couldn't reach you, Craig!' He turned to face me, staring into my eyes, snowflakes melted by tears. 'You were just hanging there out of reach. I tried. I really tried. I was going to get help.' He grabbed my shoulders with a powerful grip. 'I was going to tell you, I never meant to…'

'You wrote a bloody best-seller!' I said.

'I was protecting you.'

250

'Me? How me?'

He met my eyes and shook his head slightly. His hands dropped away and he turned to face Sarah. 'Turn that bloody camera off. Now!' He took a step towards her and she stepped back. The red light continued to blink. Another flash burst across the sky, lighting us up.

'Doug, what the hell do you mean?' I yelled.

He looked back at me. 'You don't remember, do you? Not even now? Here?' He spread his arms out. 'You told me what happened, Craig. Lying in that hospital bed. How can you not know? You told me about *him*!'

A loud crack came from above. I looked up. Far above, through the swirling sleet I saw a new threat; a blackness growing and filling the chimney. For a moment time seemed to stop. We were a tableau; like three actors frozen on stage, depicting an image to be discussed, analysed, remembered. Myself pressed against the rock, hands and back and leg trying to melt into the wall behind me. Sarah stood square to us both, face impassive, unaware of the impending danger, filming us. Doug caught in motion, arms outstretched, hopelessly off balance, throwing himself, as though in fury, at her.

And then time restarted. Sarah's face now barely registered the change in her status from persecutor to victim as Doug's full weight collided with her. She stumbled backwards then, with a look of surprise, flew over the edge. If Doug's purpose had appeared to be as an assailant only milliseconds later that all changed as a huge stream of dark rubble crashed into his back, ripping him away into the dead, howling air. I stood, stunned by the empty ledge before me where my companions had been only an instant before. The sounds of an army of ricocheting stones receded below me, its battle won. I was left with only the wind and snow for company.

251

It seemed like an age that I remained there, stunned at what had happened, as immobile as the mountain itself, but it can only have been a second before I looked down. One of the ropes threaded through my belay device had simply disappeared; the other was running through fast. I instinctively grabbed it and locked it off. The force of this yanked me towards the edge until my protection pulled at my back, knocking me over and twisting me around so I was splayed out, arms extended, hands holding the rope, face skywards as snow fell down on me.

I regained my breath whilst trying to make sense of what had happened. I had somehow survived the rock fall purely by the random gift of a few inches of space. How suddenly everything had changed and now I was alone on this cold, unforgiving mountain. It was then I felt the pain in my fingers. My hands were gripped around a thin rope that was slipping away—Sarah. I peered over the edge. Sure enough there she was, hanging ten metres below me. Perhaps alive.

'Sarah, Sarah!' I shouted. To my huge relief I saw her stir. 'Are you okay?'

She didn't reply. She was still descending slowly down as the rope slipped through my cold hands.

I recalled the dark and the cold of 1990, a rope running through my fingers into the darkness. A memory I had sought hit me with such force I gasped. I finally had the truth, but at so high a price. The pain of it tore through me, forcing tears down my frozen cheeks even as I lay there, holding this woman's life in my hands.

The rope slipped a little more and I was dragged ever so slightly towards the edge. Just how good was the anchor I had placed? Think. Act! She was out to destroy us, both of us, not only Doug. Now Doug was dead, of that I had no doubt. He had died saving her. Twenty-five years ago, he had lied about rescuing me in order to protect me, because I hadn't told Cassie about what had happened.

I felt the rope in my hand. If I let go, she would fall like her father before her. The image came to me, of me letting go, the rope out of control, rushing through my hands, faster, faster. And when the stop knot finally reached me, that instant force, that brake pulling through every bit of fibre between her and me, would all end up in a small piece of metal I had quickly jammed into a tiny crack in Fitz Roy's endless granite. For sure we would both be ripped from the mountain and our secrets would be safe.

My arms and hands were tiring. So was I.

But it was time those secrets died; for Cassie, for Bob. With all my strength I pulled on the rope and tied it off. She was safe.

CHAPTER SEVENTEEN

It was Piotr who rescued us both in the end. He made his way through the snow and climbed the two pitches up to me so we could lower Sarah safely and then tandem abseil her down to the bottom. She had come round but with a broken arm was not capable of much. Doug's famous rescue was at least feasible over two pitches. We didn't speak much, just the basics, enough to make sure we were all safe. The storm moved westwards and the sun came out once more as we turned our backs on the mountain.

We found Doug at the base of the chimney. He was lying with his back to the cliff, as though gazing out over the beautiful valley. Sarah crouched down and kissed his forehead, then removed her camera and hurled it into a crevasse. 'Piotr, you too.' Piotr unclipped his camera and handed it to her, which she dispatched.

'Thanks,' I said.

She didn't reply, but drew a cross in the ground next to him.

We trudged down through the snow to our camp where we lay and slept.

The next few days were spent retrieving Doug and on police reports. Sarah was treated at the local medical centre before travelling up to the hospital in Rio Gallegos. I stayed on to see Doug could be returned home, to Linda. I called her from El Chalten. It was a brief conversation, just the nuts and bolts. He had died a hero, saving another climber at his own expense, that was all she needed to know for now at least. But there were two other women who needed to know more first, they had been waiting a lot longer.

I found Sarah in a modern ward, on the edge of the town. She was ready to be discharged, fine other than a few broken bones, her head thankfully uninjured. Piotr was by her side, holding her hand, when I entered, but he offered to get us both coffees and left. Sarah smiled at me and for the first time I knew it was genuine.

'He's a good guy,' I said.

'I know.'

'How long you been together?'

She smiled. 'A couple of years. Piotr's long-suffering.' I wasn't going to argue about that. 'You know, Doug and I…'

I waved my hand away; I didn't need or want to know the details. I sat down next to her.

'Why did you do it? Was it revenge?'

She closed her eyes and lay back in her pillow, then started to speak. 'It wasn't like that, not at first. I just wanted to know what happened to my dad. I came out here three years ago with that book.' Her eyes opened and she turned to me. I nodded; I knew which one.

'I had some sort of idea I could find him if I retraced his steps. Dumb really. But it was soon obvious to me that Doug's version of events made no sense, geographically I mean; Mom had told me where she found you and it was on the wrong side of the mountain—that's a hell of a distance. His story was impossible. I was amazed it hadn't been spotted, but when I asked around in some of the bars down here, no one had heard of it, or if they did, they didn't care as it brought in tourists. Seems his fame was just a northern hemisphere thing.'

'And that's when you smelled a rat?'

'You mean I realised Doug was a liar? I figured the only way you, Craig, could have got out of that fix was by descending yourself, or someone else saving you. So, I had

255

you down as a liar too, I just didn't know what you were hiding.'

'Why didn't you call and talk to us?'

She sighed. 'C'mon, Craig! It was his life, his reputation at stake. No way was he talking.'

'And me?'

She remained silent for a moment, then said, 'Yes, you…I visited your shop two years ago, but there was some woman running it; you were out. I could see though it hadn't been such a money pot for you, that accident. I talked to her; she told me a bit. Sounded real fond of you. I wondered though, why you were covering for him, why you'd gone along with it all.'

'And the film?'

'Yeah, an exposé. That was the plan. I had finished a cinematography course and had a chance to make something really low budget to get my name out. I'd been following SummitSeeker and when the job came up, it was like a dream come true, like some higher presence was rooting for me. I never expected him to throw all that money at it, that was never part of the plan. I had wanted some interviews and landscape shots; I thought I could build them into a sort of documentary. It all got a bit out of control. I can't believe he's dead. I'm so sorry.'

'But to burn down my bloody shop!'

Her expression changed to one of utter puzzlement and she tried to sit up. 'What?'

I lowered my voice. 'The bloody fire that destroyed my business. Petrol—gasoline—through the letter box.'

'I know what petrol is but I have no idea what you're talking about. I had nothing to do with it.'

I shook my head slowly. She was telling the truth; I had seen enough lies from her to know the difference. 'Must be some other psycho then,' I said.

'I'm really sorry, Craig. You must think I'm such a prime bitch. I know I have been but I never meant it to turn out like this. I never wrecked your shop. I am really sorry. Honestly, you have to believe me…'

I did. I didn't need to know any more; how she had plotted, led Doug on, wrecked his marriage. We'd all done bad things. Now we needed to forgive. I needed absolution.

It was my turn. 'I need to tell you what happened, what really happened.'

She nodded and lay back and listened with eyes closed as I finally told her my recollections.

When I finished, I said. 'Doug wasn't the villain, not really, it was me. It's up to you what to do with the truth. But let me tell your mother. I owe her that. After, you can do as you see fit. Probably a film in it for you if you want it.'

Sarah shook her head. Her eyes were wet with tears. She sucked a breath in and then rested her hand on mine. 'You know, Craig, the first time I met you, you said, "A great climber died that night." When you said that, I should have realised you were a good guy. You are, Craig. It wasn't your fault, it's a dangerous sport. My dad chose to climb, no one made him and he wouldn't have wanted anyone to. I'm sorry about what I did. I think it's time now for you to forgive yourself.' She looked up as Piotr arrived back holding two cups. 'We've deleted the films and SummitSeeker fired me. I'm going home to my mom, but we'll search for my dad first, one last time.'

'I wish I could tell you where he was.'

'You've said enough, we'll find him.'

'Goodbye, Rebecca.' I kissed her on the cheek and shook Piotr's hand, then left. I had a plane to catch. A lot of planes.

CHAPTER EIGHTEEN

January 1990, Southern Patagonian Icefield, Argentina

Bob cursed as the rotten ice fell from his left boot. He adjusted his balance and breathed in hard. One, two, three…he pulled himself up onto the next small shelf and another rest. He cursed again, but not because of a poor hold or a momentary misjudgement of how to move. He cursed because he had left her behind, alone, because of pride. Because he 'needed' to do this before fatherhood. As though his world would end just because a child came along. Selfish, fuckin' selfish.

But what a view. Below him sat glaciers, forests and lakes, an expanse that stretched towards the Pacific to the west and the Southern Ocean to the south. The sun was shining, the air fresh in his lungs, he was half way up this bitch, half to do, thirty raps down and they would be reunited and he could say *sorry*, a thousand times *sorry—I love you and I won't leave you again.*

He grinned to himself. Of course, he knew that wasn't true anymore than she would want it to be. Hell, maybe next time it would be her doing some crazy solo ascent, God knows she was good enough. He squinted looking down, trying to pick out her tiny tent, some sign of life on the glacier. But there was nothing, just ice and water; blues, greens and greys.

It was mid-morning and he needed to press on. He had been lucky with the weather, if you could call holing out in a hostel for three weeks waiting for a break lucky. Waiting with his new wife, and those Brits…Just thinking about them sent a spasm of tension down his back. He needed to forget about it and summit. So, they had appropriated his route (that was the word that snob,

Doug, had used, wasn't it? 'Appropriate?'), but he was supposedly on a safer, easier line now, after all, the Franco-Italian route was the first. Nothing on Fitz Roy was remotely easy, of course though. He had been up here two years before with Nick and Scott and they all vowed they would never set foot in Patagonia again after that. How time erased memories though, or at least dulled them. Bob was terrible with names, with faces, with math, history, languages. All in all, he was a flunk-out. Mrs Erikson had said he would amount to nothing but she was already wrong about that. Because one thing Bob didn't forget were routes. Show him a photo of a piece of rock he had ascended five years ago and he would name it and describe every hold, every step in the darned thing. The time he had set off, the descent, how many pitches, the gear, the lot. That was why *Climber* magazine had given him a column and that was why he didn't fail. Ever.

He turned back to the case in hand. He could still make the top and get much of the way down in daylight. He could then bivvy out or do the final raps in the dark. He'd decide that one later. But he had to summit first, while Mother Nature was being kind. He flexed his arms and checked his boots. It was time to go.

To stand on the summit of Fitz Roy was to stand in a corner of heaven. The cold, hard but most beautiful corner there was. He turned through a complete arc and took a few snaps, a memento for his wife and his child. This was a personal climb; it wasn't about sponsors or magazines. He had regretted it almost from the moment he left her down by Laguna Sucia and even now, in this icy paradise, when he should be feeling elation, only felt the need to hurry back to her. Most accidents happened on descents; he knew that like every climber. The weather

259

had held for the day but he wasn't certain from looking at the horizon that would remain so. The ice on the summit was untouched. He wasn't surprised he had beaten the Brits up here; it was a tough mountain and their route was more ambitious. It would have been nice to have seen someone though, as unlikely as that prospect was. He wasn't a solo-junkie like some of his friends and those guys hadn't been so bad, just a bit pig-headed about their plans. If they could see him now, they would have realised they could have trusted him and together made the whole adventure a bit safer for all of them. But they hadn't and that was that. They could meet up, shake hands and swap war-stories later. A gust of wind suddenly shook him making him realise how vulnerable he was.

Was it the momentary dimming of the light, or the dip in the temperature that had first made him aware of the change? His subconscious had absorbed the information, had locked it in, had made him push on harder, faster. To be solo was to be fast, unencumbered by a partner extracting gear, or working at a different pace. But the light, it had dropped again, this time for a few minutes and on looking south he saw the change he had dreaded and hoped he would escape. Cassie would have seen it too and known what it meant. He had been through this before with the other guys and he had the means to see it out for a few days if necessary. Some food, some liquid, a tiny tent and bag. He could hunker down on the mountain and hope it would pass swiftly. But he had to get off the top, and fast.

Then he found the man, a broken figure lying on a ledge, fifty metres below, his rope trailing away into another gully. At first Bob thought the figure was asleep. He looked around for someone else, and listened. There was nothing, just the moan of the wind around the rock and the slap of the first few flakes of icy sleet on his cheek. It took him ten minutes to get down there, the descent not aided by it being well off his preferred route. The snow was flying in now, biting into his skin whenever he faced the wind. The temperature had plummeted and his fingers ached with every grip. He touched down on the ledge and pulled his rope through making ready for the next move. Crouching down he saw it was Craig, one of the Brits. He gave the man a rough shake and shouted into his face. 'Craig, Craig, are you okay?' knowing what a ridiculous question that was. Blood stained Craig's forehead but he was breathing and there were no other obvious signs of damage. The helmet had probably saved him, for now at least.

Bob looked around. Craig had somehow fallen onto this ledge, perhaps three-quarters of the way up the mountain, how the hell he had done that and where his companion was were questions he didn't need answers to now, they were both in a very dangerous situation. Bob knew he could get off Fitz Roy in one piece, even in this weather, but Craig's chances were slim. In fact, they were as close to zero as they could be unless he helped out. But then that would seriously endanger himself.

And Cassie was waiting for him. His unborn child was waiting.

Shit.

He shook Craig again; if the guy didn't come round he wasn't going to leave Bob a lot of choice—no way could he get an unconscious guy off the mountain.

'Dou…Doug, wha—'

'Hold on, Craig, you're going to be fine. Took a little tumble.'

Craig moved his head to one side and his eyes rolled upwards, but then his breathing rate increased and he moved his arms as if to sit up.

'Hold it there, man. Take it steady. Anything hurtin' ?'

Craig rolled into the foetal position.

Bob looked to the heavens, into the swirling snow and ice and cursed. It was even worse, the guy wasn't up to rapping down. Bob hugged himself, he was getting cold. This storm might last an hour or a week but it was getting dark. No way was he descending in the dark and in a storm with this guy. He pulled out his bivvy bag; they could both fit in it and would be all the warmer for the company.

It seemed to take an eternity to get them both inside out of the wind, but somehow he did it. They lay, huddled under the thin fabric as it rattled in the wind and the light outside died. Next to him Craig drifted in and out of consciousness. Bob tried to sleep knowing he would need all his energy and wits about him if they were both to survive. He wasn't sure of his companion's head injury, removing the helmet could make matters much worse, but he knew enough to run through the options. The best route down was the way he had come up providing Craig recovered enough to control a rope. There were perhaps twenty pitches before they even got to the glacier. If he left Craig here, the man would die, that was a certainty, but trying to bring him down could cost them both their lives. That's what he should do, leave him. If the roles were reversed it's what he would expect Craig to do. Climbers understood this but whilst there was a chance, he would give it a go.

Somehow, despite the wind howling and shaking the tiny bivvy, Bob slept. He awoke to Craig talking, asking where he was. Bob turned on his headtorch. Craig blinked hard in the light.

'We're in deep shit, Craig, but we can make it out of here if you are willing to try. How you feelin'?'

'Sore. Bust some ribs I think.'

'Anything else?'

'Fucking cold.'

Bob grinned. 'Yeah, me too. You want to get out of here?'

'Yeah,' Craig said with a weak smile.

'Try to sleep, we're going to need everything we've got when it gets light.'

As if in answer to him, Craig's eyes rolled up into his head and he passed out.

Bob turned off the torch and lay back. He couldn't get back to sleep but instead listened to Craig's irregular breathing over the sound of the gale. He knew they were safe for now, roped hard to the rock, but it didn't make the feeling any more comfortable. Knowing sleep wouldn't come, instead he brought up the map of the route in his head, remembering his planned descent and trying to figure out, without seeing outside, how they could get back onto it. Considering the rock, concentrating on it, brought a calmness back to him and a sense of purpose. This was going to be the biggest challenge he had ever faced. It wasn't a cup he had chosen but one that had been passed to him. He wished it could pass by, all the time knowing the impossibility of that. He would do his best, no one, no god could ask for more.

The light slowly grew and with it the wind died down fractionally. Bob was very cold; they had to get moving. He rummaged around, waking Craig in the process and collected together the gear they had; at least Craig brought with him part of a rack and a rope should they need it. He then opened the door. They were under a layer of snow that filled every crack in the rock, only broken by the rime

263

ice that had grown out of the granite. Whilst the rock gave him a hard security, off the ledge was just swirling cloud, obscuring everything fifty metres above and below. At least the incessant pressure of the wind had relented to strong gusts. Bob gathered snow and melted it over the stove. With two of them he had enough fuel left for the day. They needed to stay hydrated and warm. He filled his bottle and searched for Craig's. There was nothing, his pack had some food in it and an extra layer. They were travelling light, but his bottle must have been lost in the fall. That limit of how much water they could carry would be a problem, as if there weren't enough piling up on them. He made some coffee, filled the bottle and then got Craig to drink it. The hot liquid revived them both and so before the boost could be lost, he dragged Craig outside, tied them both in, packed the bivvy and readied to set off. Then it was time to see what shape Craig was in, would he be in a state to be lowered down, or would he have to take him down in a slow, tandem abseil?

Craig pushed himself to his feet, wobbling all the while. He clawed for the cliff behind as though looking for a hold in the snow. This was no A grade climber but they would just have to cope.

'How about your hands?' Bob asked.

Craig flexed them and mumbled. It was enough for Bob. He set up the abseil and secured Craig so Bob could do most of the work but Craig could help out. Ascending back onto the route was impossible but Bob had calculated how to descend. There were risks of course, but no choices to complicate matters.

They started their descent; pitch after pitch over ice and rock. Craig remained semi-lucid, enough to do his bit. When he passed out, his broken ribs crashing into the rock was enough to wake him. The day passed and the storm came and went. The limited food and water were shared though Craig showed little interest. Bob became increasingly thirsty until he had to stop to melt more snow. He had lost track of how many pitches they had gone through; was it fifteen, twelve, eighteen? No not eighteen, that was wishful thinking.

'Come on, buddy.' He pushed Craig into a hollow in the rock and made them both safe. His arms ached as he slowly pulled the rope back in. He could sleep now. Just grab a few hours of rest...

'You alright, Doug?'

Bob looked up at Craig, whose head was lolling to one side.

'I'm fine, we'll both be fine. You're doing great.' He wasn't going to correct him; he didn't have the energy to go through that again. He set up the small stove and pushed a mound of snow into the pan. The gas started and the flame lit, but then in front of his eyes, died. No more water, eating snow was for the damned.

He stood and roared into the wind. His eyes welled at the thought of their predicament. All around was cloud; thick, grey, damp air, spinning, turning, slithering across the mountainside. Where was Cassie? Where was his love? He checked his watch; it was four o'clock, they had a few more hours of light but they couldn't stop now, even if darkness came. They were so close and to stop without water, fuel or food. He didn't want to think what that would mean.

The cloud, snow and wind failed to abate further but they pressed on. As every pitch passed, Bob's spirits lifted. Perhaps they really were going to both make it out unscathed. He knew he was exhausted, dangerously so, but he doubted Craig would survive another night. He was pale and his skin was clammy to the touch. They needed to get off this endless cliff. But it was so, so cold. The temperature seemed, even now, to be dropping further and every gust that came drove right through him a little more than the last, as though a sabre was being sharpened.

By the time darkness came, Bob had lost all notion of how many pitches they had completed, or where they were. Their rate of descent had slowed down with tiredness at each change of pitch. He was now fumbling the ropes like a complete beginner and it was almost miraculous there had been no accident. Craig had done his bit, stoically bearing the pain he must be in, but Bob cursed him and his idiotic companion for putting them in this situation then cursed himself for doing so, as that other climber, Doug, was probably dead.

And then they came to the wall. It was dark once again but the dirty clouds had lifted and occasional moonlight fleetingly revealed the glacier below. It was so close now, a couple of pitches perhaps. But they had hit a serious problem. Craig sat next to him shivering as Bob flicked his torch back and forth across the cliff below. He knew he was well off the route and it looked as though they had hit some sort of overhang. To abseil straight off it was a risk that he couldn't take; they could be left hanging there until the ice crept over their lifeless bodies. To the left was a short traverse and what looked like a resumption of a cliff at a more forgiving angle.

They needed to traverse across this section, but was Craig up to it? They were so fuckin' close now...

He shone his torch once more across the rock as a gust of wind ripped through his jacket. They had to keep moving.

'Okay, Craig, sorry, pal, but something a bit different.' He grabbed Craig's harness and set up a belay on it, tying himself into the other end of the rope. 'Need you to belay me.' The wind whipped the words away and he had to shout them again. Craig seemed confused but then nodded. 'You can do this, just a short hop now. Got to get across that gap, we're nearly down.'

Craig nodded and pulled the rope in.

'When I get past the overhang, you follow. I'll give two tugs to let you know I'm tied in.' Bob looked down at Craig, who nodded back at him again. His companion's fingers loosely held the rope, ready to feed it through. Bob crouched down. 'You can do this. We're nearly there.'

Bob breathed in deeply and set off, edging along the ledge. It narrowed to a crack, thinner and thinner. Bob searched for a placement for protection, but found little that was convincing. He was also seriously short of gear. He prayed this was the last pitch.

The crack was now almost non-existent and ahead of him was just a wall of thin, slimy ice. He put his foot out and kicked in. The ice shattered and tumbled into the darkness. Useless. He started to back up, this wasn't going to work. The protection rope was slack behind him; Craig wasn't feeding the belay properly. He felt his legs begin to shake. God, had he tied Craig in to the other end?

Craig opened his eyes. Through his blurred vision he looked out across the valley to indistinct greys beyond. It was light now and the storm had passed. He was overwhelmed by acid dryness in his throat that drowned out the biting cold and the pains in his head and chest. He scraped some snow and put it in his mouth, instantly regretting the pain it inflicted. He breathed in and tried to remember what had happened.

The man had left him in the dark and he had been supposed to do something. He looked down at his lap. The empty belay device hung from his harness.

267

'Hello?' The croak that came from his mouth sounded like someone else. He called again, 'Hello?'

The only answer was from a gust of wind pulling at his jacket.

The man had left him alone, tied to a cliff, with just a rope that lay in a frozen bundle by his side. Craig's hands were empty. He knew he should have stopped that sudden rush of rope; the most basic of basic duties. It was his fault the man had gone. Now he would die here, like that man who had left him in the dark.

He beat his chest, a surge of pain rocking through him, waking him one last time. Out below him the ice glistened. His eyes weren't working properly but even in this state what he could see was more than a pitch away. But next to him was a rope, he could abseil off this, better to die climbing than by freezing. But it was more than a pitch away. He turned and searched for the end of the rope, then slowly, clumsily, unpicked the stop knot.

He pushed off over the cliff. The rope rushed through his frozen palms, the sudden heat melting the ice that held them solid. In front of him granite whistled by upwards then the rope was no longer in his hands and he was tumbling over and over, across ice and rock until he was moving no more, laid out like a corpse awaiting burial.

That's how Cassie Green found him two hours later, another two hours and he would have been dead.

EPILOGUE

I'm looking out through a smart shop front into the street beyond. It's August, the height of the season and it's busy, we've hardly had a moment all day. Sue turns around as the last couple leaves. She smiles at me, sharing a private joke. Through the back of the shop I hear Lottie barking, ready for her tea and afternoon walk.

It's taken a year, but I'm back where I want to be, with who I want to be with. The insurance paid out eventually; the police had nothing on me and with the help of a solicitor we got Alan to find something more interesting to do. I contemplated a change of career, moving away, but this is my home and this is my livelihood. I'll not be bullied from it.

I saw Lewis down the pub after I came back, Lewis who told me to tell the debt collectors where to go, Lewis who dropped a very subtle hint that perhaps someone, a mate, had done me a favour with the petrol followed by some disparaging comments about the Sergeant. I'll probably never find out for sure who lit the match but it was struck out of friendship, that much I do know.

I was lucky to get Sue back working for me and luckier she was so right about her internet ideas. In truth I work for her now more than the other way around. I'll leave her to what she's good at—managing the shop and focus on what I'm good at—climbing. I've got an evening session down at Plas y Brenin to run, I need to get going if I'm not going to be late.

Sue's finished arranging the new SummitSeeker display, their top end, the BG. No one has asked what BG stands for, or rather who it stands for, and I haven't discovered how Doug got that branding set from beyond the grave. But that was Doug, and this range is dedicated to the greatest climber I ever met.

Acknowledgements

Thanks to the team at Black Pear: Tony, Polly and Charley for all the work in publishing the book; thank you for supporting me in bringing this story to life. To Nick Munn and James Weaver for all the invaluable help with constructing the accident and checking the climbing mechanics. To Catherine, Nick, Rebecca, Robert, Alison, Tim, Mikki, Georgina and Felicity for reading early drafts and encouraging me to the finish and finally to Annie for giving me my writing mojo back.

About the Author

Dunstan Power is a Worcester-based author and adventurer. He has previously had short stories and award-winning flash fictions published in genres ranging from historical fiction to SF. *The Empty Rope* is his debut novel, inspired by travels in Patagonia in the early 1990s and his passion for rock-climbing and hill-walking.